THE OUTCAST: CODE APACHE

THE STORY OF A HOTSHOT CREW FIGHTING FOREST FIRES IN THE 1980S

KIRK KRUTILLA

The Outcast: Code Apache
The story of a hotshot crew fighting forest fire in the 1980s

by Kirk Krutilla

E-book ISBN: 979-8-9946878-1-9

Paperback ISBN: 979-8-9946878-0-2

FORWARD

This book is dedicated to the temporary forest firefighters of the late 1970s and 1980s, who performed at an exceptional level despite receiving little support from an employer that had created a toxic environment. Some of the individuals and events in this book are real; others are fictional and included to support the book's themes.

CHAPTER 1
THE CREW

"Experience should teach us to be most on our guard to protect liberty when the Government's purposes are beneficent. Men born to freedom are naturally alert to repel the invasion of their liberty by evil-minded rulers. The greatest dangers to liberty lurk in insidious encroachment by men of zeal, well-meaning but without understanding." *Olmstead et al. v. United States, 1928. SCT. 456 Sec 144 (1928). Brandies dissenting.*

The storms in the summer of 2000 marked a significant moment in the struggle against nature's fury. Lightning pounded the rugged ridges of Montana with relentless intensity, forked bolts slamming against the jagged terrain above Cedar Creek, where a long-lost miner's cabin still stood. Locals claimed the ghost of a Chinese man—a gold miner who once sought fortune in the unforgiving wilderness—roamed the quiet wind in search of dreams left behind.

By July, the waters of the Clark's Fork River had dwindled, depleted by an unrelenting drought, leaving behind a parched and cracked landscape. The river struggled to maintain its identity, flowing weakly toward the headwaters of Flat Creek, where an old mine now leaked arsenic, a toxic reminder of past endeavors that once promised prosperity. I stood there, watching a ridge ignite in a sudden explosion of flames, as the fire consumed everything in its path, transforming the land into a hellish tableau. Helicopters and retardant planes appeared overhead, unleashing chemical payloads that drenched the ridge in bright red, trying desperately to tame the ferocity of the inferno. I observed, both mesmerized and horrified, as flames tore through the drought-stricken landscape, the deafening roar of fire mingling with the howling wind that echoed through the canyons.

In 2001, the advancing fire threatened the town of Superior, falling from snags and trees perched precariously on the ridges above. The flames cascaded down into the low valleys, exploding with terrifying force that echoed through the mountains and sent animals scrambling for safety. That year, the Bitterroot burned, leaving a scar on the earth that would take generations to heal. It was the year the so-called "ship of fools" was forced to evolve, adapting to the harsh realities of a new century where nature's wrath could no longer be ignored.

Amid this destruction, I sat in my cabin by the side of the Clark's Fork, working on a brief for the Montana Supreme Court. Beethoven's *Fifth* played through my headphones, its rhythmic precision a stark contrast to the wild symphony outside. My two dogs—one sleek and black, the other a warm reddish-brown—brushed against me. The adrenaline from the sight of the fires pulled me back into memory, back to another time of fire and fury.

In 1987, the whirling blades of a helicopter sliced through the smoke that choked Briggs' Ranch on the Rogue River-Siskiyou National Forest, its rotor roaring through the haze. The first group of hotshots, faces worn and etched with fatigue, leapt to the ground. They squinted through the gray as their watering eyes stung in the acrid air. As they landed, they surged forward, emerging from the smoke in quick, practiced motion, their movements a mix of determination and adrenaline. Behind them, the helicopter vanished once again into the murky sky. In the heart of that fleeting chaos, a strange and quiet silence followed.

The fire they faced, the Silver Fire, stretched across 30,000 acres, hurling firebrands ahead of its front. In some areas, the Illinois River served as a natural barrier. However, in its drought-stricken state, it resembled a shriveled version of its usual, rushing self. The once-mighty stream now flowed low and slow.

The Silver Fire advanced toward the Kalmiopsis Wilderness, a region known for its rugged, untamed beauty. This wilderness formed a tapestry of deep canyons, sharp rock ridges that clawed at the sky, and clear, rushing streams and rivers that had so far withstood the onslaught of flames. Named for the rare shrub *Kalmiopsis leachiana*, which bore a delicate purple flower—a living relic from before the Ice Age—the area seemed to embody a spirit of resilience. An ethereal aura from the early Pleistocene clung to the deep gray smoke, as if the land itself whispered tales of survival against impossible odds.

The Silver Fire became more than a test of flame; it was a crucible that challenged the spirit and resolve of the crews gathered there, demanding every ounce of strength and courage they could summon in the face of nature's wrath.

Earlier that August, a venomous sky threatened southern Oregon. Dark clouds rolled through the water-starved oak, fir, and cedar along the coast, over the thirsty ponderosa pine lining the browning slopes of the Cascades, and into the brittle sage and lodgepole pine of the eastern high plateaus. The clouds darkened, then split with forked lightning, igniting fire after fire.

The blazes began in old snags, dropping fire into dry needles below. Flames climbed through the branches, igniting brush and brittle limbs, reaching into the drooping boughs of pine and fir. The wind carried the fire from tree to tree, sparking a relentless chain reaction that spread like a contagion. By early September, fires littered the desolate, dry land from Northern California through Southern Oregon and across into Idaho.

Before positioning themselves on the Silver Fire, the crew had worked the Tiller Complex. That fire, with its fierce infernos, primarily raged through the dense, once moisture-rich fuels of the western forests. It was a stark contrast to the dry, brittle conditions now facing them at Briggs Ranch, some fifty miles inland from the quiet, picturesque resort town of Gold Beach. At Tiller, towering firs and majestic cedars loomed overhead, casting long shadows across the forest floor. Yet the underbrush told a different story. There, a chaotic tangle of logging slash lay dried and ready to burn, creating a volatile foundation that fed the flames. As the fire spread, this debris fueled an increasingly dangerous environment for the firefighters.

The Tiller Complex, a relentless battleground of flames and smoke, nearly claimed Grimaldi, who stumbled into a hornet's nest and suddenly found himself surrounded by furious hornets. They stung him relentlessly as they swarmed over the dry, scorched earth, leaving him reeling in shock and panic. He, Berkson, and Thomas had strategically positioned themselves along a small, meandering creek, using its cool waters as a natural fuel break to help contain the advancing flames.

Suddenly, a piercing scream shattered the tense atmosphere. "Owe!" the cry rang out, raw with panic and pain. Berkson and Thomas exchanged worried glances, their faces etched with concern. "Dude, are you okay?" they shouted in unison, their voices cutting through the crackling of distant flames and the rustling underbrush.

Before they could get an answer, Grimaldi burst from the tangled weeds—a whirlwind of frantic energy. "Bees!" he shouted, his voice pitched high with alarm as he swatted wildly at the air, desperate to escape the swarm.

It was chaos. Grimaldi stumbled forward, his skin already dotted with angry red welts where the hornets had struck. The sight sent a chill through Berkson and Thomas; they both knew all too well that Grimaldi had a severe allergy to bee stings. The absence of an EpiPen hung heavily over them—a grim reminder of the stakes they faced in this unforgiving landscape.

Berkson had grown up in a university town in the heart of Illinois, where academic life thrived and both his parents were professors. It was in another academic haven that we first crossed paths—our friendship began during college in a farming community in Iowa. It took root during long, spirited debates on politics, often held in the cozy, bustling pizza shop Berkson proudly opened—a local hotspot for students and residents alike. Over hot slices and late nights, we explored our beliefs and ambitions, anchoring memories in the warmth of shared ideas. I often returned to that college town during the off-season, drawn back by friendships and the nostalgia of fields, farms, and youthful dreams.

"Owe!" the scream echoed again, raw and urgent. Without hesitation, both men sprang into action, instincts sharpened by experience. Thomas, who always thrived under pressure, didn't hesitate. Years later, he would recall the time a man fired a gun at him—how, with quick reflexes, he'd disarmed the shooter and ended up sending him to the hospital. But now, his focus narrowed to one goal: saving Grimaldi from the onslaught of stinging hornets. With practiced urgency, he called for a helicopter drop with an EpiPen.

They moved toward Grimaldi with resolve, their hands moving in practiced unison as they began to swat away the persistent bees. As they worked to free Grimaldi from the swarm, the heat of the flames seemed to intensify, creating a suffocating atmosphere that made it hard to breathe. Sweat dripped from their brows, mingling with the dirt and ash that had settled on their faces. They sensed the urgency in the air, a tension that urged them to act quickly, as Grimaldi's frantic movements began to slow, his energy visibly waning. Time felt suspended in that moment, each passing second weighed down by the knowledge of how quickly things could turn dire.

The air thickened with the scent of charred wood and the oppressive heat. Above this chaotic scene, a recently dropped first aid kit dangled precariously from the gnarled branches of a massive fir tree. The kit swung just out of reach as a faint wisp of smoke curled upward from a charred hollow deep within the tree's core—a reminder of the devastation that surrounded them.

Thomas stood a short distance away, assessing the Douglas fir that loomed over the landscape, dwarfing its companions and reaching heights well above one hundred feet. The massive tree leaned slightly, its heavy canopy creating a dense roof that filtered the sunlight in scattered beams, casting eerie shadows on the ground below. He worried that the tree holding the first aid kit would need to break through that canopy; if it didn't, the kit would remain stuck out of reach. To fell a tree, one must make a face cut—two cuts: one straight in and the other slanting downward to connect with the first. Then, a back cut is made from the opposite side to a point where enough wood remains to form a hinge, like a door opening and closing. The hinge prevents the tree from falling outside its intended lay.

With grim determination, Thomas positioned himself to one side, his mind racing with the implications of what could happen if the tree became entangled with another as it fell and the first aid kit was trapped. He took a deep breath, then swung his chainsaw into action, the sharp teeth of the chain biting into the wood with a satisfying growl. He worked quickly, intent on avoiding a barber-chairing scenario—a dangerous situation where the tree could split and swing toward him, causing serious harm.

As he cut, the tree groaned and creaked ominously, a sound that echoed through the heavy silence of the forest. The massive tree swayed, caught briefly in the branches above, creating a spectacle of splintering wood and cascading foliage. Suddenly, it broke free, plummeting toward the ground in a swift descent. With a thud, the tree struck the earth, sending up a cloud of dust and debris that hung in the air before slowly settling.

Berkson, who had been anxiously waiting nearby, sprang into action, rushing over to administer first aid to Grimaldi, whose condition had become life-threatening. The urgency of the situation sharpened amid the chaos surrounding them. At last, Grimaldi began to recover—probably because of the Brundle Tea he had drunk earlier—and they all breathed in a fresh gust of air as the wind shifted.

Ford, another crew member, along with Grimaldi and Thomas, would mix their coffee, salt, pepper, and sometimes the Tabasco packets from their MREs into a single water bottle, passing it around between them. They called it "Brundle Tea," a quirky nod to the movie *The Fly*. The concoction gave them strength and energy, a ritual that had become part of their daily routine. (In the remake, Jeff Goldblum played Dr. Brundle, who transported himself from pod to pod. Unfortunately, and unknowingly, he also transported a fly, which merged with his DNA. He gained incredible strength, heightened clarity, and power, but his lifespan became that of a fly.)

CHAPTER 2

BRIGGS RANCH

From the Tiller Fire, the crew moved to the Silver Fire. On the Silver Fire, Briggs Ranch served as their base camp. It sat six miles from Oak Flats, the main fire camp. The ranch sprawled across a picturesque valley carved by the flow of the Illinois River. The once-lush grasslands—once vibrant and green—now lay dry and brittle, a mere shadow of their former vitality. Each step into the heart of the ranch revealed remnants of a bygone era: a short walk to the south uncovered old feeding and watering troughs, their wood weathered and gray. Around them, the ground was littered with white paper sleeping bags, carelessly strewn across the dying, decaying grass.

The ranch's atmosphere thickened with smoke and melancholy, hauntingly reflecting what once was—a space where laughter and life had flourished, now overshadowed by the relentless march of time.

As the expansive ranch disappeared into the rise of a distant ridge, a group of firefighters gathered nearby, gently petting a tame deer driven from the flames, seeking refuge in this unexpected haunt. Smoke curled and danced through the air, casting a hazy veil over the scene, as if nature itself mourned the devastation.

Suddenly, as if conjured from the swirling smoke, Uphoff emerged with a determined stride. His appearance evoked memories of the ranch kid who once faced the difficult decisions, forced into the harsh realities of life to help his struggling family survive the grind of their circumstances.

As he pressed forward, memories flooded his mind—vivid recollections of his time in Job Corps, where he diligently honed his skills and tirelessly trained with heavy machinery, striving to carve out a future in the world of equipment operations. The long hours spent in the training yard, learning the ropes and mastering the controls, had instilled in him a deep sense of purpose.

He recalled the adrenaline rush of a fateful day in 1985, when he sped to the crew in his shiny new blue Firebird, the engine roaring to life as it tore down the road. The car felt like a symbol of his newfound independence—a reminder that he was more than just a kid from the ranch. He was ready for the fight.

Now he stood as the intrepid warrior of the crew, embodying the spirit of resilience and determination. Rather than yearning for the sweet smell of dry mop or the sour scent of wet mop, Uphoff craved the burn of the hot line—the visceral rush of adrenaline that came with confronting the flames head-on. His mind drifted to the Savage Peak Fire of 1985, memories flooding back as a poignant reminder of the battles fought and the lessons learned in the flames.

The remnants of a grueling ten-day stint just before the Savage Peak fire at the Lake Mountain fire punctuated the stillness of the morning. The inversion layer, a stubborn barrier, held the smoke close to the ground, keeping the fire contained beneath a deceptive veil of calm.

The Savage Peak fire. Uphoff's saw, the Husqvarna 181, shone with a vivid, bright orange finish. It stood as a remarkable piece of machinery, boasting 4.9 cubes of screaming intensity, perfectly suited for the fierce demands of firefighting. Slung confidently over his shoulder, it felt like an extension of himself—light yet powerful. The camp at the Savage Peak fire, set in the already-burned area, served as a temporary refuge—a fragile oasis surrounded by devastation. Fallen, blackened trees lay sullenly strewn across the scorched earth. The line had blown out behind them, a harsh reminder of fire's unpredictable nature; someone had succumbed to fatigue and fallen asleep at the pump along a small stream, now choked with brush.

The flames had surged through the tortured Alpine Firs, their limbs—once vibrant and green—now dropped lifeless to the ground. The trees stood stripped, their trunks tapering upwards. As the fire raged, it had dropped low, consuming fine fuels like pine needles and aspen leaves, while also lingering beneath rotted logs and tangled roots, where the cool humidity of the night had slowed its advance.

On the Savage Peak fire, the crew rose from their paper sleeping bags as the fire began to stir, creeping back to life. As they prepared to depart their temporary refuge, they watched the flames lick at the forest's edge, insidiously weaving through fallen needles and remnants of Ponderosa and Lodgepole pines. The fire gradually crept into denser stands of Alpine Fir, which dotted the terrain before giving way to vast Alpine meadows that stretched far above. The crew stayed alert, knowing the battle was far from over; the ground beneath them was a cauldron of danger.

They soon arrived at a critical spot where the fire's relentless advance had been temporarily checked by a talus rockslide cascading into a spur ridge, forming a natural barrier. Here, at this pivotal anchor point, they began their work cutting the fire line. Hunt, the experienced assistant superintendent, gazed upward toward the endless rise of the spur ridge looming above them. It was here, at this strategic location, that they would carve a path up to the main ridge—where they would continue their essential work, fighting to hold back the encroaching inferno.

He reflected on the precarious positions he had found himself in over the course of his seven years with the Hotshot crew—a tenure filled with moments that tested his courage and resolve. Memories flashed through his mind, recalling the adrenaline-fueled days battling wildfires, where every decision could mean the difference between life and death for his team. He also drew on his experience as a winter ski patrol member, where he had honed his lifesaving skills under the treacherous conditions of avalanche terrain. Those long, cold days navigating the slopes—ensuring the safety of skiers and snowboarders amid the ever-present threat of snow slides—had ingrained in him a sharp awareness of risk and the importance of staying composed in the face of danger. Each memory added depth to his understanding of peril, shaping him into the courageous, even-tempered firefighter he had become.

Uphoff stood firm, surveying the line stretched out before him—its path indirect and meandering, deliberately veering away from the encroaching fire. Not one foot in the Black—the area already consumed by flames and ash, considered safe for cutting line. This was an indirect line: strategically necessary, but also the most perilous type to cut. Unburned fuel lay between him and the fire, concealing unseen dangers, ready to ignite and surge forward with deadly speed. For now, the graying talus rockslide—a rugged barrier of stone and debris—served as his safety zone, a temporary bastion against the chaos that threatened to erupt at any moment.

Ahead of the crew, Hunt moved with purpose, flagging the line and scouting for potential safety zones. These zones were critical—areas where fire couldn't burn—natural refuges, such as rocky outcrops or meadows, where a crew could escape if the flames suddenly flared beyond control. He paused briefly, his gaze shifting to the side. A hundred yards away, a meadow sprawled in the sun, lush and vibrant. The sight was a relief—a perfect safety zone standing in stark contrast to the encroaching threat. Bright green grasses and a kaleidoscope of wildflowers created an inviting sanctuary, a refuge of life in a landscape marked for destruction if the fire jumped the line.

With a sense of urgency, he marked the escape route with blue flagging, guiding the crew toward the path they should take if the inferno threatened to overtake them. The flag, a lifeline, fluttered in the breeze, its bright hue a beacon pointing the way to safety.

As a light breeze stirred, it lifted the smoke from Uphoff's face, offering a brief reprieve from the oppressive heat and choking air. He gripped the pull cord of his saw, feeling the familiar tension in his muscles before yanking it with determination. The saw roared to life, its powerful engine cutting through the dense silence of the forest. He cut now, focused and deliberate. Each stroke required care, ensuring that every tree fell in the right direction—away from the fire and toward safety, outside the established line.

The saw purred rhythmically as white chips of wood flew in a flurry, some catching in his beard. The first tree began to fall—teetering at first, then slowly descending down the line. It found its resting place on the swing Dutchman, spinning gracefully outside the line. This was critical; any heavy fuel on the fire side posed a major risk of the flames crossing back over.

"Down the hill!" he bellowed—a warning that a tree was falling. His voice cut through the tense atmosphere as he maneuvered the trunk using a step Dutchman, guiding it safely away from the ridge and the advancing fire. His command echoed across the mountainside—a clarion call for precision and caution. The wood creaked under the strain before the tree hit the step Dutchman and launched down the slope, far out of the fire's range.

Beside him, Pearson—the other sawyer—mirrored Uphoff's movements with impressive synchronicity, their teamwork operating like a finely tuned machine. Pearson, who had spent his formative years scaling the steep slopes of Mount Hood, carried a deep-rooted understanding of a mountain's temperament and secrets. His childhood was filled with the lessons learned helping his father rig houses during frigid winters, all while honing his skiing skills amidst swirling snow.

Tall, lean, and athletic, Pearson moved with a natural agility that allowed him to sprint ahead of the crew during their grueling power hikes, capturing the landscape's raw beauty with his camera as he went. He moved with a grace that belied the exhaustion always looming, pausing only long enough to snap a photo of a breathtaking vista or an intricate natural detail before dashing back to rejoin his weary companions. Each return brought a renewed burst of energy and enthusiasm to the crew.

Uphoff's gaze shifted downward into the canyon below, where the breeze had strengthened, carrying off the smoke that once hung low and heavy—a ghostly shroud that had obscured their vision. With each passing moment, the tension in the air thickened, a constant reminder of the fire's volatility and the relentless battle they fought as it began its ominous crawl, moving deliberately through the carpet of dead needles scattered across the forest floor. Brittle needles crackled underfoot—haunting reminders of the dryness.

As the wind picked up, a sudden gust swept through the low branches of a solitary alpine fir. The tree had a robust crown, its thick, lush branches reaching skyward in a spire-like formation. The green needles glistened in the sunlight.

Suddenly, the lower branches—still untouched by flames—began to smolder, releasing wisps of smoke. Once vibrant, they surrendered to the heat, their edges darkening as the fire overtook them. Moments later, the tree erupted in flames, crackling and popping, a raw display of nature's fury.

Uphoff, keenly aware of the danger, narrowed his gaze at the thickening smoke billowing below him—a dark, swirling mass that shifted ominously with the breeze. He jerked the pull cord of his saw. With skilled hands, he jammed the saw dogs into the silver, thin bark of the alpine fir, feeling the vibrations reverberate through his body. The saw's teeth plunged in, ripping, pulling, and chewing through the wood with fierce determination as it spat out wood chips in a dramatic spray, each flake cascading slowly to the ground.

With a practiced eye, he assessed the depth of the face cut, urgency coursing through his veins. He slapped a back cut into the tree, feeling the tension build as the trunk began to yield. It tipped slowly at first, then gained momentum and crashed down.

The crew resumed cutting line. Black line. Safe line. One foot in the black, burned fuel. Nothing left for the fire to burn. A hot line, where Uphoff now worked, methodically facing each tree and felling it away from the fire. He felt the hot, nasty heat press against his face as he looked up from a face cut. The crown of the tree he was felling had caught fire, now threatening the line.

A quick face cut in the opposite direction, a wedge driven in by me, and the tree tumbled back into the fire.

Back on the Silver Fire at Briggs Ranch, as the crew stirred from their slumber, the last remnants of the night's humidity clung to the air, slowly dissipating under the gentle embrace of early morning light. Shafts of sunlight pierced through a warm haze of smoke—thick enough to feel, but not so heavy as to choke the breath from their lungs. Echoes of lingering coughs hung in the stillness.

The crew lingered momentarily in their camp—a fragile safety zone nestled within the chaos of the surrounding fire. One by one, the sawyers hoisted their saws over their shoulders, the weight of their tools a familiar comfort. Following close behind, the rest of the crew—clad in bright yellow and green Nomex, their fire-resistant garb—marched in line against the backdrop of impending danger.

To the sound of heavy, labored breathing that seemed to resonate within the trees, Uphoff was suddenly thrust back in time to 1987 and the Silver Fire, his mind leaving Briggs Ranch behind as they headed toward that day's starting destination—until a branch slapped him in the face, jolting him out of his reverie. A quick, instinctive right turn later, Uphoff and the rest of the crew found themselves ascending the Silver Prairie Trail, a rugged path winding through the wilderness, broken by patches of brush sweeping low across the ground.

They had been following the Illinois River Trail—a route they had hoped would be a reliable companion through the chaos of the firefighting effort. It was a well-maintained trail, one that had seen its fair share of boots over the years.

CHAPTER 3

THE SUPERINTENDENT

As he trudged forward, Uphoff wiped the sweat from his brow, his skin glistening with effort, and cast his gaze over the top of the ridge, where the fire was supposedly contained. Uncertainty crept into his thoughts as he wondered what truly awaited just beyond that ridge. Did the fire merely lurk, preheating the fuels above, biding its time? Would it wait for the afternoon sun to beat down and the upslope winds to whip it into a ravenous frenzy, driving it toward the ridge and throwing firebrands to ignite spot fires? Or had it met its end—snuffed out in the shadows among the gloomy oaks, where dry moss and Goatsbeard dangled from their limbs?

In a sudden rush, the crew reeled forward, the sharp snap of brush against their skin echoing the urgency of their mission. The coolness of morning still lingered in the air—a refreshing contrast to the heat they knew would soon engulf them. A thin wisp of smoke filled their lungs, a sharp reminder of the fire's ever-present threat. Lost in thought, surrounded by the rhythm of heavy breathing, they felt a quiet tension begin to build. It wasn't fear that gripped them, but a deep-rooted awareness of life itself—a recognition of the dangers ahead, a stark contrast to the kind of overconfidence that invited death.

"When you lose that feeling, it's time to leave the show," Hunt said, his voice steady and unwavering, heavy with experience. McCollister nodded in agreement, a silent understanding passing between them. Ford, tall and lean, wore his characteristic grin, adding a spark of levity to the tense atmosphere.

A rugged ridge gradually revealed itself, rising from the landscape. The air grew thicker, the smoke swirling around them in a haze that stung their eyes and clogged their throats. It was the dry smoke of the aging oaks that dominated the terrain, their twisted branches reaching out like skeletal fingers. Beneath the ancient trees, Goatsbeard smoldered on the branches, releasing puffs of smoke into the breeze—a sign the fire had already passed through.

As the crew pressed on, they came to an abrupt halt, hearts pounding as they took in the scene ahead. Standing before them were the Mt. Adams crew, their faces set with determination, and the Boise Hotshots, equally resolute—both groups awaiting their next move.

The crew's superintendent stood tall against the backdrop of the late autumn sun, which cast a warm hue over his sweat-slicked skin. He felt the weight of his experiences bearing down on him—each year he had dedicated to his work a testament to his unwavering commitment to understanding the fine line between light and dark, between victory and defeat. Clutching a well-worn Bible in his hand, he raised it high above his head, using it as both a shield and a weapon—an emblem of his deeply held beliefs and unyielding conviction in the face of adversity that threatened to engulf him. Perched on a rough-hewn stump, he cut an imposing figure—lanky and striking, his blond ponytail cascading down from beneath his hard hat.

This was the first year he had joined the Hotshot crew, and he took immense pride in his role as the new and emerging vision of trust and leadership within the agency. Eleven arduous years spent in the timber and brush disposal business for the agency had imparted valuable lessons—one of which insisted that a good Bible could defeat any obstacle, any fire, a mantra that had served him exceptionally well throughout his career.

However, the crew stood before him like a canvas of imperfections, marred by streaks of dirt and disarray. His keen eyes took in every detail—a scowl creeping onto his lips as he assessed their lack of discipline. Ford's Nomex shirt—a material with exceptional heat and flame-resistant properties—had come untucked during the arduous hike to the fire, a minor infraction that set the superintendent's teeth on edge and sent a shiver of irritation coursing through him. He noticed the smudges of dirt marking McCollister's face, and the way the crew had strayed from the perfectly straight line he had drilled into them time and time again. The image they presented was crucial—not just for their safety but for their professional advancement. As the agency had long insisted, being proactive remained paramount, and something as simple as shirts tucked in neatly could reflect that proactive spirit.

"Proactive, proactive, proactive," he asserted, the words rolling off his tongue with fervor as he repeated the mantra three times, as if the rhythm itself might solidify his resolve and reaffirm his authority. He believed he was three times more proactive than the best in the agency. See, he had proved it to them. Had he not just said *proactive* three times? A swell of confidence rose within him; he was doing much better now than he had been just over a month earlier, when despair had threatened to overshadow his ambitions. The dream job he had longed for had slipped through his fingers, but he knew now that his inaction had sealed his fate. Repeating *proactive* again, he reveled in the belief that he stood clearly above the rest—if only they could grasp the brilliance of his insights. Nothing could stand against him; his ideas and plans were invincible, a vision of success he felt destined to achieve.

Yet beneath the surface, a disquieting feeling began to churn—an uncomfortable sensation that gnawed at his composure like a persistent insect. He thought, *Look good, act good, work good,* a mantra that had echoed through his mind countless times before. He recalled the days of his youth, trailing behind his father, a traveling salesman whose livelihood depended on convincing homeowners to invest in new siding. Each house they visited testified to varying degrees of neglect, and he remembered the way his father brazenly pointed out their dilapidated state, declaring them unsightly with a bluntness that bordered on cruelty. The words had rolled off his father's tongue with a confidence that left an indelible mark on the boy's psyche.

He could still vividly picture the expressions on the homeowners' faces—some embarrassed, others defensive—as his father, with unwavering conviction, articulated their shortcomings. He remembered feeling a surge of disgust not only at the houses, with their peeling paint and crumbling facades, but also at the people who lived within them. Their inability to maintain their properties struck a chord in him, mirroring the disdain his father had felt. That shared sentiment forged a connection between them, albeit a twisted one, as they judged the world through a lens of superiority that was as harsh as it was illuminating.

The superintendent's gaze fell on me, Krutilla, who had packed eight fuzees into the canteen holders of his web gear, and the sight sent a sharp spike of irritation jolting through him. A fuzee was a torch that could be used to ignite fuel that needed to be eliminated. Had he not laid out a clear plan just weeks earlier during the Tiller Complex operations? Four fuzees were the correct number to carry; anything more felt unnecessary and reckless. Krutilla clearly did not adhere to the principles of proactivity he had tried so meticulously to instill in the crew.

As he watched Krutilla, a fire ignited within him—a growing resentment fueled by the realization that Krutilla seemed to be attempting to usurp his authority once again. The beefy foreman remained an imposing figure, undeniably powerful, with a physique capable of bench-pressing well over 300 pounds and deadlifting nearly 500. However, the very muscle that granted him strength also weighed him down and slowed him, especially on steep inclines. The superintendent grimaced inwardly, grappling with both envy and disdain. Krutilla's physical prowess posed a threat, but it was the foreman's blatant disregard for protocol that truly stoked the superintendent's simmering anger, boiling beneath the surface like an uncontained blaze.

He considered himself vastly superior to Krutilla and to the rest of what he deemed a scummy crew. In his mind, the superintendent represented a powerhouse—powerful, successful, and undeniably attractive. The fact that he could function without a full night's sleep proved his superiority. Just look at him; he hardly needed rest to maintain his edge. He shoved a handful of M&M's into his mouth. The colorful candy offered a momentary distraction from the tumult of his thoughts. He reminded himself that he had been thriving on a mere two hours of sleep a night for how long now—two weeks, perhaps even longer.

As he glanced into the reflective surface of his compass, he admired his finely chiseled chin, the sharp angles of his jawline accentuating his self-perception of excellence. A face like his belonged to someone of consequence—someone as talented and multifaceted as he believed himself to be. It was a visage meant to command respect, to make destiny itself bend to his will. Each feature, honed by both nature and nurture, served as a testament to his belief in his own greatness.

He straightened his posture and quickened his purposeful gait, showcasing a confidence that radiated from him like the sun illuminating the forest. With a slight nod of his head, he asserted his presence—a silent proclamation that he was indeed special, a beacon of superiority in a world of mediocrity he found increasingly intolerable.

He harbored an overwhelming disdain for Krutilla, a contempt that surpassed his feelings for the rest of the crew and, indeed, for firefighters in general. To him, Krutilla's foolishness stood out like a sore thumb; he seemed too dim-witted to follow the meticulously crafted plans the superintendent had devised, including the precise number of fuzees to carry on the line. In his mind, Krutilla embodied sheer stupidity, incapable of recognizing the brilliance of his superiors. The thought irritated him further.

A sharp twinge of pain pierced the haze of his thoughts, reminding him of the pressure mounting within as he grappled with the reality around him. The tension in the air thickened, underscoring the stakes they faced, and he felt it wrapping around him like the smoke lingering beyond the trees—a suffocating blanket of uncertainty.

CHAPTER 4

THE AGENCY

The plan for the day was to improve the rugged trail leading to Silver Prairie and establish a brush line along it. Eventually, the goal called for extending the well-worn path all the way down to the banks of the Illinois River at Conner's Place—a broad, flat clearing that opened gracefully along the river's edge. The crew would tackle the dense brush tangled with poison oak, its glossy leaves a deceptive threat lurking in the underbrush. Towering oak trees, draped in soft green moss and delicate strands of Goatsbeard, stood sentinel along the route, their gnarled limbs stretching over the line. Amid these trees, occasional old Ponderosa Pines rose majestically. Lodgepole pines, more numerous, also littered the trail to Silver Prairie.

The Mount Adams crew, equipped with their Pulaskis—an ingenious tool that combines the sharp edge of an ax with the flat surface of a hoe—worked to bring the trail down to mineral soil. The mineral soil line would prevent the fire from creeping through it, helping to keep the fire contained. These tools carved through the undergrowth, shaping the rough trail into a more navigable path. Meanwhile, the Boise Hotshot crew undertook the critical task of burning out the line, a technique that involves the cautious ignition of dry fuel during periods of low-intensity fire. This meticulous burning was essential to reduce the flammable material between the fir and the fire line in a controlled, strategic way.

As my squad and I prepared for the day's labor, they positioned themselves strategically to throw the brush far to the side of the line, ensuring their work would be both effective and efficient. This marked my seventh year on the Hotshot crew. Yet despite my commitment, I knew deep down this would be my final year in the field I loved. The thought weighed heavily on me.

I had persistently pursued a permanent firefighting position over the past four years, only to face rejection after rejection. Although I had earned accolades for excellence in fire management and received awards recognizing my skills, the elusive title of permanent firefighter—with its accompanying health and retirement benefits—remained just out of reach.

It signaled changing times, I realized, reflecting the growing challenges that had become the norm in our line of work. In 1991, after four long years of futile attempts, I finally made the difficult decision to give up and redirect my path toward law school. There, I discovered a surprising truth: navigating the complexities of the legal system, winning cases in a State Supreme Court, and serving as *amicus curiae* in the United States Supreme Court proved far more straightforward than securing a permanent position within the firefighting organization I had once yearned to join. In that realization, I found a bittersweet comfort—a new direction forged from the embers of past ambition.

I felt an unsettling sense of disquiet settling over me like a shroud, my thoughts drifting between the rhythm of tossing brush and the weight of my worries. Time seemed to stretch in a certain way while I engaged in the methodical tasks that defined much of my firefighting life; it was almost as if the work itself became a meditative practice. The woods—rich with the scent of pine and dry earth—served as a sanctuary for poets, philosophers, and deep thinkers alike.

GOING COYOTE ON THE SILVER FIRE

Zigzag Hotshot Crew
Kalmiopsis Wilderness

I follow Krutilla's single head-lamp beam
beneath ghost big leaf maples and madrones,
as our boots remember our ash-gray bodies back

inside this landscape of smoke, forgotten by stars
and sky, whose air gags us and hides a thin wafer
of sun, up where silhouettes of old cedar hiss yellow flame.

Abandoned by screams of helicopters that first night
on initial attack below Silver Prairie seems so long ago.
When Rambo ripped open the front of Mulligan's leg

with his Husqvarna. He had just dogged his face-cut
into a big bucksin snag. Its top was on fire, leaning out
over the crew. Above us, the canyon's sky turned red

and started to suck fire down the crowns of every tree.
We could hear the yells from other crews. Gleason tried
to get them on his radio. As Rambo coaxed the shriek

of his chainsaw into the waist of that tree, pieces
of neon-orange embers began snowing sideways out
of the night. Onto our skins. Mulligan, Rambo's swamper,

tried to sweep them off his back when the machine's bar
exploded into his shin. Berkson, our EMT, said the saw teeth
were colored with blue muscle and tiny white pieces of bone.

Then, the day of the blow-up, Elise and J.D. got lost and saw
the dead burning bear. Back-burning the next afternoon
the bald-faced hornets got Grimaldi. We were contouring

above the river in these steep sun-brown stringer meadows
when he jammed his lit fusee into their hidden ground nest
and hundreds of them—like in a cartoon—chased him past us,

disappearing down into thick manzanita. When we finally
found him, his face welts were big as jawbreakers. Belly
up in the duff, he had pissed and crapped his pants too.

Berkson put a needle in him. Kept him in the creek all day.
The next day, Grimaldi was pounding hot line, singing
Doors songs with Bougar Bill in head-high poison oak. Now

we have no radio contact. No food. When we can, we sleep
on the ground until our dreams, once again, realize
the sound of the flames. Then, when we hear the heart

of the fire make its terrible runs up Silver Creek
everyone cheers. If you have ever fought wildfire
you understand. You want to be here.

Paul Keller

The hours spent mopping up hot spots, meticulously cutting line down to mineral soil, or hurling brush into growing piles felt like an eternity of introspection. Though these moments lacked the exhilarating thrill of flames dancing dangerously close as we carved out a hot line, or the heart-pounding adrenaline that accompanied dropping a burning snag with widow makers poised to fall, this quieter work possessed an undeniable gravity. It offered time uniquely suited to reflection and contemplation.

As I threw the brush, my mind wandered into deeper territory. *Where does Greek logic fit with Judeo-Christian faith?* I wondered, my brow furrowing as I wrestled with the contrast between the two philosophies. At first glance, they seemed to stand in stark opposition. Yet, I could not shake the feeling that humanity had been conditioned to embrace both. *Isn't there an internal conflict at play here?* I asked myself, the forest sounds fading into a muted backdrop for my internal dialogue.

My thoughts continued to braid themselves into new complexities, drawing in DNA and genetic predisposition. *Instincts for survival,* I thought, *interfere with the already contradictory synthesis of logic and faith.* The ideas swirled in my head like lingering smoke after a fire was contained, each thought an ember struggling to stay lit amid the encroaching darkness of uncertainty.

Some of those days in the heart of the forest proved to be the best of my life, filled with camaraderie and the thrill of battling nature's fury. Yet even in those moments of joy, when I became lost in the maze of my own thoughts, I had to remain perpetually alert to the ever-present danger lurking among the trees. My mind often drifted, spiraling into uncharted corridors of contemplation. I became acutely aware of the contradiction: despite my deep love for fighting forest fires, I could never build a sustainable career in this work. The realization nagged at me, and I kept searching for reasons to justify it—reasons ultimately unrelated to the truth of my situation.

I wondered whether my offhand comment about the meteor during a briefing—or perhaps the philosophical musings about Aristotle— had inadvertently sabotaged my chances. In truth, it was neither. But I would only come to grips with the obvious truth of that realization many years later, when the chaos of my thoughts had settled and the clarity of hindsight provided a sharper focus.

I recalled a conversation with the head personnel officer of the Forest Service, a man whose perspective on experience struck me as decidedly unconventional. He proclaimed, with an air of authority, that one year of fighting fires equated to ten years of experience fighting fires, arguing that ten years of performing the same work merely repeated one year ten times. The absurdity of this logic sparked my curiosity. I began to speculate wildly—wondering if, then, one fleeting second of actual firefighting experience could stretch to equate to ten years, considering that ten years represented simply one second of action repeated an astonishing 35,360,000 times—not even factoring in leap years or the time I had spent sleeping when I wasn't actively battling flames. Fires had varied by fuel type—brush, timber, grass—and the flammability of those fuels. Weather, too, had shaped the many fires I'd faced over seven years, each one different from the last. This wasn't a philosophy. It was just an excuse for a deadly policy of hiring inexperienced firefighters. A system willing to confuse spectacle for substance.

Amidst my convoluted thoughts, the personnel officer confidently assured me that this bizarre equation held true. This tall, thin man, with a gaunt face that seemed to echo the weariness of his spirit, appeared destined for a long career with the Agency. At fifty years old, he epitomized loyalty, even when he found himself at odds with decisions made by those higher up. In his youth, he had been vibrant and full of life, but a crashing realization had left him hollow, knowing that nothing would ever change within the system he served. With a resigned sigh that seemed to echo through the trees, I dismissed the encounter, allowing a thought to drift through my mind—hidden deep within the shadows of rationalization—as I pondered the futility of it all.

I took a deep breath, steeling myself as I voiced concerns about the dramatic shifts occurring within the Agency. I pointed out, with growing exasperation, that government bureaucrats were carelessly discarding the foundation of two thousand four hundred years of Western learning, rooted firmly in Aristotle's philosophies. I referenced Aristotle's concept of knowledge tied intrinsically to experience, a principle I believed should guide their actions and decisions, citing the ancient text *Metaphysics* as a cornerstone of my argument. Yet my words fell on deaf ears, as I learned the Agency sought the "cream of the crop"—a phrase that rang hollow in my ears. I received the unsettling finality of being told that someone with my genetic makeup could not meet their lofty standards, despite my unique blend of attributes and experiences.

This formed part of a broader civil rights policy dictated by the federal agency, which, despite its noble-sounding intentions, felt more like a cold dismissal. "We are looking for the cream of the crop, so men need not apply," the personnel officer stated bluntly, his eyes devoid of empathy as he delivered the verdict. The same officer later asserted that Agency policy held greater authority than the rulings of the United States Supreme Court. I referenced *Johnson v. Transportation Agency, Santa Clara County*, 480 U.S. 616 (1987). He dismissed it with a wave of his hand, as if it were a mere footnote in a much larger game. It was too bad. I believed the law in *Johnson* was sound. If an underrepresented group was equal or nearly equal, they should get the job.

As I stood there, absorbing the weight of this bureaucratic absurdity, frustration surged within me. The personnel officer looked at me, a flicker of impatience in his eyes, as though he silently wished I would stop talking—just shut up and accept the reality thrust upon me. But the words stayed lodged in my throat, a tangled mix of disbelief and indignation, as I grappled with the absurdity of being judged not by character or capability, but by a metric that felt utterly contrived and unfair.

Or was it the meteor comment made earlier at the forest-wide safety meeting that did me in? At the meeting, the tension in the room felt thick enough to cut with a knife—or perhaps it was the sight of the safety expert, a representative from industrialized Europe, standing confidently at the front of the room in his impeccably tailored three-piece suit. This man, in a crisp white shirt and a carefully knotted tie, had come to instruct us on how to operate safely in the unforgiving wilderness, drawing parallels between the strict safety protocols of European heavy industry and the unpredictable environment in which we worked.

The expert issued a provocative challenge to the full auditorium of Agency employees, his eyes sweeping the crowd with measured certainty. "There is no accident that could not be prevented," he declared with unwavering confidence. While he may have been technically correct, it sounded more like something suited to a sterile office than the rugged, chaotic reality we inhabited. I couldn't help but think the only way to achieve such safety would be to stay inside the station all day—wrapped in a metaphorical straitjacket—completely detached from the realities of our work.

Then, an employee from the back of the auditorium, perhaps emboldened by the absurdity of the statement, raised his hand and asked, "But what if a deer jumps out of the woods and right into your vehicle?" The question hung in the air, laden with genuine concern and a hint of sarcasm. The expert, undeterred, replied with an air of condescension, "Well, you should be driving slower." His response did little to ease the unease settling over the audience. I exchanged glances with my colleagues, each of us silently questioning the practicality of such advice in the face of real-world dangers.

"What about meteors?" I shouted. "What if I'm driving down the road and a damn meteor pops out of the sky and crashes into my vehicle?" I could see the expert silently wishing I'd just shut up.

"Watch out for meteors!" Cassady bellowed with a wild grin as he made his way out of the auditorium, his voice echoing off the walls and slicing through the heavy tension. The absurdity of the comment lingered for a moment—a bizarre reminder of the chaos woven into our daily lives. From that day forward, whenever anyone from the auditorium caught sight of me, they would chuckle and shout, "Watch out for meteors!"

Cassady stood as the outcast among them—an anomaly in a sea of seasoned firefighters who had dedicated their lives to mastering the art of battling blazes. With one year under his belt at the prestigious U.C.L.A. law school, he had chosen firefighting instead. His four years of experience on the hotshot crew granted him valuable insight into the unpredictable and often treacherous nature of our work. Still, it wasn't enough to save him from the whims of fate and the bureaucratic tides that swept through the agency like a relentless storm.

After the tumultuous end of the 1983 season—marked by both triumphs and tragedies—Cassady mysteriously vanished from the hotshot crew, leaving behind a trail of whispers and unanswered questions that hung in the air like smoke from a long-extinguished fire. Though he still held fire-related jobs, the raw adrenaline and exhilarating thrill of being a hotshot were forever denied to him, leaving a void he could never quite fill. Instead, he drifted into odd roles—jobs that felt like faded echoes of his former self: delivering pizzas where the cheese was conspicuously absent, setting up carnivals that lacked real rides or excitement, and spending long, meandering days at beaches dishearteningly devoid of sand, the vast stretches of water offering little solace.

Yet, despite the strange and often disheartening trajectory his life had taken, Cassady possessed an undeniable boldness that set him apart from his peers. He had the courage to step forward when others hesitated, to voice his concerns when something felt amiss, to challenge the status quo even when it meant standing alone against the tide of conformity. In a world governed by arbitrary rules and stubborn traditions, Cassady remained a beacon of unpredictable energy—a light amidst the chaos of our reality. His spirit, though battered, refused to be extinguished, reminding those around him that perhaps there was still room for audacity and individuality in the face of overwhelming odds.

Inexplicably, Cassady held a firm belief that the most authentic route to a meaningful firefighting career involved immersing himself in the act of battling blazes. He believed that by learning about fire—understanding the intricate dance of flames and smoke—he would prepare himself for the weighty responsibility of safeguarding human lives. Yet in the harsh light of reality, Cassady had it all wrong. Even those in positions of authority—the Superintendent, with his ever-growing list of quirks, and the Personnel Officer, who maintained a stoic demeanor—recognized the naiveté of that notion.

If Cassady had truly aspired to a career in fire management, he should never have set foot on the fire lines. Risking everything before even submitting his application was, ironically, the exact thing that disqualified him. In an era marked by bureaucratic absurdities, a law degree seemed to serve as the golden ticket to fighting fire. At that point, he would be recognized as a professional and, inexplicably, gain exemption from the fate that ultimately befell him. "See, there is no discrimination," they would proclaim, their voices dripping with a blend of arrogance and ignorance. To them, the solution for being deemed genetically inferior was to acquire a professional degree—an absurd, yet unchallenged, reality.

In an alternate universe, Cassady might have roamed from California to Montana, leaving trails of destruction in his wake, and most likely would have risen through the ranks—earning promotions along the way. He would have seamlessly fit into the Agency's vision, which prioritized individuals who looked good on paper, regardless of their true capabilities or intentions. The irony struck me: I mused bitterly that one could not extinguish a fire with mere paper. The Agency, with its bewildering policies and arbitrary decisions, baffled me to no end. If only Cassady had been savvy enough to purchase an indulgence, perhaps he would have secured a job that aligned with his passion—instead of being relegated to the shadows of what could have been.

Cedar burning in the center,
Olympics 1985

Shaniko Butte fire 1982

Krutilla Triple

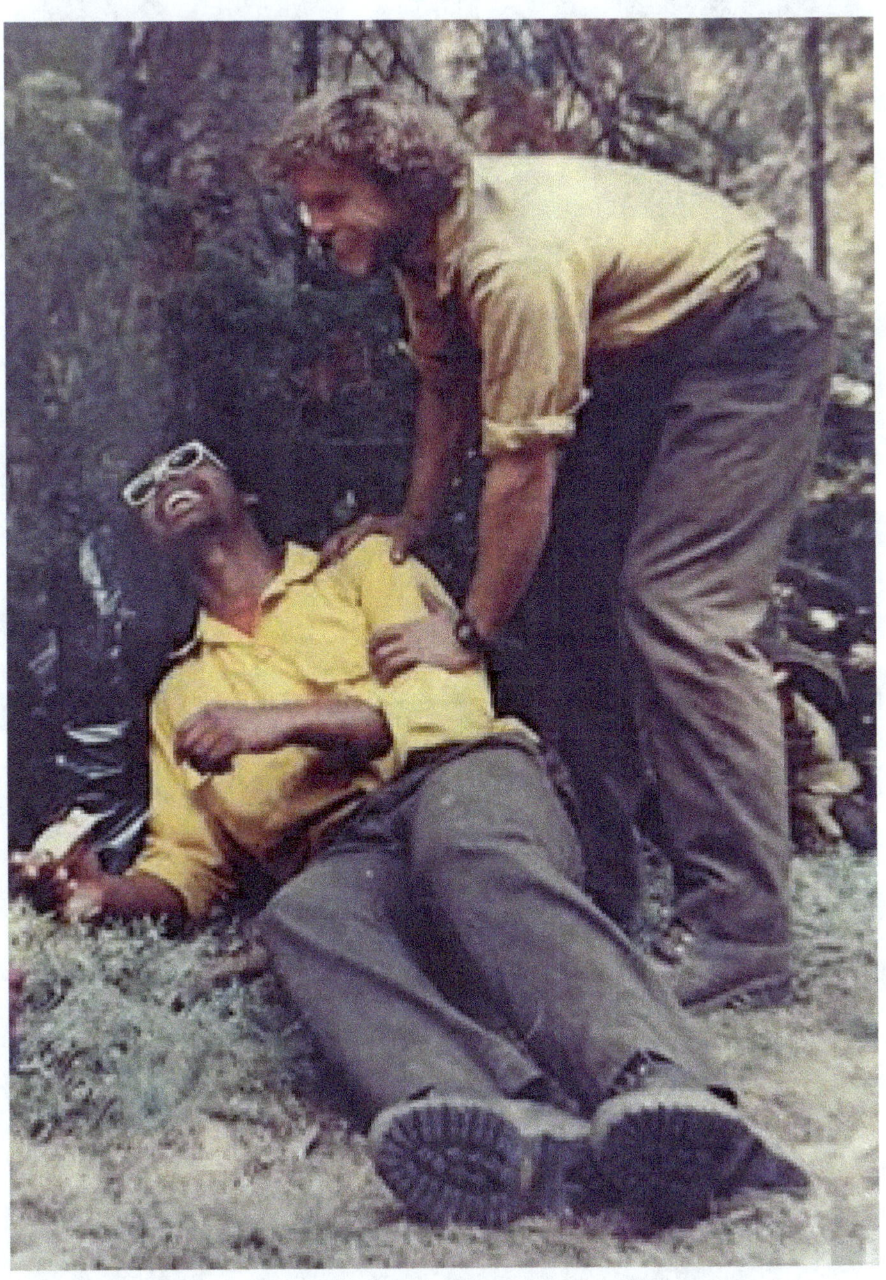

Glenn drying clothes on the Silver Fire

Kay and Carol

Krutilla Hunter, McAllister and
Keith 1982

Mary, Juan Romeo, Hunter,
Dinardo and Krutilla 1984

Lake Mountain fire where Gracie ran from the flames with the rest of the crew

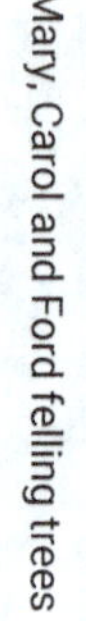

Mary, Carol and Ford felling trees

McAllister cedar tree-Green
Canyon campground

McAllister cedar tree-Green
Canyon campground

Cassidy, Dinardo Rozenburgh, Two individuals enjoying the night at heli-spot 42 on the Silver Fire

Alaska 1985

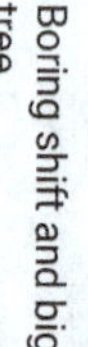

Boring shift and big tree

Saving 9 house on the Centennial
fire, Montana 1984

Big Phil giving instructions on the Football Fire-1982

Football Fire 1982

CHAPTER 5

PAST FIRES

I found myself transported back to the blistering summer of 1987, standing amidst the chaos of the Silver Fire. I gazed up the line, where the sawyers worked with frenetic intensity, their chainsaws roaring against the backdrop of a hot, dry day that parched my lips. The sun beat down relentlessly, casting harsh shadows, and sweat trickled down my back, soaking into my shirt.

With steadfast determination, I fought the oppressive heat as my squad of seven, and I labored diligently, straining our muscles to haul away the downed brush and scattered wood from the fire line. Each movement was deliberate and careful as I navigated through tendrils of poison oak that thrived in the sweltering conditions, their glossy leaves glistening like a warning in the sunlight. By that point in the day, I had grown indifferent to the irritating presence of the poison oak; I was so blistered and raw from previous encounters that any additional exposure felt inconsequential—almost trivial compared to the larger battle we faced against the encroaching flames.

The itch and burn of the rash blended into a familiar discomfort, merging seamlessly with the sweat that trickled down my thighs, creating an unbearable sensation—like I was slowly melting in the heat of the moment. Lira, the husky Latino firefighter, had shared that antihistamines helped cool the relentless itch that poison oak induced. The antihistamine worked to dull the pain.

As we worked, the sun continued its arc across the sky, casting long, ominous shadows that heightened the tension in the air. I shook my head slightly, trying to dispel the thoughts of loss and injustice that threatened to distract me. I refocused on the task at hand, determined to maintain my vigilance and protect my crew, even as the heat bore down on us.

I took a moment to check the fuzees tightly packed in the covers of my canteen, ensuring they remained secure and ready for use should the need arise. My gaze dropped to the slope down the ridge, where I knew the fire lurked just out of sight. Though thick smoke hung heavily along the ridge, obscuring my view of the flames, I sensed the fire's presence. I inhaled deeply, the smoke filling my lungs—a reminder of the danger that surrounded me. Lifting my canteen to my lips, I took a long, refreshing drink of water and felt it cool my throat, momentarily washing away the grit of the day.

Time rushed forward into the afternoon, casting a warm, golden hue that enveloped the landscape. A gentle breeze swept across my face—a welcome relief amid the oppressive heat. The up-slope winds, born from the heated valley floor below, rose along the ridge, carrying with them mixed sensations: warmth and a hint of danger. With every gust, I knew that while it cooled my skin, it could just as easily awaken a dormant fire, igniting the stillness into chaos. Weather and topography shaped fire; a dry cold front could fuel a super blaze, pushing the head of the fire forward as the winds shifted with the front.

Methodically, I tossed the brush aside as we worked to clear the line. My gaze shifted to where the sawyers had gathered for a brief respite, their bodies leaning against trees, visibly fatigued. The sound of saws biting into wood had slowed—a sign that even the most skilled among us—Gale, Grimaldi, Thomas, Ford, and Berkson—were feeling the weight of the day. Our saw squad was no longer as deep as it had been, and that realization sent a ripple of concern through my mind.

I recalled how I had run the saw squad earlier that season, feeling the rush of adrenaline as we worked in unison, cutting through the dense forest with ease. Now, however, Uphoff and I led separate squads, and Pearson, after facing discouragement, had seemingly vanished—retreating into the shadows of the past. My thoughts drifted back to the Lake Mountain Fire, when our saw squad had been ten strong, slicing through the woods with intensity and precision that now felt like a distant memory.

The Lake Mountain Fire of 1985 marked a pivotal event—a series of infernos that sent Gracie running, her Dolmar, a container carrying fuel for the saws, left behind as she dove into the safety zone, flames licking at her heels. Before the Savage Peak fire, a fierce blaze had already ravaged the land, culminating in the infamous Boise Bar fire, where a relentless downpour of hypothermic rain miraculously extinguished the flames that had threatened to consume everything.

On the Lake Mountain Fire, I fixed my gaze on the remnants of the blaze, which had initially murmured along the forest floor, weaving through needles and twigs before erupting into chaos by early afternoon. What had once been a subtle whisper transformed into a thick, boiling column of smoke and flame, twisting and writhing in response to a wind that howled in fury. The flames danced wildly, leaping hundreds of feet into the air—bright and feral—as they licked the sky above the tormented trees, which bent and swayed under the relentless onslaught. Their crowns merged into a continuous blaze that threatened to consume them entirely.

Meanwhile, Mary worked hard, her focus unwavering as she executed a perfect face cut beneath the lean of a towering tree. With grace and precision that spoke to her years of experience, she swung the saw like a maestro, expertly guiding the blade into the back of the tree while simultaneously clearing the holding wood—leaving more holding wood on one side to guide the fall of the tree away from its lean. I watched intently, my heart racing as the back cut took shape. The tree began to sway slowly toward the fire line, its movements deliberate and ominous. The tension in the air thickened as it swung away from the line, narrowly avoiding the inferno.

Suddenly, from above, Carol's voice cut through the chaos—a warning that rang loud and clear: "Tree coming down!" Mary, ever vigilant, continued her cutting, her senses heightened, fully alert to the dangers that lurked above. In this environment, she knew the slightest distraction could mean the difference between safety and disaster.

Mary hailed from the serene yet rugged landscapes of upstate New York, where rolling hills framed the backdrop of her youth. She had carved out a space for herself among the vibrant rhododendrons blooming along the slopes of Mount Hood, where nature thrived in its most stunning forms. This lush environment not only invigorated her spirit but also became the stage for her remarkable physical prowess.

Being in exceptional shape came naturally to her—a fact born of relentless dedication to working at a bustling ski area that thrived during the winter months. Day in and day out, she navigated the slopes with grace and agility, honing her skills as she skied through fresh powder and raced down mountain trails. Each winter, she immersed herself in the thrill of outdoor challenges, embodying a lifestyle that was as exhilarating as it was demanding. That connection to the wild mountains forged her into a formidable firefighter and sawyer, capable of tackling even the most daunting challenges the forest presented.

Meanwhile, Carol diligently cut into the tree that leaned heavily toward the fireside of the line, its massive trunk almost groaning under the tension of the moment. Just a minute earlier, the falling boss had delivered a stern lecture, warning that there was no way she could bring down a tree with such a pronounced lean in the opposite direction. He spoke from limited experience, a truth that rang in his voice as he stressed the importance of understanding a tree's natural inclination.

Despite the odds stacked against her, Carol remained undeterred. Her determination shone through as she made the back cut—slowly, methodically—with the precision of a skilled artisan at work.

Kay, her steadfast friend, pounded wedges into the back cut of the tree with a rhythmic intensity that echoed through the tense atmosphere, each strike creating a thunderous heartbeat that matched the urgency of their situation. The air thickened with the scent of charred wood and the distant roar of the fire, but her determination held firm. Both she and Kay hailed from the rugged Upper Peninsula of Michigan—a place where the wildness of the Great Lakes had infused their spirits with an indomitable zest for life.

Together, they had ventured westward, leaving behind the familiar landscapes of their youth—but not the cherished memories of their shared past. They often reminisced about evenings spent with friends from back home, feasting on Swedish meatballs, savoring the rich flavors of potato sausage, and indulging in Kalv sylta—a dish that brought them straight back to the heart of their home. Laughter always followed, especially over bowls of rice pudding, the sweet final touch to those carefree gatherings.

Kay, with her exceptional skills, never played a passive role in this dangerous operation. She often took on the challenge of falling a burning snag herself—a testament to her courage and expertise. It was that fearless spirit, combined with her unbreakable bond with her partner, that drove them both to face the inferno with tenacity, ready for whatever obstacles lay ahead.

Her EMT bag strapped tightly across her back, Kay kept the wedges about six inches apart, deliberately choosing the spacing to maintain stability as the tree began to respond to the pressure. Sensing the shift, she doubled down, adding two more wedges—one plastic, one metal—stacked to prevent slipping. The combined strength of the wedges worked in concert, and slowly, the tree transitioned from its precarious angle to a vertical stance, as if obeying a silent command.

Then, with an exhilarating rush, the tree fell cleanly into its intended lay—away from the fire—its crash sending a thunderous boom through the forest. The falling boss, unimpressed and perhaps irritated by the unorthodox success of the operation, stomped off, leaving a trail of frustration in his wake.

I, meanwhile, on the Silver Fire, found myself deep in it—throwing brush for this saw team, making sure they had the space and safety to operate. I had directed the saw operations with a sharp eye, maintaining unwavering focus as I orchestrated the crew's movements. Uphoff and Pearson served as my main sawyers—two of the best in the business—backed up by Gale, Ford, Jim, Mary, LeRoy, and Carol. Each member stood ready to step in when needed, prepared to lend their strength and expertise. Together, we were a cohesive unit—a Hotshot crew forged in the fires of experience and companionship, willing to face whatever the day would bring.

Alongside Pearson, Mary, and Carol, the entire crew keenly felt Jim's absence. His cheerful demeanor and infectious energy had always motivated them; his presence was like a missing piece in a complex puzzle. A former Marine with impressive physicality, Jim had effortlessly sprinted up steep mountainsides, and his winter ski patrol experience had only amplified his already remarkable conditioning.

He hadn't been just any firefighter; he had excelled with a saw, wielding it with an expertise that set him apart even among the best. It was as if he'd been born with the saw in his hands, every cut precise and intentional. Even while carrying a grueling 70-pound pack, he had kept pace without breaking stride, as if the weight was nothing. Jim's unique balance of strength and skill made him a true powerhouse in the field—and his absence echoed like a heavy loss in the hearts of those who had worked beside him.

Back on the Silver Fire, the sun moved steadily across a vast expanse of cloudless blue, casting a golden hue over the rugged terrain. His thoughts drifted to Mary and Carol, two formidable women who had once played an integral role in the crew but no longer stood by his side. A wave of nostalgia washed over him; he couldn't shake the longing for their companionship and skill. He missed the strength and determination they had brought to every task, meeting every challenge head-on.

They had chosen to start families—a decision he respected deeply. Yet, it left a noticeable void in the team dynamic. Spending sixty out of sixty-one days on fires didn't lend itself to nurturing a family, and he understood their decision to prioritize their new roles as mothers. Still, their absence weighed on him, a constant reminder of the sacrifices made in the name of personal growth.

His mind wandered back to the Hotshot superintendent workshop earlier that year, where discussions had flared over the topic of affirmative action. The women leading the session had boldly asserted that, even if women didn't possess the ability to run saws, they still needed inclusion on saw squads. When he pointed out that he'd shown slides of women effectively running saws, the response had been sharp: he was "setting women up to fail because women did not have the ability to run saws."

The words struck a deep nerve, igniting a fury that hadn't left him since. He had muttered under his breath, "I call bullshit on that," his words heavy with frustration and disbelief.

I caught the tail end of Keller's question when he asked, "You call bullshit on what?" His voice remained calm—a stark contrast to the emotions swirling within me. As the sun dipped below the ridge, its last rays painted the sky in deep orange and purple hues. A thin veil of smoke began to cool the sun that September night, casting an almost ethereal atmosphere.

Keller, the poet—ever the contemplative soul—slipped into deep thought, likely pondering my frustration and the complexities of our world. He reflected on the slow, cold suns and the myriads of different times we had experienced together—each moment in the field a testament to resilience and shared purpose. In that fleeting silence, he felt the weight of his choices, the challenges ahead, and the undeniable bond that had been forged amid flames and ash.

As the last remnants of daylight faded into the horizon, Keller lost himself in thought, letting his mind drift through verses of poetry that danced like shadows in the twilight. Meanwhile, I delved into my own philosophical musings, contemplating the intricacies of my role as a foreman on the hotshot crew—feeling the weight of responsibility and the ever-present threat of danger. The rest of the crew, each absorbed in their own reflections, shared a silent camaraderie that spoke volumes in the stillness of the evening.

The cold sun, once a fierce and relentless orb, surrendered to the encroaching coolness of the September night, casting a serene air over the land. Darkness settled over us like a soothing blanket, bringing peace after the chaos of the day. One by one, the crew gathered their sweat-soaked tools, the soft clinks and rustling sounds echoing in the quiet. They took one last swig of water, savoring the refreshment that quenched their thirst and offered a brief moment of respite.

Keller remained lost in thought, pondering his poetry.

ON THE CLOVER-MIST WILDFIRE
YELLOWSTONE NATIONAL PARK

> *"Grizzly Bear: Omnivorous, fearless—without anxiety—steady—generous—contemplative—relentlessly protective of the wild."*
>
> Gary Snyder

We do not think
about the flames

as they curl
arm and beard
hair black.

We do not worry
about the flames

that explode
in these trees
all around us.

Our minds forget
about the flames

that chase us
back down
Clover Creek.

Our fears here
in this forgotten
Absaroka Range

dance only with
the great dark shape
and telltale stink

of bear.

Paul Keller

Krutilla reflected on his philosophy. The rest of the crew lingered in their own minds. The cold sun disappeared into the cool September night. It was dark and quiet now. The crew collected their tools, took one final drink of water, and began the walk back along the line of mineral soil that had been carved earlier by the Mount Adams crew. Down the slope they streamed toward Briggs' ranch.

They paused where the Boise Hotshot crews had burned out, lighting up the night. Goatsbeard and dry moss blew gently over the line, sparking small spot fires that the crew quickly snuffed out with their tools and the last of their canteen water. The fire cooled.

The Superintendent called Krutilla on the radio. "Do you think we should stay on the line?" he asked.

I radioed back that I would stay a bit longer. "The Goatsbeard's still throwing small spots over the line," I said.

The Superintendent relayed to the rest of the crew that we were pulling out immediately. We made our way down to the Illinois River Trail—a stream of headlamps cutting through the dark—until we came to rest in the fields of drying grass, hanging low and mournful at Briggs' ranch.

It was another restless night for me in that paper sleeping bag. As I warmed up, poison oak burned into my legs, across my chest, and down my arms, until I finally crept out into the cool night air. I stayed out until I froze, the cold dulling the pain, then slipped back into the bag. I heard coughing and hacking as the cold we'd brought from the Tiller Complex spread through the camp. We woke to a meal, huddled around the heat of diesel-burning smudge pots, eating breakfast that had been warmed in five-gallon cans.

CHAPTER 6

LAPINE

Smoke hung low over Briggs Ranch, a thick blanket of gray cloaking the landscape in an unsettling haze. In the distant dark, figures slowly emerged from their sleeping bags, silhouettes shifting cautiously in the dim light. At first, they appeared only as shadows against the swirling smoke, but as they shuffled toward the flickering smudge pots, the faint glow revealed their outlines. Each movement was deliberate, as if they were navigating a dream—hesitant yet determined. The smudge pots kept them warm against the morning chill.

A simpler time? The question lingered in the air, heavy with a sense of nostalgia. But they didn't just recall a simpler time; they remembered one fraught with complexities that seemed only to deepen. When faced with obvious wrongness—like the crackling roar of a forest fire consuming everything in its path—and when so much was at stake, they tried to obscure the truth. In such moments, clarity became a luxury, and they summoned smoke and darkness to veil what they could not bear to see.

"Ask the stupid question," one figure murmured, their voice barely audible over the crackle of fire and the distant thunder of flames. "Ask it like you seriously want an answer." The urgency in their tone carried a desperate need to avoid confronting the harsh realities just beyond the smoke.

"Keep attacking," another voice called out, rising above the quiet. "Keep attacking. If they're too busy defending themselves, they might miss the hitch in the goose steps." The words hung in the air like a challenge—a rallying cry to stay vigilant amid the chaos. The figures pressed closer to the smudge pots, their faces illuminated in flickering shadows, revealing expressions laced with fear and determination. Each knew the battle for survival had only just begun.

Years later, after the relentless flames had finally subsided and the devastation began to blur in the collective memory of those who endured it, the Agency's chief found himself wrapped in a thick fog of lament. He sat at his desk, papers strewn haphazardly across its surface—each crumpled sheet a stark reminder of the dire reality looming over them.

The weight of his responsibilities pressed heavily on his shoulders as he contemplated the grave issue at hand. The Agency was grappling with a significant and alarming dearth of strike team leaders—those critical figures who held the front lines together in the fight against the fires devouring vast swathes of the western landscape. Each leader served as a linchpin in the intricate machinery of firefighting, and without them, chaos reigned. As he sifted through the disarray of reports and memos, his mind churned with the implications of their absence, the thought beating like a war drum: how could they possibly face nature's fury without the seasoned guidance of those who had led before?

The fires blazed with unrelenting ferocity, consuming everything in their path, while the crews meant to battle them languished in camp—idle, restless—because there was no overhead structure to guide them into action. The chief furrowed his brow, frustration knotting in his gut, as the question pounded in his thoughts: Why were no strike team leaders available to mobilize the crews?

Suddenly, from the quiet of his own home, my voice rang out—sharp, cutting through the air like a blade. "You don't have any strike team leaders because you fired them all, you dumbshits!" I shouted, my words soaked in disbelief and contempt. The absurdity of it stoked my anger. Of course, the Agency hadn't fired them outright—that would've been too blatant, too dishonorable. Instead, they had laid them off, sidelined them, and left them without a place in the system. And if any dared to return, they faced the bitter truth that "their asses would be nailed to a cross," a fate that felt more real than metaphorical.

In firefighting, strike team leaders were vital. They coordinated two crews simultaneously, forming the essential bridge in the command structure. Without them, disorder took root, leaving crews exposed and adrift. My mind raced, haunted by the consequences of that gaping absence, knowing full well that survival on the line depended on strong, competent leadership.

Back in 1986, the freeze on hiring permanent employees had lifted. But a logjam of qualified men created a barrier that kept many from landing the coveted positions known as "permanents" within the Forest Service. These roles came with fire retirement—shortened due to the brutal wear on the body—and health insurance. But the bottleneck blocked the agency from hiring its so-called "cream of the crop," who, by definition, were not men. They couldn't meet their "hard target" in hiring, which amounted to an illegal quota. By the end of 1987, the purge of seasonal male employees was in full swing, and those with the most experience and qualifications carried the biggest targets on their backs.

"Atta Boy." I felt the warm hand against my back. It was a familiar phrase. The engine forewoman's hand gave me a hearty pat just as I emerged from the cramped confines of the bathroom. The forewoman, a robust woman with husky blonde hair framing her face, had just returned from a series of fire assignments. While she was out on fires, I remained behind at the Ranger station, tethered by what they deemed my "value" as a GS-4 temporary worker—too valuable to join the crews facing down the burning infernos out of state, where the money was and the fires more extreme.

Instead, I picked up the slack, filling in for the GS-5s, 7s, and even 9s on the Lapine district. During their absence, I took it upon myself to mentor the new temps, imparting my extensive knowledge about the intricacies of firefighting. I taught them the essentials of the trade—how to pump water effectively, how to draft from various sources, how to lay hoses efficiently, and how to identify the telltale signs of a fire, even before it became visible.

However, the engine forewoman struggled with some of these fundamental skills, having never received proper training in the art of firefighting. This lack of experience left her feeling indignant, an emotion that only intensified her frustration. Although her supervisors explained that they thought she possessed these skills when they hired her, she remained upset. Recognizing her predicament, the supervisors decided it was my responsibility to take her under my wing and guide her through the learning process.

With each lesson, I felt the reassuring pat on my back—a gesture of encouragement that became a recurring motif. "Atta Boy," I heard again as I patiently taught her the intricacies of pumping, demonstrating the mechanics with a steady hand and clear instructions. "Atta Boy," I heard once more as I guided her through the drafting process, a method of filling the engine from a stream. "Atta Boy," echoed again when I showed her the proper way to lay hoses. "Atta Boy," she said as I taught her to run the pump on the back of the engine she drove, each step reinforced with careful explanations and supportive words.

There was one area where I didn't need to intervene: finding fires. The forewoman possessed a peculiar "psychic" ability that, according to her, would quickly kick in, allowing her to sense fires before they became visible to the naked eye. This unique talent served as a point of pride for her, a special gift that set her apart from others in the field. Ironically, she never found a fire that year.

As a result of the low morale permeating the ranks, the Ranger—the top bureaucrat at the agency—had recently instructed supervisors across the board to offer their workers "Atta Boys," a simple yet "very important form of positive reinforcement." With that thought lingering in my mind, I made my way toward the district meeting. "Atta Boy." I felt the pat on the back from the assistant fire manager as I entered the building.

The year was 1989, a time marked by significant change and tension within the ranks of those who fought the relentless forces of nature. I now found myself in a role that felt worlds apart from the fierce and fiery battles I'd once engaged in as a firefighter. I was part of a brush disposal crew—a position that felt more like a shadow of my former self. The only other member of the crew was my supervisor, Weinrich, who oversaw our operations with quiet efficiency.

"The vehicle is brain dead," Weinrich announced over the crackling radio, his voice tinged with laughter. We were marooned on a winding mountain road, surrounded by towering pines that swayed gently in the breeze. The vehicle, a sturdy workhorse that had clearly seen better days, had come to a sudden halt—stubbornly immobile, as if it had decided it would go no further. The tow truck driver, a burly man with grease-stained hands and a weary expression, delivered the disheartening diagnosis: the vehicle's brain was not functioning.

"Yes," Weinrich reiterated over the radio, "the vehicle is indeed brain dead. We need someone to pick us up." His tone was clipped, but the underlying humor didn't escape me. I couldn't help but chuckle at the absurdity of the situation.

It had been a long, challenging day that left me both drained and accomplished. The day before, an agency man had asked, "How long will it take you to do the project he described?"

"I don't know," I replied, feeling uncertainty settle around me. I'd have to see it. He laughed, revealing he'd already asked Weinrich the same question—clearly trying to pressure the ever-diligent Weinrich, whose legendary commitment struck me as a bit ironic.

The project involved pulling a light brush load away from a designated line. As the agency man explained the details to Weinrich, I sprang into action. I methodically maneuvered the brush, the crunch of twigs and leaves beneath my feet as I dragged it into place. I kept about 100 feet behind the agency man, who was too absorbed in his explanation to notice.

As the agency man wrapped up his explanations and took his leave, Weinrich turned his attention back to me, instructing me on how to execute the project—just as I put the finishing touches on the task. With a burst of enthusiasm, Weinrich grabbed the radio, his voice brightening as he called the agency man. "We are done! Any more week-long projects you want us to do this morning?" he asked, a playful challenge embedded in his tone. He flashed a grin and gave me a conspiratorial wink.

Together, we completed in two months what was initially expected to take two years of labor by a six-person crew. That team had already dispersed to other jobs by the time we wrapped up the task.

Despite our efficiency, I grappled with the reality that my role felt far removed from the adrenaline rush of confronting wildfires. Vivid, haunting memories lingered—racing toward the heart of a blaze, every second stretching into eternity, the heat enveloping me like an all-consuming embrace. Instead of wielding tools and instincts honed through years of experience, I now bore the responsibility of teaching engine foremen the intricate and nuanced techniques of fire management and suppression.

I remembered the days when the very air seemed to crackle, the world blurred in smoke and flame. I stood at the center then—a warrior facing the elements head-on. Each instruction I gave to eager recruits became a bittersweet echo of those lost moments, a reminder of a kind of purpose that only comes from being immersed in the fight. The weight of my current responsibility pressed heavily on me, a constant reminder that while I now stood on the sidelines, the fire still raged—waiting for no one.

This duty, though undeniably crucial to our firefighting efforts, felt like an immense burden—heavy, unyielding, wrapping around me like a dense fog. Each day, as I navigated the complex work of passing on knowledge to eager novices, I wrestled with the realization that I was now guiding others through the very skills that once defined my own fierce, adrenaline-fueled battles. Those wildfires, wild and untamed, once demanded everything I had. Now, they seemed barely a footnote in the agency's larger agenda.

The thought of standing before eager, hopeful faces—eyes filled with ambition, determination, and dreams of heroism—fills me with a profound longing. A longing that reaches beyond the dangerous beauty of flickering flames. I miss the camaraderie I shared with my fellow firefighters. I yearn for the thrill of rushing into the inferno, the shared surge of adrenaline, and the undeniable sense of purpose that came from standing shoulder to shoulder in the fight against nature's fiery wrath.

Each time I instructed inexperienced crew members, I remembered the heat that once wrapped around me like a second skin—the acrid smoke that stung my eyes and made my throat ache, the heart-pounding rush that came with every successful maneuver to tame the wild forces of nature. These memories swirled in my mind—vivid and tantalizing—stark against the reality I now faced, where I stood more as a mentor than a warrior. I felt more like a teacher than a combatant, and the fire that once fueled my spirit now flickered in the distance—tantalizing, yet frustratingly out of reach.

Each lesson reminded me of what I once was. While I understood the importance of passing on my knowledge to the next generation of firefighters, I couldn't help but feel like I was fading into the background. The weight of that realization settled heavily on me, like a cloak made of lead, as I stood before their eager faces, offering wisdom that echoed my past with bittersweet clarity.

My knowledge had become invaluable, often indispensable, as I was frequently the first person called to respond to local blazes. It was a role that pulled me back into the line of danger, where the thrill of facing the flames again felt both intoxicating and terrifying. I remembered the heat licking at my skin, the smoke burning my lungs—memories that flooded my senses with nostalgia and dread. Each call to action brought back the fierce rhythm of past confrontations with nature's fury. And while I relished the chance to fight again, I couldn't shake the gnawing sense that I had been relegated to a role where I must teach rather than lead—a reality that clung to me like a persistent itch.

Still, I couldn't ignore the irony of my situation. I was no longer classified as a firefighter in the traditional sense. That title now belonged to the so-called "cream of the crop"—an elite group composed of a few genuinely skilled individuals and many who fell far short of the lofty expectations assigned to them. These so-called elites often lounged in the warehouse, radiating smug superiority, while I labored in the field, extinguishing flames and managing nature's aftermath—overlooked, undervalued.

As I watched this dynamic unfold, resentment simmered beneath the surface. The agency's shifting hierarchy had created a world where experience and grit seemed secondary to arbitrary classifications—classifications that elevated the unworthy and diminished those who had earned their place. The contrast between my hard-won knowledge and the complacency of those resting on unearned laurels weighed heavily on me—a constant reminder that the line between worthy and unworthy had blurred in the shifting sands of agency politics. I was left grappling with a sense of disillusionment that wrapped around me like a heavy shroud.

In 1990, a significant case emerged—*Bragdon v. Yeutor*—a case that many would struggle to uncover without the aid of the Freedom of Information Act. The court ultimately ruled that the agency in question could not engage in discriminatory practices against men. The ruling, however, sparked a frenzy of confusion and frustration within the station where the ranger—the top administrative officer—presided, and where I now worked in Montana.

She darted about, her high-pitched voice piercing the air as she exclaimed, "How can we meet our hard target if we cannot discriminate against men?" The words echoed through the hallways, laced with a bewildering mix of panic and desperation, revealing her struggle with a concept that felt utterly foreign. The idea of a civil rights policy that didn't permit discrimination against a particular group baffled her; nothing in her graduate school coursework had prepared her for this.

The agency brought in its think tank, and the following year, she proudly announced, "People hired to fight forest fires do not have to fight forest fires." She had clearly taken the same college classes as the Lapine Ranger. Despite her confusion, the agency navigated the convoluted legal terrain. By 1991, they arrived at a startling conclusion: individuals hired to combat wildfires didn't need any actual experience or knowledge of firefighting—because they weren't required to fight fires.

Hiring someone inexperienced over a seasoned firefighter no longer constituted discrimination. This policy shift opened the door for anyone to be thrust into the hazardous world of wildland fire, much to her delight, as it enabled her to meet what she called her "hard target." By the 1990s, crews began to burn up again, unlike in the 1980s.

Overall Fatality Trends: The USDA Forest Service notes a general downward trend in wildland firefighter fatalities from the 1930s to the 2000s, though significant year-to-year fluctuations occurred. The 1990s, in particular, saw a spike in fatalities due to a few major, tragic events.

As I stood there in the dim light of the night, I couldn't help but reflect on my own journey—recalling the days of my youth when I passionately circulated open housing petitions and accompanied my mother, a dedicated Head Start teacher, to segregated schools. Those moments sparked something in me—a fire for civil rights that continued to burn brightly as I confronted the rampant anti-gay sentiment of 1981.

I fought against the odds, breaking barriers by including women in my saw rotation—a bold move that challenged the status quo and defied those who believed women lacked the strength or capability to operate chainsaws. The memory left a bitter taste in my mouth as I thought back to the cat pile fire in 1989.

CHAPTER 7

CAT PILES

It was in 1989, working for LaPine, that my most recent memory of working alongside a Hot Shot crew occurred. I joined the brush disposal crew, tasked with burning a logging unit located in a different district.

I walked the line around the unit—a small area of about three acres above a road—scanning for potential hazards and inefficiencies. That's when I spotted the hoses, those vital lifelines soon to assist in containing the fire. They lay haphazardly across the ground, tied in knots—a disarray that sent a shiver down my spine. It was an ominous sign, one that could spell disaster. I approached the individual in charge, a firefighter who exuded a blend of authority and weariness, and voiced my concern with urgency: "Where I come from, tied hoses mean bad hoses." My words hung in the air, heavy with the weight of unspoken truths.

With determination coursing through me, I took it upon myself to re-plumb the entire unit with high-quality hoses, ensuring everything was set up correctly and methodically untangling the chaos before me. All the while, a Hot Shot crew stood nearby, watching with a mix of curiosity. Despite their reputation as the best of the best, they chose to observe rather than engage today—their confidence in their own abilities rendering them passive in the face of the challenge.

Once I completed the task, my next assignment involved supervising the holding operation on the far side of the unit. But as the minutes ticked by and conditions remained unfavorable for ignition, it became painfully clear we couldn't get the unit to burn as planned. The anticipated flames stubbornly refused to ignite. In a sudden shift of roles, I found myself not only overseeing the holding operation but also stepping into the role of a lighter, prepared to ignite the fire myself. I embraced the challenge, though I knew splitting responsibilities was never a good idea.

When I finished, I found myself in the throes of what could only be described as a classic Hot Shot moment—I heaved, my body rebelling against the sweltering heat and the strain of my labor. With sweat dripping down my brow and the acrid scent of smoke thick in the air, I knelt on the ground beneath a towering column of smoke, my hands pressed to the gritty earth as I searched for any hidden spots that might flare unexpectedly. The ground was rough and unforgiving beneath my fingertips, the heat radiating from the fire creating an oppressive atmosphere that made it hard to focus amid the chaos.

Suddenly, the sharp crackle of the radio broke through the tension, accompanied by a panicked voice that sliced through the air like a knife, urgently declaring, "There is a spot fire." A spot fire is a fire at a distance from the main fire, caused by sparks or airborne embers from snags or other burning material. I paused for a moment, straining my ears as I awaited a response from the Hot Shot crew, who had stationed themselves at the top of the unit, entirely secure in their position. These crews, known for their swift reactions and teamwork, seemed unusually silent, leaving me with a growing sense of unease—a gnawing worry that something was amiss.

After what felt like a short eternity, I took the initiative and pressed down on the radio key with a firm grip, my voice steady despite the chaos around me. "Where is the spot fire?" I inquired, trying to keep my tone calm and assertive, as I sensed the urgency of the situation. The same frantic voice crackled back through the static: "It is over there." The lack of clarity hit like a wave, and frustration followed close behind.

Realizing the futility of trying to communicate any further over the radio, I decided to take matters into my own hands. I pushed myself up from the ground, determination fueling my movements as I made my way toward the place where the smoke column had been bending ominously—a telltale sign of dropping embers.

Upon arriving, I spotted a cat pile ablaze among others that had not yet ignited, the fire flickering defiantly in the distance, about a quarter to a half mile away. It felt both familiar and unsettling—a sharp reminder of fire's unpredictability. I assessed the situation and concluded the best approach was to let the pile burn out while preparing for the worst. I brought down bladder bags, ready to handle any new spots that might ignite nearby.

About two hours later, the Hot Shot crew ambled into the spot fire—now burned out. Lost in the moment, I drifted back to a vivid memory from 1985. The recollection washed over me like a warm wave, bringing with it the sights and sounds of that summer—a time when the world felt simpler, yet still fraught with danger. I could almost hear the crackle of the underbrush and feel the cool mountain breeze against my skin, a bittersweet reminder of days gone by.

That year proved particularly busy, and the crew buzzed with energy as we joined another team on the Hubbard Creek Fire. I took on the role of crew boss, a position I often held that season, remembering the adrenaline as the other assistant crew boss from this Hot Shot crew and I flagged a fire line along an alpine ridge. The cool night stood in sharp contrast to the day's heat, the starry sky above twinkling like burning holes in the darkness—showcasing nature's beauty and its peril.

In that moment, standing in the present, I reflected on how quickly time passed—and how each fire season brought new challenges and a constant dance with danger. Now, at the spot fire, I faced the former crew boss of the Hot Shot crew, the tension palpable in the air.

The recently demoted assistant crew boss, now working on an engine, leaned in slightly, a furrow forming between his brows. "I've heard your name. I know I've heard your name before," he said. His voice, though steady, carried a hint of curiosity laced with unresolved annoyance—a flickering ember of tension igniting beneath the surface.

I responded with a calm yet pointed tone, "That's because I applied to your crew, asking for a grade GS-2 or above. I didn't even get a call from you." The words hung between us, heavy with frustration. I felt it boil just beneath the surface—the effort I'd put into that application, the anticipation met with silence, a stark reminder of the bureaucratic indifference that often defined our world.

He crossed his arms, irritation flickering in his eyes. "This crew is going to burn up," he said. "They had to hire seven people with no experience. They shifted me to an engine foreman." The implications of his words settled heavily between us—a grim reminder of what was at stake, a reality none of us could afford to ignore. "I'm quitting and taking a job with a helicopter in Alaska." His final words lingered in the air, a declaration that left little room for argument, the uncertainty of the future looming over us like smoke before a flare-up.

That night in 1989, under the oppressive cloak of darkness, I stood at the edge of the dying fire in the cat pile, watching the crew waddle up, their heavy footsteps echoing hollowly in the stillness. The fire had dwindled to wisps of smoke, the last few sparks whispering into the night—a ghost of the chaos that had once raged.

A gnawing thought twisted in my mind, relentless and foreboding: *this crew is going to burn up.* It clung to me like smoke, a dark premonition that would prove tragically true just two years later, when disaster struck in Montana—claiming the lives of many members of that Hot Shot crew, along with members of a Smokejumping crew that tried to help them.

CHAPTER 8

BACK TO BRIGGS

In 1989, as I stood at the edge of the dying fire, a shiver coursed through my body—a visceral reaction to the chill of the night air. The last embers of the cat pile surrendered to the stillness of the dead night, leaving behind a haunting silence. The surrounding darkness pressed in, and the starlight that had once brought comfort vanished, devoured by the thick smoke hanging in the air.

In that moment, I felt overwhelmed, choking and hacking uncontrollably as the oppressive smoke clung to me—a stark reminder of the chaos that had unfolded at Briggs Ranch two years earlier. At Briggs, my crew bustled around me, their movements a flurry of activity as they filled their water bottles with fresh, cold water. I heard splashing mingled with the low murmur of voices drifting through the air. I tightened my web gear and adjusted our headlamps, their beams flickering to life in the dim light of dawn. Web gear is what we wore to hold our canteens and meals.

The sun had yet to rise, casting the world in a heavy darkness, thick with foreboding. The crisp morning air bit sharply against my skin as I braced for the challenges ahead. The rugged terrain of the Illinois River Trail stretched before me, the ground hard and unforgiving beneath my boots. A stream of headlamps snaked around the bend toward the Silver Prairie Trail, the lights fading into the smoke that clung to the ridge, shrouding our path in an eerie haze.

The crew paused briefly at the spot where the fire had slopped over the containment line—right where I'd suggested we stay the night before. It wasn't an extreme slop-over. Sparks from Goatsbeard had crossed the line, dropping fire to the ground. Within a few hours, we lined it and continued from where we'd left off the day before.

As the first rays of sunlight pierced through the thick smoke, casting a dim glow over the landscape, our determination intensified. The faint golden light caught our faces, creating a surreal contrast against the swirling gray. With renewed focus, we plunged into cutting line; the saws bit into the brush, carving out a narrow path that would serve as a crucial barrier against the encroaching flames.

Just as we found our rhythm, the Mt. Adams crew—a neighboring unit—arrived to lend support. They quickly assessed the situation and determined that only three individuals needed to dig down to mineral soil, freeing the rest of us to concentrate on clearing brush. The collaboration unfolded seamlessly.

The saw squad faced an overwhelming challenge. Despite their efforts in wielding their saws, they quickly realized the saw squads were simply not deep enough to handle the sheer volume of debris hurled around by seventeen other individuals. The atmosphere transformed into a congested whirlwind of limbs and fallen branches, creating a chaotic ballet that threatened to ensnare anyone caught in the fray.

Suddenly, the superintendent grabbed a saw, his determination evident as he cut with a frenzy that bordered on reckless. The saw ripped through the holding wood, sending the trees spiraling backward toward the crew, a scene unfolding in slow motion. The holding wood acted as a hinge, directing the fall of the tree.

I instinctively pulled my squad back, my instincts screaming to create distance from the falling danger. The superintendent, oblivious to the risks, noticed and quickly assumed that Krutilla was once again sabotaging him. Why would Krutilla be pulling people back?

He believed he was being safe—clad in goggles, protective chaps, and earplugs. In his eyes, it was Krutilla who was being reckless. Hadn't he lectured him earlier about the importance of earplugs?

I cast a glance toward the superintendent, who tried to comfort Juli, who had barely escaped a falling tree, the fear still etched on her face. Trees lay scattered in different directions, creating a chaotic landscape that would take time to clean up—a mess that reflected the turmoil of the day. Krutilla placed a wad of Copenhagen in his mouth, watching as the crew's momentum slowed to a crawl, the energy draining from their bodies like sunlight fading from the sky. I gazed over the Kalmiopsis wilderness, where the peaks of the Big Craggies rolled endlessly toward the horizon, a reminder of the vastness of nature. Despite the turmoil around me, I savored the moment, knowing it would be one of my last.

Recognizing the escalating risk around me, I took swift action, making a decisive call that shifted the course of our efforts. My voice cut through the clamor as I gathered a portion of the crew, led them away from the chaotic fray, and guided them up toward the relative safety of Silver Prairie—an area where we wouldn't need saws to cut line. The path to Silver Prairie was steep and uneven. Upon reaching the clearing, I met Hunt, the assistant superintendent, who took on the vital role of lookout for the crew. Hunt's watchful eyes scanned the horizon for any signs of danger—a vigilant guardian in the face of the unpredictable fire looming just beyond our reach. He would let us know if the fire blew up and threatened us.

In this more serene setting, my crew and I prepared to cut line down to Conner's Place, buoyed by the relative calm. The line we had established earlier began at the far edge of Brigg's Ranch, a few days before our arrival, tracing a winding path up the ridge toward the expansive openness of Silver Prairie. Conner's Place, a significant landmark in our operations, lay approximately six miles upriver from Brigg's Ranch—a sharp contrast to the chaotic scene we had just left behind, where danger had felt immediate.

When we completed our work, we created a substantial triangle of unburned area amidst the encroaching flames, forming a strategic barrier against the destruction threatening to consume everything in its path. The winding Illinois River Trail formed one side of this triangle, elegantly snaking through the landscape. We stretched the second side from Brigg's Ranch up the ridge to the picturesque Alpine Meadow. Finally, we connected Silver Prairie to Conner's Place, enclosing the triangle. That night, the night crew burned out the area of unburned fuel between the main fire and the fire line. When the humidity was high, the backfire lacked intensity, eliminating the unburned fuel between our line and the main fire.

Unlike the cacophony of saws relentlessly cutting through dense brush, a peaceful silence enveloped us, wrapping around the crew like a warm blanket on a cool evening. This tranquility was broken only by the occasional clanging of hand tools as they struck hidden rocks while we dug toward mineral soil—the metallic echoes resonating softly in the stillness. Intermittent, brief conversations flickered in and out, but these exchanges remained utilitarian. As we dug the line, we prioritized speed and efficiency, with little room for socializing. Moments of connection and laughter were reserved for the slower, more tedious mop-up process, when the urgency had passed and the work allowed for a brief respite.

Except for the bear grass, with its thick roots, I found the grass easy to remove. The line to mineral earth stopped the fire from creeping over. We made quick progress as we followed a spur ridge down toward the Illinois Gorge. Jeff flagged the fire line along the spur ridge to Conner's Place. Grimaldi took over as lookout; from where he stood, he could alert either crew to potential problems.

In front of Hunt, Silver Prairie spread along the mountainside in red, white, and blue. The red-orange flame of Indian Paintbrush contrasted with the white of bear grass and the blue of wild chicory mixed among its blades. Purple aster dotted the flag. No fire hung on this side of the ridge. The air felt sweet and cleared our lungs of smoke. The

Illinois Gorge lay below, with mountains stretching in a panoramic view toward the Pacific. The vision remained clear here.

As the rest of the crew diligently tied the brush line into the sprawling expanse of Silver Prairie, a sense of accomplishment settled over us like the gentle dusk creeping in, softening the edges of our world. With each stroke of our tools, we further defined and completed the line through Silver Prairie, creating a tangible testament to our hard work and perseverance in the face of adversity. Below the vastness of Silver Prairie, the vibrant green oak leaves that once dominated the landscape gradually gave way to towering Ponderosa pines, standing tall and proud against the backdrop of the evening sky. The rich scent of pine needles mingled with the coolness of the air, creating an invigorating atmosphere that sharpened our senses and reminded us of the beauty we fought to protect.

We labored tirelessly, steadily making our way down toward the Illinois River, which lay below, slumbering in its rocky bed, quietly anticipating our arrival. We carved the line out of the wilderness with determination as the waning light of a late Indian Summer afternoon cascaded around us, gradually yielding to the cooler embrace of evening. The sun, now a fiery orb dipping behind the horizon, cast a golden hue across the landscape, painting everything in warm shades of amber and bronze as we completed the task before night fully descended.

As the sun dipped behind the darkening ridge, it cast long shadows across the rugged terrain, and I reluctantly pulled away from my strenuous labor. A collective hacking and coughing echoed through the fading light, testifying to our fatigue and the toll of the day's work. The relentless chill of evening took its toll; colds crept among us like unwelcome intruders. The antihistamines I had on hand eased the worst of the symptoms—offering relief from the painful blisters on our sunburned skin and soothing the swelling around our eyes, which threatened to shut from the persistent irritation of poison oak.

Lost in thought, Keller pondered his poetry, while Krutilla considered his philosophy, and the rest of the crew drifted into their own reflections.

Thomas wrote songs in his head that he would later revise:

We came from all around
To fight the fire on the ground
We trained hard every day
Don't let that fire get away

We left our homes behind
To battle nature's worst design
A season at her best
Storm King Mountain was their test
The front page told the rest

(Chorus)
Oh... they were Hotshots, proud to be
Part of the Region 6 IHC
They risked their lives almost every day
To keep Mother Nature's flames at bay
Until that day

Oh... they were Hotshots, proud to be
Part of the Region 6 IHC
Too much smoke on too much angle
They got caught in the fire triangle

The cold sun disappeared into the cool September night. It was dark and peaceful now. The crew gathered their sweat-soaked tools, took one last swig of water, and walked back along the line of mineral soil we had cut. Down the crew streamed toward Brigg's Ranch.

We stopped where the Boise Hotshot crews had burned out, their work illuminating the night. Goatsbeard and dry moss drifted gently over the line, causing small spot fires that we quickly extinguished with our tools and the last of the water in our canteens. The fire cooled. The superintendent called Krutilla on the radio.

"Do you think we should stay on the line?" he asked.

I radioed back that I would stay a bit longer. The Goatsbeard was still causing small spots over the line. The superintendent then radioed the rest of the crew to inform them that we were pulling out immediately.

We pulled back down to the Illinois River Trail, a stream of head-lamps flowing through the dark until we came to rest in the fields of drying grass at Briggs' Ranch, hanging low and mournful.

We made our way in the dark to the camp that awaited us, the atmosphere thick with fatigue and a lingering discomfort that hung heavy in the air. Donna, brimming with her usual spirited determination despite our ailments, partnered with me. She busied herself filling canteens with fresh water—the cool liquid glistening in the dimming light like liquid glass—while I set off in search of cold medicine and additional ointments to combat the effects of poison oak, which had wreaked havoc on our skin, leaving it red and inflamed.

Meanwhile, I noticed Keller and Donna, who had suffered most from the relentless grip of the poison oak, their faces blotchy and red—stark reminders of the invisible enemies lurking in the under-brush, waiting to ambush any unwary soul.

As we gathered in the dim light of the camp, the flickering fire cast dancing shadows around us. A sense of companionship began to form, binding us through our shared struggles and the quiet hope that tomorrow would bring relief. Stories and laughter fell short, cut off by exhaustion. But even so, we drew strength from one another, fortifying our spirits before giving in to the rest we desperately needed.

CHAPTER 9

TO CONNER'S PLACE

All truth passes through three stages:
first, it is ridiculed;
second, it is violently opposed;
third, it is accepted as self-evident.

Arthur Schopenhauer

What a beautifully crafted spin on the narrative. The federal government came crashing down upon us—a relentless force of nature, showing no mercy and offering no compassion to those of us who risked our lives daily. We constituted the entrenched good old boy power structure. Our privilege stood out so plainly that, even after a grueling decade of labor in the perilous world of firefighting—where we oversaw life-and-death situations day in and day out, often clinging to little more than a flicker of hope—we received a meager wage of just $7.28 an hour. It was a paltry sum, a cruel joke, especially considering the physical and emotional toll the job exacted from us.

To make matters worse, the system left us without health insurance or any semblance of retirement benefits to support us in our later years—an unforgiving reality that loomed like a dark cloud over our futures.

It was almost ironic—tragically fitting—that the government chose to remedy this profound injustice not by rewarding our sacrifices and unwavering dedication, but by denying us the benefits we had seemingly earned. "Thank God" for that, one might say, as we were transformed into the well-deserving scapegoats of the people—a reflection of society's need to blame and vilify rather than uplift and support those who risked everything for the greater good. The irony stung, a bitter aftertaste that lingered long after the discussions had faded.

The new day dawned, casting a golden hue across the rugged landscape and bringing with it the promise of challenges, as Hunt strode purposefully toward Conner's place—a modest, deserted homestead nestled in the vast Montana wilderness. The sun climbed higher, illuminating the dust motes dancing in the air, as Hunt—the veteran fireman—led the way, embodying the strength and determination that had defined him over the years. He walked at a steady pace, neither hurried nor lethargic, exuding a quiet confidence that inspired those around him. As the heart and soul of the crew, he was more than just a member; he stood as their unspoken leader, a guiding force who carried them through the tumultuous years from 1984 to 1987—years filled with trials that would have broken lesser men. His experience was marked by intense moments, such as those he faced during the harrowing Lake Mountain Fire and the Centennial Fire, where he stood resolute against raging infernos that threatened to consume everything in their path, including the homes of innocent families. With a fuzee in hand, he boldly confronted the fiery demons, his heart pounding as he battled the flames that roared like a beast unleashed. In those moments of bravery, Hunt solidified his role not only as a firefighter but as a protector of the community.

As I walked alongside him, he felt the hot wind whip against his face—a fierce gust carrying the scent of impending danger, a warning that resonated deep within. The wind rushed past, bending the yellowed cheatgrass that grew wild and untamed across the rolling hills, which stretched endlessly toward the distant horizon of Havre, Montana. Havre itself, swept by the same wind, seemed to exist in a vast expanse of nowhere—a quiet settlement marked by isolation and resilience. Each step we took felt heavy with the weight of responsibility, yet a thrill of purpose coursed through us, binding us together as we prepared to face whatever challenges the day might bring.

A column of thick, ominous smoke bent and swirled with the capricious wind, weaving its way toward the solitary house that stood resolute among the towering ponderosa pines. The rich, earthy aroma of the trees—usually so invigorating—barely registered now, overpowered by the smoke thickening the air, wrapping itself around everything like a suffocating shroud.

But the future loomed, and in just a few short years, 1987 would arrive with a harrowing twist of fate. I would vanish from the world of firefighting, never again holding a fire job, leaving behind a legacy shrouded in mystery. As the smoke billowed and spread across the horizon, it swallowed the last vestiges of a setting sun, darkening the sky and transforming it into a foreboding canvas of gray and black—a portent of the chaos that lay ahead.

In the eerie silence where I stood near the weathered house, the stillness broke only with the occasional rustle of leaves and the distant crackling of branches. The air thickened with tension, each moment stretching into eternity as I felt the weight of impending danger settle heavily on my shoulders—an oppressive reminder of the stakes at hand.

The thick, sour smoke—relentless and invasive—crept insidiously through the tinted lenses of my sunglasses, curling around the edges and filtering through the fabric of the bandana I had tightly secured around my mouth. It seeped in, a tangible reminder of the peril we faced, a physical manifestation of the chaos closing in. Just ahead, Mary, McAllister, Carol, and McCollister approached, their faces set with determination and urgency. Each wielded a garden hose, the nozzles aimed with precision as they sprinkled water onto the parched grass, creating a fragile barrier against the advancing flames. The sound of water hissing against dry earth offered a brief reprieve from the suffocating heat—a small oasis of hope amid the encroaching inferno.

Behind the trio, Dinard, Carol, and Roby worked in near-perfect harmony, synchronizing their movements as they laid out fire with a fuzee—a specialized tool used to unleash flames that roared back toward the main fire with ferocity. The flames leapt skyward, their fiery tongues licking hungrily at the dry brush. With every flicker of the blaze, glowing embers spiraled into the darkening sky, becoming tiny stars against the backdrop of impending night—a stark contrast to the destruction they fueled.

Roby, the fearless firefighter known for her unwavering spirit, sprinted down the escape route amidst the raging chaos of the Shaniko Butte Fire. Flames licked hungrily at her sides—a terrifying wall of heat and light that threatened to envelop her entirely—yet she pressed on, determination etched across her face. In front of her, I stood poised and ready, my eyes sharp and unyielding, prepared to leap into the heat and grab her at a moment's notice should she falter.

Roby's roots ran deep in the wild plains of South Dakota, where the vast expanses of land breathed life into her adventurous spirit. The sounds of ducks splashing in nearby marshes and the gentle caress of the wind weaving through her hair were memories that played like a soothing melody in her mind. Those tranquil days had shaped her, instilling a profound respect for nature's unpredictable temperament. Later, she ventured far from home, joining the Peace Corps in the Philippines, where she invested her time and energy teaching sustainable farming methods to local communities. It was a transformative experience—one that deepened her understanding of resilience and the strength that comes from unity.

After years of hard work on a brush disposal crew, Roby finally found her place among this elite group. Now, as she battled the ferocious flames for the third year on the Hotshot crew, she felt a sense of belonging that resonated deep within her soul. Each moment spent fighting alongside her teammates reminded her of the purpose that drove her—an unwavering commitment to protect the land and the people she loved from the encroaching darkness. In the face of the inferno, Roby stood tall, embodying the spirit of a true firefighter, ready to confront whatever challenges lay ahead.

As they carefully applied the fuzee, the air around them crackled with energy. Heat radiated off the ground, enveloping them in a stifling embrace. Dinardo's sharp, focused eyes scanned the environment with an expert's gaze, ever aware of the threat posed by the approaching flames. With each calculated move, Roby deftly guided the fuzee, igniting patches of grass that caught fire with a ferocious hunger, transforming the landscape into a chaotic dance of fire and smoke—a reflection of the turmoil within their hearts.

They worked swiftly, knowing every second counted. By wetting the nearby cheatgrass, they created a thin line of moisture—a precarious defense, a last-ditch effort they hoped would hold against the relentless advance of the inferno. The flames roared down the ridge with a ferocity that mesmerized and terrified, spitting out fifty-foot tongues of fire that rolled ominously toward the house—the very structure where the firefighters had set up their makeshift camp. In that moment, as the heat intensified and darkness encroached, the crew stood united, each member a vital thread in the tapestry of resilience they had woven together, ready to confront whatever fate lay ahead.

The house, once a sturdy refuge, now teetered on the edge of calamity, trembling in the face of the oncoming threat. The firefighters felt the heat radiating off the flames, a searing reminder of nature's volatile power. The urgency of their task weighed heavily on them. Each crackle and pop of the fire echoed in their ears, a constant reminder of how quickly they had to act to protect their camp—and each other—from the all-consuming blaze.

Elsewhere, Hunt, Gracie, and Juan put in a small handline uphill with a pond as their safety zone. Hunt made sure Gracie was monitoring our escape route. Everything was swirling around them. Gracie and Juan lit off the line. The burnout did not burn as cleanly as they wanted, yet they still had the pond as their safety zone. The evening was arriving, and with higher humidity, the burnout, though not complete, still saved the house from the fire.

Gracie and Juan then went to the third house Dinardo had saved from the fire. The owners arrived with ashen faces, saying, "Thank God." Gracie said, "Thank Dinardo."

Earlier that day, the crew had arrived on the fire, marking their journey with a frantic plane trip to Havre, followed by a bone-jarring bus ride to the Centennial Fire. They reached a disheveled fire camp, scorched and burned over, a haunting testament to the fire's destructive force. The heat threatened the wooden structures of the houses. As the urgency intensified, a heated discussion broke out at a fork in the road. In that chaotic moment, McAllister—driven by gut instinct—impulsively decided to steal a pickup truck loaded with essential tools. The situation left no room for hesitation. As the bus and truck sped toward the first of the threatened houses, McAllister felt a surge of adrenaline. He seized the vehicle because, in his eyes, the houses were under immediate threat while everyone else stood frozen on the road, paralyzed by indecision.

McAllister, a strikingly muscular Black man with a model-like face, vanished from the agency's ranks after the tumultuous year of 1986. He became an enigmatic figure, serving as Hunt's de facto assistant during their time together, seamlessly blending strength with intelligence in a way that commanded respect from his peers.

As the situation escalated, Hunt ignited the burnout from the rear of the house with his fuzee, sending a wave of heat and light cascading outward. Within minutes, the landscape transformed into a blackened wasteland—a stark contrast to the vibrant natural beauty that had once thrived there. The fire surged through the cheatgrass with insatiable hunger, racing back toward Havre as if on a mission to consume everything in its path. Yet, amidst the chaos and destruction, the charred expanse became their makeshift safety zone—a paradox of devastation offering a fleeting sense of security.

Mary, brimming with determination and armed with a garden hose, focused on a critical task. She worked diligently to create a wet line around the house, spraying water with precision to form a barrier she hoped would hold back the encroaching flames. A short distance away, Dinardo, Jeff, and McCollister joined forces, their fuzees crackling with fiery magnesium as they ignited the far end of the water line. The flames danced wildly in the air, illuminating their determined faces against the darkening sky and revealing their unwavering resolve to protect what remained.

"Get your crew the hell out of there!" a safety officer shouted, his voice cutting through the thick, acrid smoke hanging in the air like a heavy shroud. Despite it being his first encounter with such a volatile situation, he had already earned the title of Agency fire expert—a title he wore with a mix of pride and trepidation. His "expertise" stemmed from a two-day training course that supposedly prepared him for the unpredictable nature of wildfires. He stood resolutely on a narrow, dusty dirt road barely twenty feet wide—a path that felt perilously insufficient against the fifty-foot flames roaring from the dry cheatgrass like a wrathful beast unleashed.

"All stations, Code Apache!" Dinardo shouted, his voice rising above the cacophony of crackling flames and distant calls from his crew, resonating with an urgency that could not be ignored. The thick smoke swirled in a chaotic dance, stinging eyes and choking lungs, making every second count. Krutilla, fueled by adrenaline and determination, shouted directly at the safety officer, urging him to get the hell out before the flames engulfed him.

As the flames closed in, licking hungrily at the dry grass and underbrush, the firefighters lit the backfire, drawing in the surrounding heat. The fire consumed the fuel in a sweeping rush, creating a protective barrier as the flames split laterally around the charred remnants—ultimately safeguarding the house from the raging inferno.

With their hearts pounding and the intensity of the situation driving them forward, the crew pressed on. Their efforts were rewarded as they managed to save not just one, but nine additional houses that day. The battle against the wildfire had been fierce, but their collective bravery and rapid response turned the tide. "Code Apache" came through again, serving as a rallying cry that resonated with the spirit of the firefighting community, echoing the courage that defined their mission.

"What does 'Code Apache' really mean?" the head Agency man yelled, confusion and irritation mingling in his voice as it echoed through the smoky air, his words directed sharply at McAllister. The crew around them paused, thick tension hanging in the air as they gauged the outcome of this unexpected confrontation.

"It means absolutely nothing," McAllister replied truthfully, maintaining a calm demeanor that starkly contrasted with the agitated energy radiating from the Agency man. Frustration deepened the latter's furrowed brow as suspicion mounted; in his mind, a conspiracy was unfolding right before his eyes. "Code Apache" morphed from a mere phrase into something far more sinister—an enigma that demanded unraveling.

The origins of this so-called conspiracy proved innocuous enough. It had all begun when Krutilla noticed Dinardo, deeply engrossed in an article about a shoe called the "Apache," at the dimly lit bar known as the Inn Between—a watering hole nestled in the shadows near their home base. The bar, with its worn wooden counters and flickering neon lights, often served as a refuge for weary firefighters seeking solace after grueling days of service. The air was thick with the scent of stale beer and the low murmur of conversation, creating an environment ripe for unexpected ideas to take root.

Intrigued, Krutilla snuck around the corner of the dim bar where Dinardo sat and, with a mischievous glint in his eye, keyed his radio and declared, "All stations, Code Apache." Dinardo, startled by the sudden broadcast, picked it up on his own radio and found himself pondering the curious association between the code and the article he had just read.

As fate would have it, later that same year, amidst the chaos of another fire, Dinardo found himself wide awake at three in the morning, adrenaline coursing through him like electricity. Without warning, he spontaneously radioed Krutilla with the same phrase: "All stations, Code Apache." This seemingly meaningless transmission sparked a wildfire of a different kind among the Fort Apache crew, who, upon hearing it, began broadcasting "Code Apache" far and wide across the fireline, turning it into a rallying cry that echoed through the smoke-filled skies.

The Agency man, a figure draped in a veneer of authority yet steeped in self-serving ambition, overheard the murmur of "Code Apache" and felt a chill run down his spine. In that moment, he became acutely aware that he had stumbled upon no mere coincidence; he stood witness to a conspiracy brewing right under his nose. His disdain for Dinardo intensified—Dinardo, who always exhibited a stubborn independence and a propensity for questioning orders. The opening Dinardo had unwittingly provided seized the Agency man with gusto, transforming "Code Apache" into a clandestine signal—a lifeline for the crew to operate beyond the watchful eyes of the Agency.

This code signified more than just a phrase; it represented a rebellion, a rallying cry for those moments when the crew had to prioritize saving homes over adhering to bureaucratic red tape—moments when the instinct to protect the vulnerable outweighed the rigid protocols imposed by the Agency. The very essence of firefighting, the heart and soul of their mission, was encapsulated in that phrase.

On the Centennial Fire, a "Code Apache" challenge awaited the crew as they prepared to traverse a cat line that stretched perilously over a hidden yellow jacket nest. The nest, with its buzzing inhabitants, posed a veritable minefield of stings and pain, and the resident yellow jackets eagerly defended their territory. Their angry buzz filled the air, warning anyone who dared to approach.

Once the crews successfully navigated out of the area, leaving the danger behind, Dinardo approached the nest with a purposeful stride. He carried a gallon of saw fuel mixture—a potent concoction that could turn the nest's occupants into embers in an instant. With a steady hand, he poured the flammable liquid into the nest, ensuring every crevice was soaked with the volatile mixture. Yellow jackets stormed from the nest only to collapse after absorbing the fuel. Then, with a sense of anticipation, he laid a line out to McAllister, who stood ready and waiting to ignite the concoction.

As McAllister struck the match and lit the line, a brilliant flame erupted over the nest, shooting skyward like a fiery fountain and illuminating the dusky sky for a fleeting moment. The crew watched in awe as the fire danced and flickered. Just then, the Fire Boss—a figure of authority and experience—arrived on the scene, surveying the situation with keen eyes.

Caught up in the exhilaration of the moment, Dinardo pointed toward the remnants of the yellow jacket nest and declared, "Yellow jackets' nest." The Fire Boss, recognizing the significance of their actions and the pain they had neutralized, responded with a double thumbs-up—a gesture of approval that conveyed all that needed to be said. With a satisfied nod, he then drove on, leaving the crew to bask in the glow of their small victory against nature's fiercest defenders.

As the Agency man's paranoia grew, Dinardo's determination to wield "Code Apache" as a symbol of defiance intensified. Each time he repeated the words, he stoked the flames of dissent, fanning the embers of rebellion that had ignited among the ranks of the Fort Apache crew. The more the Agency man feared the implications of "Code Apache," the more Dinardo leaned into it, using it to galvanize his comrades.

Before long, the situation morphed from an innocuous signal into a full-blown conspiracy, one that the Agency man began to label the "power triad." This trio—Dinardo, Krutilla, and McAllister—shared a fellowship he deemed a direct threat to his authority. In his mind, they plotted to undermine his position and dismantle the very fabric of the Agency's control over the crew.

In a fit of creativity, Dinardo even went so far as to craft a secret handshake. This playful yet defiant gesture carried no real operational significance but served as a symbol of unity against the Agency man's oppressive oversight. The escapade only exacerbated the Agency man's growing anxiety, which ultimately led him to sever ties with the crew entirely, unable to withstand the pressure any longer.

The tides of fate, however, proved relentless. Dinardo vanished after the tumultuous 1984 season, leaving behind a void that echoed with whispers of what had been. By 1987, the only remnant of the "power triad" conspiracy was Krutilla. As the Agency descended into what could only be described as a Stalinist purge, it carried out a calculated and ruthless operation targeting anyone who challenged authority or deviated from prescribed protocol. Krutilla, too, was swept away in the chaos, caught in the crossfire of a power struggle that left no room for dissent. He became a casualty of the relentless machinations of the very system he had fought to protect—a system that had once stood as a beacon of hope and safety but had twisted into something shadowy, more concerned with control than with the well-being of the firefighters who put their lives on the line each day.

Back on the Silver Fire, the crew moving toward Conner's Place became enveloped in a haze of introspection, their minds drifting to places only they could reach. The trail, a gentle ribbon of earth, ran level alongside the river, its surface dappled with sunlight filtering through the leaves of towering trees that stood as silent sentinels. As they walked, the acrid smoke from Briggs Ranch gradually dissipated behind them, replaced by the fresh, invigorating scent of the surrounding wilderness. Hunt strode confidently at the front of the line, his posture exuding an unshakable sense of purpose, while I lingered at the back, my thoughts a whirlpool of reflections and worries.

The coolness of the morning air brushed against their skin—invigorating and refreshing, like a gentle breeze carrying the promise of a new day. It wrapped around them, soothing the weariness clinging to their muscles after relentless days spent battling the fire. I took a moment to adjust my hard hat, which had grown increasingly loose after days of grueling work. As I tugged at it, the helmet slipped down over my matted hair—a constant reminder of the harsh conditions we had endured together on the fire line. With each passing day, it felt as if the hard hat had grown more ill-fitting, almost as if my head had inexplicably shrunk in response to the intensity of our work and the weight of the challenges we faced. The absurdity of the thought brought a quiet chuckle to my lips—a small moment of levity amidst the chaos.

Turning slightly to my right, I leaned forward, lowering my voice to a conspiratorial whisper meant only for Christine, who walked just ahead of me, her thoughts momentarily interrupted by my presence. "Christine, did you ever notice that the longer you work for the Agency, the more your head shrinks?" My tone was light, laced with humor—an invitation to smile, a small attempt to lift the mood.

She glanced back at me, her expression brightening as the words sank in. Her laughter rang out like a buoyant melody, breaking the tension that sometimes hung heavy in the air. "My hard hat is loose also!" she replied with a playful grin, our shared laughter echoing through the trees and weaving itself into the fabric of our journey. In that moment, surrounded by the beauty of the wilderness and the bonds forged in fire, the burdens of our work felt just a little lighter.

Ford, always attuned to the banter drifting through the air, overheard the exchange. With his signature sharp wit, he called out to Berkson, the crew's resident genius, his voice bouncing off the trees. "Why do people's heads shrink the longer they work for the Agency?" The question hung in the air—playful, yet tinged with the truth of their experience.

Berkson, never one to shy away from a challenge, yelled back with enthusiasm, "It's all about fluid displacement! Your brain's just trying to make room for all that knowledge!" His response sparked a chorus of laughter from the crew.

As they continued their six-mile trek to Conner's Place, the rhythmic sound of their boots striking the earth harmonized with their shared humor, transforming the arduous journey into something almost enjoyable. Their thoughts may have wandered, but the bond they shared remained unbreakable—a lifeline in the chaos they faced.

"Why does Uphoff remain so calm all the time?" Christine inquired, furrowing her brow slightly as she watched the foreman's serene demeanor amid the chaos of the crew.

"Quaaludes," Ford replied with a sly grin, his deep voice carrying a hint of mischief. "He's a Quaalude addict. He can't function well without them, but that calm exterior he puts on? It's just a façade. It's quite sad, really, but we've all learned to put up with it. You might even be able to help him out—who knows?"

With a chuckle, he continued, "I once hid his stash, thinking it might do him some good. But the look he gave me was wild, crazed, like a cornered animal. I honestly thought he might take it out on McCollister."

Christine nodded, recalling the confusion she felt when she first joined the crew. It had taken her a solid few months to realize that the very straight-laced Uphoff, who always seemed so composed, wasn't actually on Quaaludes at all. Over time, she began to understand the layers beneath his calmness—the struggles he faced and the strength he drew from his quiet resolve.

Eventually, her heart softened toward him, and they found common ground in their shared experiences. In a twist of fate, the two of them ended up together, forging a bond that blossomed into deep love and culminated in their marriage—a testament to the unexpected connections that can form even in the most demanding of circumstances.

CHAPTER 10

ATTRITION

However, upon their arrival at Conner's Place, the atmosphere shifted dramatically. The coolness of the morning air brushed against their skin, invigorating and refreshing, like a gentle breeze carrying the promise of a new day. It wrapped around them, soothing the weariness clinging to their muscles from the relentless days spent battling the fire.

Conner's Place sat along the banks of a meandering river, a tranquil setting that whispered of its once-vibrant past. The remnants of the homestead stood as a somber testament to better days, with only meager signs hinting at the life that had once flourished there. Now, it clung to the landscape—a lonely clearing stretched along the thirsty river. The gentle sound of flowing water contrasted sharply with the ruggedness of their task, offering a momentary distraction as the crew gathered their tools and gear.

At Conner's Place, the crew broke into four saw teams, each tasked with the vital job of cutting the brush line. The air thickened with the scent of pine and fresh earth, filling their lungs as they prepared for the labor ahead. The Mt. Adams crew received the assignment to dig down to mineral soil and assist with the brush line, ensuring a clear path for the firefighting efforts to come. Krutilla paired with the seasoned Glenn, who brought a wealth of experience to the team, along with the physically imposing Gale as the main sawyer and the capable reserve sawyer Lira—both of whom excelled in their craft.

As they set to work, Krutilla's team plunged into the task with infectious energy, making rapid progress that echoed through the dense forest. The rhythm of their saws reverberated in the air like a well-rehearsed symphony. The sharp, keening sound of metal teeth biting into wood punctuated the occasional pause as they exchanged knowing glances and nods of encouragement.

Gale, with his keen eye and steady hand, took the lead, making precise cuts that radiated confidence. He expertly directed the fall of each tree, his movements fluid and sure—as if he had danced this dance a thousand times before. Each trunk landed in its intended lay with a satisfying thud, leaving little to no extra work for the brush throwers.

Gale, whose roots traced back to the scenic town of The Dalles, Oregon, had spent his formative years in the shadow of the majestic Columbia River—a natural artery coursing through the landscape, nurturing the salmon that echoed the vitality of the region. This river was more than geography; it had witnessed his early adventures, where the air filled with the rich, earthy scent of pine and the distant calls of wildlife mingled with the sound of rushing water. He knew the rugged terrain of the East Side fuels intimately, particularly near Duffer and the Barlow Ranger Station. Here, the dry-side fuels posed both challenges and opportunities—and Gale had honed his skills extensively among these trees. His expertise in felling large Ponderosa pine reflected his deep understanding of East Side fuels.

However, as often occurs in the untamed wild, not all tasks unfolded straightforwardly. One tree posed a significant challenge: a formidable oak leaning heavily over the line. The team exchanged concerned glances as we assessed the situation. I stepped forward, brow furrowed in thought, contemplating the best approach to tackling the giant that stood stubbornly in our path.

Gale, a pragmatic problem-solver, faced the tree away from its lean, analyzing the situation with a practiced eye. Lira stepped in, deftly placing wedges and double wedges into the back cut—a vital step to shift the weight. Yet, despite their careful preparations, the tree's weight still didn't shift over the face, creating a tension that hung heavy in the air. With a determined glint in his eye, Gale decided to put another face cut into the tree, this time three feet above the original. The team held their breath as he expertly maneuvered. A wedge slid carefully into the back cut of the new face. With a satisfying creak, the weight shifted dramatically. The oak finally succumbed to gravity, falling gracefully to its intended lay—a triumphant moment that underscored their teamwork and skill amidst the wild surroundings.

After a while, they reached an area where the trees grew sparse, giving way to a small clearing bathed in the soft glow of the morning light. The coolness of the air brushed against their skin, invigorating and refreshing, like a gentle breeze carrying the promise of a new day. It wrapped around them, soothing the weariness that clung to my muscles from the relentless days spent battling the fire. The scent of earth and pine needles filled the air.

Amidst this charged environment, my saw team passed the superintendent's location, our movements purposeful and focused. As we navigated the uneven terrain, we soon encountered Berkson and Grimaldi's saw team. They were wrestling with a tree precariously lodged in the branches of another, creating a hazardous situation that demanded immediate attention. We quickly assessed the scene, realizing we needed an additional wedge to dislodge the entangled tree before it caused further complications.

After a few tense moments of careful maneuvering and deft adjustments, we drove the wedge into place with precise force, securing its hold against the encumbered tree. We collectively applied steady, measured pressure. Finally, our efforts forced the trapped tree—teetering dangerously in its entangled state—to surrender. With a loud crack echoing through the surrounding forest, it gave way and cascaded down from its precarious perch above the ridge. I watched it land safely on the ground, the thud reverberating through the earth beneath my feet.

I exchanged uneasy glances with Grimaldi and Berkson as they posed a question that weighed heavily on our minds. "Should we follow the ridge or stick with the flag line?" they asked, their voices tinged with uncertainty. The flag line, though generally aligned with the ridge in most sections, diverged significantly in this area, veering off toward a spur ridge that reconnected to the main ridge just a few hundred feet ahead. I believed the directive instructed us to adhere to the ridge unless told otherwise, so a surge of concern gripped me at the conflicting orders they presented.

I listened intently as they shared that Hunt had explicitly advised them to follow the flag line—a choice he made to ensure our saw teams connected seamlessly to the starting point of the other crew. Mulling over the situation, I weighed the benefits of sticking to the ridge. It typically represented the safest and most defensible option when battling a fire, forming a natural barrier against unpredictable flames. Yet the flag line's deviation at this point sparked questions I couldn't dismiss.

I speculated that the flagger might have intentionally avoided the ridge for reasons not immediately clear to us sawyers. What if hidden obstacles, such as rocky formations or dense brush, lay out of sight and complicated matters if we remained on the ridge? Alternatively, perhaps someone had marked the route down the main ridge, only to lead us into a steep drop-off that required a shift to the spur ridge. There was also the possibility that the decision had been based on fuel assessments—maybe the flag line was laid out to steer us away from a patch of heavy, flammable material, reducing the risk of a flare-up.

My gaze fell on the ridge, the fire line targets, and a clear logic began to dawn on me. Cutting a line parallel to where the other crew had started would lead to inefficiencies. Not only would we need more line to connect the segments, but it would also create doglegs and hooks—treacherous spots for holding fire. Hunt's reasoning resonated with me. It meant we'd need to cut a wider line in this area, so I signaled Grimaldi and Berkson's team to move ahead, taking charge of cutting the line. Besides, I had complete trust in Hunt, who was flagging the route.

About half an hour later, my attention snapped to the sound of screaming below. The Superintendent raged at Grimaldi and Berkson, a storm of fury painting his face beet red. They hadn't adhered to the ridge. The hiccup stemmed from the non-Agency division boss requesting the Superintendent to have his crew follow the ridge. The division boss, flustered, apologized to the saw teams for the chaos he had unwittingly triggered. The saw team shrugged it off, saying they were used to the Superintendent's antics. Krutilla shouted down, defending Grimaldi and Berkson, asserting it had been his call. In that moment, he recalled a heavy weight of dread—a biblical reference about passing through fire. The Superintendent stomped away, seething.

Gale, feeling the weight of his spirit drained, handed the saw to Lira. He no longer felt like sawing.

An hour later, Grimaldi's chainsaw gash in his leg served as a painful reminder of the day's dangers—a deep wound that throbbed insistently and demanded immediate attention. With urgency in his voice, Krutilla radioed for a helicopter to evacuate Grimaldi, fully aware the injury couldn't be ignored. Berkson swiftly moved in to bandage Grimaldi's leg, his hands working with practiced efficiency as he applied pressure and gauze to staunch the bleeding. Once the makeshift dressing was secured, he supported Grimaldi, guiding him carefully down the rugged terrain toward Conner's place, where the helicopter waited. Grimaldi's face remained a mask of determination, even as the aircraft lifted off toward the hospital—a place he would remain for three long days before beginning his own new adventure.

With Grimaldi taken care of, the rest of the day unfolded much more smoothly for my team—a welcome change from the earlier chaos. We were fortunate to have Mike and Laurie from the Mt. Adams crew join us, two seasoned firefighters known not only for their excellent work ethic but also for the fellowship they brought wherever they went. As we threw brush aside with practiced ease, we reminisced about the past year, sharing stories of fire and survival—each tale a vibrant thread that connected us in the challenging, often perilous world we navigated together.

Lira, ever the steady worker, cut through the wood with a consistency that spoke of his unwavering focus. The rhythm of the saw in his hands was comforting, almost meditative. As he worked, his mind wandered between vivid memories of past adventures and dreams of future travels that beckoned like distant horizons. He envisioned himself as an adventurer, thoughts of his journeys dancing through his mind like flickering flames, igniting his imagination. He saw breathtaking landscapes stretching from sunlit New Mexico to snow-capped Colorado, where he might escape the oppressive heat of summer and find solace in the tranquil embrace of winter's chill. The rhythm of the saw matched the tempo of his thoughts—a steady cadence anchoring him in the moment, allowing him to lose himself in the task at hand.

As the day came to a close, he handed the saw back to Gale, a sense of satisfaction washing over him as he reflected on the good, consistent line he had cut. Each stroke of the saw carried the weight of their collective efforts—a testament to the bond they had forged in the face of adversity.

Unfortunately, our other saw teams weren't as lucky in their endeavors. The ominous shadow of the Superintendent, consumed by his own tempestuous fury, loomed heavily over the crew, casting a pall of unease that rippled through the air. Ford, in a split second of sheer luck and skill, narrowly escaped a catastrophic accident when the saw he was wielding veered dangerously close to his neck. The near miss left him shaken, adrenaline surging through his veins like wildfire—a stark reminder of the fine line we all walked in this perilous profession.

Thomas, while boring into a tree, experienced a jarring setback when the butt of the saw recoiled, slamming into his abdomen. The injury required emergency evacuation, and he had to be flown out the following day—another grim reminder of the daily risks we faced.

In a fit of rage, the Superintendent seized a saw to demonstrate his misguided interpretation of proper technique. The atmosphere shifted, tension crackling in the air like static. He began cutting with wild abandon, his movements erratic and frantic, sending splinters flying like shrapnel. The crew, sensing danger, instinctively spread out, their instincts sharpened by countless hours in the field. Each firefighter recognized the threat he posed. Trees splintered under his reckless assault, the sound of cracking wood echoing around us, punctuated by chaotic sprays of debris raining down.

In a heart-stopping moment, two crew members dove behind a nearby tree, narrowly avoiding disaster as a tree fell at a shocking ninety-degree angle from its intended path. The ground shook violently with the impact—a visceral reminder of the unpredictability of our environment and the hazards it concealed.

Amid the chaos, the Division boss emerged like a beacon of authority, his commanding voice slicing through the din. He bellowed at the Superintendent to pull the crew back to camp—a necessary call given how far the situation had spiraled. Still caught in his whirlwind of bluster, the Superintendent fired back defiantly, "Do you really think we need to go back to camp so early?" His words dripped with stubborn defiance, oblivious to the tension and fear thick in the air.

But the Division boss stood firm. His voice rose above the chaos—sharp, urgent. "Get the crews the hell out of here before you kill someone!" The words struck like a lightning bolt, a desperate plea for safety in the face of recklessness.

CHAPTER 11

SLOP OVER

With the fire line successfully established, the night crews methodically burned out the area between this line and the encroaching flames, intending to starve the fire of its fuel during cooler periods. The following morning, the crew embarked on their necessary patrol, navigating a tired and twisted trail that wound three miles up to what was once known as Silver Prairie. Now, they faced a darkened expanse—a stark reminder of the previous night's burnout, where the fuel had been consumed between the main fire and the line. The superintendent, spiraling deeper into madness, remained conspicuously absent from their ranks.

As they walked, the crew moved in harmony, forging a silent unity through shared purpose and mutual understanding. This was not the flat, easy terrain of the Illinois Trail; instead, they faced a steady uphill grade that demanded their focus and energy. The steepness discouraged casual conversation but allowed thoughts to swirl within each of their minds, echoing the weight of the task ahead.

This dedicated group passionately sacrificed their summers, springs, and falls for their work. With vast experience, they saved homes, protected property, and preserved lives. Despite years of underpayment, their love for the job bound them together, transcending mere financial reward in the face of adversity.

So, what do I think a rational government does when faced with challenges it cannot comprehend? It systematically degrades the very individuals who have dedicated their lives to service. It humiliates them publicly, eroding their dignity and self-worth. The aim is clear: to drive us away—to make us feel so unwelcome that we choose to leave of our own accord. Meanwhile, those who excel in this cruel game, those who most effectively degrade and humiliate their peers, receive handsome rewards. They garner accolades for sensitivity, wellness, and inclusion—awards that mock the very essence of compassion they so blatantly disregard. This conduct is not merely questionable; it is astonishingly outrageous—so extreme in its degree that it transcends all conceivable boundaries of decency. Such behavior rightly deserves the label of atrocious and utterly intolerable within a community that prides itself on civilization and a moral compass. I ponder the irony and the tragic reality of such governance, reflecting on what it means for the most civilized country in the history of the world to stoop to such depths.

The place once known as Silver Prairie now stood as a shadow of its former self—a black prairie haunted by the remnants of a once-vibrant landscape. I had completed the arduous task during the night shift of establishing a fire barrier, meticulously burning out the area from Silver Prairie all the way down to Conner's Place. Today, my crew and I embarked on the critical mission of patrolling that line, vigilantly searching for any signs of fire that might have slipped over the boundary. We remained on high alert for spot fires—unpredictable flames carried over the line by windborne embers. The weight of responsibility hung heavy on my shoulders as I navigated the charred remains of what had once been a flourishing ecosystem, my eyes scanning the terrain for the telltale signs of danger lurking just beyond the line.

As one group of firefighters and I walked the line, another team made its way to the far side of the now dreary ridge, a stark contrast to the vibrant landscape it had once been. We positioned ourselves carefully, spreading out approximately fifty feet from one another to form a grid designed to catch any elusive spots of fire that might have escaped detection. Each of us moved with deliberate slowness, our senses heightened as we inhaled the lingering scent of smoke—a reminder of the devastating blaze that had consumed the prairie, leaving behind a landscape devoid of the sun's warmth. We paused intermittently, scanning our surroundings with intense focus, searching for any signs of hidden smoke.

About half a mile down the ridge, I approached another firefighting team stationed in an area where the burn had dangerously crept over the line, spilling fire into a deep draw filled with dense brush and towering trees. Rocks dislodged from the ridge above began to cascade down the steep draw, echoing through the canyon. The thunderous noise reverberated as stones cracked and snapped against one another, crashing into trees and bouncing off their sturdy trunks. The momentum of the falling rocks finally died when they encountered the thick brush clinging to the base of the oaks.

The crew I encountered appeared visibly tense, their unease evident as they worked to suppress the slop-over fire in this precarious location. The threatening terrain, coupled with the unsettling sounds of nature's destructive forces at work, created an atmosphere thick with anxiety and caution. I felt the weight pressing down on us, knowing that one misstep could lead to an uncontrollable situation in these treacherous conditions.

Here, the slop-over presented a myriad of dangers—some glaringly apparent, others shrouded in uncertainty. Fiery embers might have drifted with delicate grace, spotting below the fire line where fuels thrived. The threat of a rapid upslope surge loomed—a violent rush of flames poised to torch everything in its path.

Loose rocks loomed ominously overhead, waiting to dislodge without warning. They would announce their descent with a terrifying, thundering crash as they careened down the ridge. Each rock, freed from its resting place, could become a lethal projectile—capable of hollowing me out in an instant if it struck true. I felt the volatility of the environment, knowing vigilance was my only defense. The fire could easily tumble down the slope in a cataclysmic rush, ready to unleash its wrath upon an unsuspecting crew caught off guard in the late afternoon. I was determined to tackle this volatile area head-on.

At the bottom of the fire, where danger surrounded me, I engaged alongside Christine. We worked in concert, digging a cup trench—a crucial defensive measure against the rolling debris cascading from above. I focused intently on carving out a small protective barrier while Christine remained vigilant, scanning the treacherous heights for any sign of loose rock that might spell disaster. As we labored, smaller rolling materials quickly filled the trench.

With her brow furrowed, Christine suggested we add more cup trenches below the original to strengthen our defenses. I nodded, and soon enough, we saw results as the new trenches held back the debris. Each scoop served as a reminder of the danger we faced.

Keller, Berkson, and Ford spread out below the slop-over, scanning the dry, brittle fuels surrounding them. Every twig and parched leaf posed a potential spark ready to ignite. Their focus remained unwavering as they prepared to leap into action at a moment's notice to stop any spot fire. Meanwhile, the rest of the crew worked hard cutting line, securing the flanks of the slop-over, and creating barriers to protect what lay below.

I watched as Christine moved with effortless grace, embodying resilience—her blond hair tossing beneath her hard hat, catching the light as she focused on the task at hand.

Christine paused for a moment and cast her gaze upward, locking onto the foreboding, abrupt ascent above us. The sun had risen, casting an eerie glow across the landscape. She wiped the sweat from her forehead with the back of her hand—a futile attempt to rid herself of the oppressive heat clinging to her skin. Her eyes stayed fixed on the perilous heights above, anxiety coursing through her veins as the atmosphere thickened with tension.

The hand crew worked with urgency, digging swiftly along the flank of the slope-over as they eyed a Ponderosa Pine snag jutting from the charred earth and ashen remnants. This snag, with its solid three-foot base, meandered skyward through the canopy of resilient oak trees, standing defiant against the devastation around it. Once it pierced through the dense canopy, the trunk narrowed dramatically to about two inches in diameter before expanding again and spiraling upward. Danger lay in its heights; the top of the snag threatened to break free at any moment—a ticking time bomb ready to crash down without warning.

Their eyes moved between the precarious snag and the line they cut—a tenuous thread of safety amid chaos. They understood all too well that the top could plummet at any moment, turning their painstaking work into a deadly game of chance. With a shared understanding, they completed the line and instinctively moved back, creating a safe distance between themselves and the unstable snag. The air grew heavy with the weight of their collective anxiety.

Gale scrutinized the Ponderosa Pine snag. He swung the massive chainsaw in his hands with practiced ease, making it seem child-sized. The saw's roar blended with the crackling fire and distant shouts of fellow firefighters.

The snag leaned precariously downhill, its age-worn bark splintered and cracked. Gale knew that if the tree tumbled, it would careen through the chasm below, potentially unleashing fire. He shifted his gaze to the side hill, where sturdy oaks stood anchored. He weighed the risk—if he directed the snag to fall uphill toward the oaks, those ancient trees could withstand the timber's weight, avoiding chaos.

With determined resolve, Gale set out to ensure the tree would fall in the right direction. He adjusted the holding wood, deliberately leaving it thicker on the uphill side—a calculated move to steer the snag's descent safely away from the volatile area below.

With a solid thud, Gale struck a nearby tree with the back of his axe, the sharp sound echoing through the forest. A faint scent of dry ash wafted through the air, a stark reminder of the destructive power of fire that still lingered nearby. He paused to survey his surroundings, nodding to his fellow crew members, who wisely moved farther from the anticipated trajectory of the tree's fall. Their expressions mirrored his own mix of focus and apprehension—fully aware of the stakes.

A quick glance at the spire of the snag confirmed its firm position for the moment, but tension crackled in the air like the fire they were fighting against. With resolve, Gale fired up his chainsaw, the engine roaring to life with a fierce growl that cut through the stillness. As he positioned himself for the top cut of his Humboldt, a face cut with the intersecting cut coming up from below -white chips of wood flew past him, bouncing off the belt of his web gear—each piece a testament to the precision and skill behind every movement. The forest seemed to hold its breath, waiting for the snag to yield—either falling safely or wreaking havoc in its descent.

As he maneuvered the saw with practiced control, his eyes locked onto the cut, his focus unwavering. The top of the snag swayed perilously above him, trembling with the rhythm of the saw's powerful vibrations. Each oscillation sent a shiver of tension through his body, a constant reminder of the danger towering above. The energy in the air grew taut with anticipation, as if the forest itself were bracing for the moment everything would shift.

When the angle of the cut aligned perfectly with the slope of the hillside, Gale began his upward cut with determination. He was completely absorbed in the task, oblivious to the wooden chips flying past his shoulder—tiny projectiles celebrating the accuracy of his work. As he carved out the bottom of the Humboldt face, his gaze flickered between the emerging notch and the swaying treetop above, fully aware that even the slightest miscalculation could mean catastrophe.

With each pass of the bar, a pie-shaped chunk of wood broke free from the snag and dropped to the blackened soil below, leaving behind a whisper of smoke and a sprinkle of ash that danced lightly in the air. The remnants of the fire clung to the ground, a poignant reminder of the destruction they fought to contain. Gale felt the weight of the moment—the intensity of the task at hand—as he pushed forward with unyielding resolve. Every swing of the saw brought him one step closer to safety—for his crew and for the forest they struggled to protect.

Meanwhile, he maintained a vigilant watch, his gaze fixed firmly on the towering top of the tree, ready to scream out a warning at the first sign of peril. He understood that if the crown began to fall, he needed to act quickly, diving to a safer area to avoid the falling top of the tree. As Gale commenced the back cut, his focus sharpened, his eyes flickering from the precise angle of his cut to the spiraled crown of the snag above, which now trembled ominously in response to the relentless vibration of the saw. There was tension in the air; the tree's slender upper section quivered and swayed precariously back and forth at its narrowest point, just below the lush oaken canopy that provided a slight respite from the harsh reality of their surroundings.

As the bar sank deeper into the wood, the sound of wood severing echoed through the forest. As the tree began to lean slowly forward, a sharp crack resonated in the air, sending a jolt of adrenaline through Gale's veins. He instinctively leapt over a recent hot spot, narrowly avoiding the danger that lurked beneath the surface. Then, in a sudden, dramatic moment, the gnarled top of the tree snapped—breaking free with explosive force—and hurtled toward the very spot where Gale had just stood moments before. The impact thundered as it collided with the ground, sending a cloud of dust and debris swirling into the air, filling the chasm with a gritty haze as the remnants of the tree shattered upon impact, scattering into countless jagged pieces that tumbled down into the depths of the canyon below.

For a moment, silence enveloped the scene, starkly contrasting the chaos that had just unfolded. Below them lay the potential for numerous fires—a grim reminder of the ever-present threat they faced in this volatile environment. Fate, it seemed, acted as an unpredictable force; sometimes, even when he did his utmost to ensure safety, the tide would turn against them without warning. With a steady hand, he completed his cuts. As the tree fell gracefully, it nestled perfectly between the sturdy oaks—a testament to his skill and the precarious balance of their dangerous undertaking.

Hunt peered down into the ravine, his brow furrowing in concern as he contemplated the potential disaster looming below. The crew stationed at the ridge had a narrow window of opportunity to make it over the ridge and into the relative safety of Silver Prairie. He knew that a quick-thinking crew could patrol down the slope. But they required unwavering vigilance and readiness to act at a moment's notice. If the fire raced toward them, their only viable escape route would lead them down a treacherous slope away from the encroaching flames. This dire situation could escalate in the blink of an eye, so they needed to form a plan swiftly and with precision.

Uphoff took on the crucial responsibility of moving down the slope with urgency, his keen eyes scanning the terrain for any signs of imminent ignition. Meanwhile, I, along with McCollister, Ray, Lucy, Glenn, Berkson, and Juli, progressed more cautiously—methodically gridding the area while staying alert for any signals from Uphoff. Our role proved vital; we had to be ready to give a timely warning to those above if the situation took a turn for the worse. As we strategized, I positioned myself in the middle of the formation, ensuring I could co-ordinate effectively, while the others spread out to cover more ground on the periphery.

"Keep an eye out for rock slides, or any place we can jump to if the fire makes a run," I shouted, my voice cutting through the tense atmosphere, laced with urgency. The gravity of the moment weighed heavily in the air, each crew member acutely aware of the stakes, our hearts pounding in unison as we braced for the unpredictable wrath of nature.

This was not the kind of carnival ride I wanted to embark upon without the invaluable experience of both McCollister and Glenn by my side. McCollister—with an impressive tenure spanning ten years on the crew—had seen it all and done it all. There wasn't a better hotshot out there with his remarkable ability to work diligently while simultaneously keeping a vigilant eye out for potential spot fires that could threaten our safety. Yet, in an instant, McCollister vanished from the scene, disappearing after the fateful year of 1987.

And then there was Glenn—another stalwart of the crew—who, despite his own decade of experience on various hotshot teams, had chosen to join us for a deeply personal reason. Glenn moved here because his wife was expecting their first child, and the crew's home station was nearby. He yearned to be close during this momentous time.

Uphoff strode deliberately down the rugged chasm, measuring his steps and maintaining a steady pace as he approached the unpredictable terrain. He considered that a slower pace might help him catch lingering embers or smoldering spots that could spell danger, but he remained acutely aware that time was of the essence. The potential for a rapidly escalating situation loomed ever-present, compelling him to maintain brisk momentum as he navigated the uneven ground. With an air of cautious anticipation, he scanned the surroundings, finely tuning his senses to detect any anomalies.

As the minutes stretched into hours, the landscape shifted around him, and three hours later, he finally reached the Illinois River Trail. The familiar sound of flowing water greeted him, providing a soothing backdrop to the urgency of his mission. He pressed on, determined to reach Brigg's Ranch, where he hoped to gather vital supplies that would sustain them through the arduous challenges ahead.

Meanwhile, my crew moved with a sense of purpose. The air thickened with tension, creating an unspoken understanding among us that silence was our ally. Without exchanging a word, we consciously suppressed any conversation that might disrupt the sounds around us. Each subtle crackle of underbrush could signal the presence of a hidden spot fire, and we remained alert, our senses sharpened.

I advanced with careful precision, covering approximately fifty feet before coming to a halt. In unison, we paused to engage our senses—smelling the air, listening intently, and scanning our surroundings for any signs of danger. My eyes darted toward the nearby foliage, and I took a long, scrutinizing look down the ridge. If I caught sight of any smoke rising from the depths below, I would need to act immediately—retreating downhill and away from the encroaching threat, fully aware I couldn't hope to outrun a fire racing uphill toward the heights above me.

To the untrained eye, it might appear that little was happening. But intensity cut through the air, sending electric jolts of anxiety through my nerves with every heartbeat. A fog of anticipation hung over me like a storm cloud. Then, the stillness shattered—McCollister's voice boomed through the quiet, demanding our attention with a sharp, decisive "Stop." The weight of his words carried urgency, and coming from someone as seasoned and reliable as McCollister, they signaled that something was wrong.

As we stood there, a delicate wisp of smoke, barely discernible against the forest backdrop, wafted through the air—curling like a phantom. I couldn't see it clearly, yet its presence felt unmistakable, a sweet smell dancing on the breeze and hinting at something burning nearby—most likely the Ponderosa Pine needles that carpeted the forest floor in a thick, fragrant layer. The Ponderosa, known for its distinctive aroma, released a sweet scent that lingered in the air, contrasting sharply with the sour, acrid smoke rising from the brush.

McCollister's keen eyes, sharp and perceptive, scanned the surrounding area as he absorbed every detail, every shifting shadow. He narrowed his gaze, searching for the source of the smoke, his instincts on high alert. Nearby, Juli, Ray, and Lucy instinctively drew closer, pulled toward the gravity of his focus. They exchanged furtive glances, each one recognizing that this subtle shift in the environment could herald a much larger threat looming just beyond our line of sight. The atmosphere thickened with an unspoken understanding—we had to remain vigilant, ready to respond should the situation escalate.

Lucy quickly shifted her gaze, scanning the vast expanse of woods around her, eyes straining to catch any sign of smoke curling lazily through the trees. Not long ago, she'd traversed the rugged terrain of Nepal, navigating the breathtaking trails of the Himalayas, where the air felt thin and crisp, filled with the scent of high-altitude flora. Just before joining the crew early this summer, she had reveled in the beauty of those mountains—surrounded by peaks that pierced the sky and valleys that whispered secrets of the ancient earth. Her abrupt, invigorating transition to life on the hotshot crew stood in stark contrast to the serenity of the Himalayas. Here, the weight of responsibility pressed heavily on her shoulders as she immersed herself in this new world, determined to prove her worth among seasoned veterans.

We began to test the wind, our senses heightened, noses wrinkling as we caught the faint but unmistakable odor of smoke. The breeze shifted, carrying the scent, and each crew member instinctively turned toward the direction it seemed to originate from. With careful steps, we closed the distance, now no more than five feet apart—attuned to each other, our bodies taut with focus.

Yet when we arrived at the spot, the telltale smell had dissipated, vanishing into the air and leaving us puzzled. McCollister's brow furrowed in concentration as he scanned the surroundings, his gaze settling on a small cluster of gnats fluttering erratically around a log that rose from the forest floor, its top half obscured by tufts of grass and debris. Something about the scene felt off.

In a deliberate motion, McCollister removed his glove and, using the back of his hand—avoiding the calloused fingers he needed to grip tools—he felt the area. We watched him, our breaths held in anticipation, each of us aware that the fate of our mission might rest on what he uncovered next.

He reached under the log with the back of his hand, brushing his fingers against the remnants of the mild humidity lingering in the shadows—a subtle reminder of the night that had just slipped away. The coolness of the earth contrasted with the warmth of the day as it slowly awakened. As a gentle breeze stirred around him, he detected the faint yet undeniable heat radiating from a concealed area beneath the log—a hidden danger momentarily shrouded from view. A sense of satisfaction washed over him, and he smiled inwardly; he had found it.

Though it might seem insignificant at first glance, he understood the importance of this discovery. He had likely averted a catastrophe that could have threatened thousands of acres within the triangle— or worse, allowed the fire to surge unchecked over the Illinois River. Left unnoticed, this seemingly innocuous spot could have unleashed a torrent of flames, with an unimpeded path stretching a staggering thousand feet up to the ridge above. I imagined the chaos that would have followed—burning logs rolling down the mountainside, igniting everything in their path and transforming the tranquil landscape into a raging inferno.

A thin, wry smile crept onto McCollister's lips as his keen eyes, sharp and focused, pierced through the thick underbrush around his aquiline nose, scanning for any signs of danger still lurking in the shadows. He didn't shout or yip; such displays weren't in his nature. Instead, he exuded quiet confidence—an unshakeable assurance that spoke volumes without a single unnecessary sound. As he knelt, he mixed the heat from the ground with the cool dirt beneath his fingers, feeling the warmth dissipate into the soil until no heat remained. Yet, despite the reassurance, he unscrewed the cap of his canteen and poured a measured amount of water over the area, ensuring any lingering embers were fully extinguished. He understood the gravity of the situation; this was too important to leave to chance.

Fast forward to a later time, a year marking the beginning of McCollister's new life with his wife, Rachel, in the picturesque landscapes of Guatemala in the 1990s. In those quieter moments, he often reflected on his time with the crew, wondering whether those experiences had been real or merely vivid dreams—or scenes from a captivating film he once watched. But the memories no longer lived as dreams; they were etched into his mind as tangible realities.

As he walked through the verdant coffee plantation owned by Rachel's parents, surrounded by the aromatic scent of rich, dark coffee beans, he suddenly caught a glimpse of smoke rising in the distance. The column bent ominously toward the plantation—a stark reminder of his past battles with fire. Instinctively, he broke into a run, adopting the long, powerful stride of a marathoner, perfected during his time on the hotshot crew. His heart raced—not just from exertion but from the urgency of the moment—as he sprinted toward the buildings, determined to protect what he held dear.

A brush and grass fire surged with alarming speed down the hillside, threatening to engulf the coffee plantation in a fiery embrace.

In an instant, McCollister's family mobilized into action, joining his squad in a desperate bid to protect their home. He rallied Rachel, his beloved wife, along with her elderly parents, both in their late seventies. Despite their age, they understood the gravity of the situation and moved with purpose, driven by the primal instinct to safeguard their land.

As they formed a line, McCollister and his squad dug in with shovels and azadonas—long-handled hoes that had seen many battles against encroaching flames. They pounded the tools into the earth, creating a firebreak—a desperate line of defense against the advancing inferno. The oppressive heat surrounded them, and the acrid scent of smoke filled the air. But they worked tirelessly, muscles straining with each swing as they tied the line into the road, hoping to halt the fire's relentless advance.

But the fire surged ahead like a wild beast, and an ominous weight settled over us. He realized the line wouldn't hold unless we moved quickly and with conviction. A determined spark ignited within him as he drew a cigarette lighter from his pocket. He had never been a smoker, yet the lighter he carried was a constant reminder of his hotshot days—when it might be needed to light a lifesaving backfire.

With deft movements, he ignited small patches of dry brush along the line, watching the flames flicker to life. The little fires grew, crackling and roaring as they rushed toward the main fire, consuming the fuel in their path and leaving behind a barren stretch of earth.

Back on the Silver Fire, perhaps guided by an unspoken understanding or shared instinct, my crew instinctively fell into formation without a command or prompt. Our movements synced seamlessly, like a well-rehearsed dance, each step echoing the rhythm of our collective purpose as we began working the fire down the steep incline. We navigated the rugged terrain with determination, calculating each step deliberately, our minds wholly focused on the essential task at hand.

Though we wouldn't dare voice it at the time, I sensed a profound respect brewing beneath the surface among us for McCollister. In the distance, the majestic mountains towered over the banks of the Illinois River, their peaks seemingly brushing against the sky. We continued on.

As we traversed the steep bluffs looming over the river, we helped one another. We formed a human link, each grasping hands with the next in a quiet show of solidarity. The person at the top of the chain found stability by hugging a sturdy tree, its rough bark digging into his side, anchoring him against gravity's pull. Below him, another crew member clung tightly to his web gear—the familiar weight offering comfort amidst the precariousness. The chain continued down, each member steadying the next until, finally, Ray—his grip strong and his resolve unwavering—reached for another tree, ensuring the chain remained unbroken. Together, we secured our collective safety, inching toward solid ground, our hearts pounding in rhythm with the survival instinct.

Ray, an artist of notable talent, stood out among us as the embodiment of creativity and strength. People often likened him to Van Gogh, a painter whose emotional depth resonated with those who understood the struggles of the human condition. Ray didn't just fight fires; he carried pride in being half Black and half Cherokee, shaping a unique perspective on life and art.

We gathered at the Illinois River Trail, a narrow path winding through the rugged landscape, surrounded by towering trees that seemed to whisper secrets of the forest. Although fatigue lingered in our bones from the long descent, the physical exertion didn't weigh us down. Instead, it was the mental strain—the intense focus on every minute detail, every decision that could mean life or death—that pressed upon us. Each team member remained acutely aware of the stakes. That shared sense of responsibility bound us together more tightly than any physical chain.

I paused for a moment to steady myself before reaching for the radio, brushing my fingers over the familiar buttons. Static crackled to life as I called out to Hunt, my voice steady and calm. "There's nothing to fear," I assured him, hoping to instill a sense of control amid the chaos of our situation. Hunt's voice came through, laced with curiosity and a hint of uncertainty, as he asked whether he should follow the hypotenuse of a right triangle down to the river or take the line out instead.

Weighing the options carefully, I answered firmly, telling him to walk the line out. Although it might be the longer route, the treacherous cross-country terrain was too hazardous. We would navigate the chasm, descending through steep bluffs and towering cliffs, all enveloped in the darkness of night. The thought sent a shiver through me, but I knew it was the right call.

Just as I finished my transmission, the superintendent's voice crackled over the radio, infused with a fervor that bordered on manic. He interjected with a flourish of biblical references, proclaiming that with his help, we could accomplish anything, announcing his plan to join the crew at the top to mop up the slop-over. He said he was going to walk down to the Illinois River Trail. I rolled my eyes, knowing his bravado often masked a growing instability. "You are sabotaging him by giving him good advice, knowing he will do the opposite," Berkson said.

By the time my crew finally arrived at camp, it was early evening, around seven o'clock. I went straight to the camp managers, urgency in my voice, and asked them to save food for another crew that would be coming in late. With the night still ahead of us, I took the opportunity to help my team restock our supplies. Our movements were efficient and practiced, a well-oiled machine pushing through exhaustion.

Around three o'clock in the morning, the superintendent and the rest of the crew finally arrived, dragging their feet from sheer fatigue, too worn out to even think about eating. With little more than a nod, they collapsed into their beds, surrendering to sleep. The sun would rise early, as it always did, and we would be up again at five-thirty, the usual time to prepare for the day ahead. Thankfully, the next day promised a quieter task: mopping up the remnants of the fire, a welcome reprieve from the intensity of what we had just endured.

CHAPTER 12

MOP UP

The following day, our task was to mop up the remnants of the backfire that had transformed the landscape of Silver Prairie. We engaged in mop-up, a critical yet labor-intensive process, to extinguish hot spots that lingered stubbornly near the fire line. This meant thoroughly mixing the heated areas with mineral soil or dousing them with water to ensure that the last embers of the disaster were completely extinguished. Our crew was now noticeably smaller; we had lost two members to saw injuries during the chaotic battle against the flames, one to a painful encounter with the relentless sting of poison oak, and two others who left in pursuit of higher education, leaving a void in our ranks.

In those long, drawn-out days of mop-up, as the sun sank lower in the sky, casting a warm, orange glow that flickered like firelight across the charred landscape, I lost myself in thought. I wondered, in the quiet recesses of my mind, why those who had once cared so deeply for one another—who had forged unbreakable bonds of trust and camaraderie while standing shoulder to shoulder against infernos that could easily consume us—were now expected to turn their backs on each other.

I felt the weight of the forest pressing in around me, as if the trees themselves were listening, bearing witness to the injustice simmering beneath the surface. It was a bitter pill to swallow: the realization that the government, through the Agency, had so callously cast us aside, treating us as mere numbers in a ledger rather than the brave souls we were. The policy—cold, bureaucratic, and calculated—embodied a reckless disregard for human life, a betrayal that echoed through the very heart of the forests we had fought to protect.

Yet despite the tragic losses we endured—friends and colleagues who died in the line of duty, their laughter and stories now just memories drifting in the breeze—no one was ever charged with manslaughter. The silence of accountability hung heavily in the air, thickening the atmosphere as I mourned not just the fallen but the fracture in our sense of unity. Each step felt like a march through a graveyard, a solemn reminder of the cost of our profession. And I couldn't help but wonder how long it would be before the scars of this betrayal faded—if they ever would.

Amid these deep and contemplative reflections, I grappled with the realization that a clear picture often eluded me in the chaotic landscape of my thoughts. Sometimes, what seemed like the most insignificant detail turned out to hold the greatest importance in the grand tapestry of firefighting. The nature of our work was steeped in nuance, requiring a trained eye and a sharp mind to truly understand what mattered most.

Any seasoned firefighter—someone who had weathered the flames and understood the intricacies of our perilous trade—would emphatically tell you that a person capable of extinguishing a tiny spark at the bottom of a ridge, one brimming with dry fuels, proved far more crucial than all the slurry planes, engines, and crews combined. This held especially true when considering the potential devastation that could unfold if such a small ember were left unchecked. Within moments of ignition, that seemingly insignificant spark could evolve into a roaring inferno, consuming everything in its path—no matter how massive the conflagration—raging across a hundred thousand acres, fueled by the relentless winds of a dry cold front.

The weight of this truth pressed on me, reminding me of the countless times I had witnessed the devastating consequences of negligence and the critical need for vigilance. In the world of wildfires, the smallest actions often lead to the most significant outcomes. Each decision made in those fleeting moments could tip the balance between safety and catastrophe, and I carried that burden with both pride and trepidation.

As I surveyed the charred landscape of Silver Prairie, I noted with relief that no smoke rose through the heavy humidity of the morning. The air felt thick, almost tangible, saturated with the remnants of the backfire. Patches of yellow ash lay scattered across the ground, and instinctively, I reached down to feel the ash with the back of my hand. It was a small precaution I'd learned through experience; if the heat proved stronger than expected and left blisters, they would form in a place that wouldn't hinder my grip on a tool.

Satisfied the area was cool to the touch, I scanned my surroundings with sharpened awareness, my instincts honed to detect even the subtlest hint of danger. Then, a fleeting whiff of smoke drifted in on the breeze, lingering just long enough to catch my attention—though no visible signs emerged from the underbrush. It was as if the smoke lurked in hiding, waiting for a single moment of carelessness to strike again.

Beneath the sprawling shadow of an ancient oak log, I uncovered another patch of ominous yellow ash, its fine particles swirling gently in the air. This time, I noticed gnats flitting about—drawn to the spot as if investigating the aftermath of a great battle. With the back of my hand, I cautiously assessed the warmth radiating from the ash. Then, peeking from behind the log, I caught it—hardly visible smoke, whispering from the earth like a secret.

Realizing the potential danger, I sprang into action, swiftly mixing the heated area with mineral soil. I worked diligently, sweat trickling down my brow as the heat gradually dissipated, surrendering its hold until it finally extinguished.

Nearby, Glenn stood among us—part of the bridge foursome on our crew—a seasoned veteran with a wealth of experience and a poetic soul. He often gathered around a table of cards with Krutilla, Berkson, and Ford during the excruciatingly long hours we spent waiting for planes to ferry us to far-flung destinations where fires burned. We played bridge, grateful for the distraction from the uncertainty of where we might be sent next. The planes soared through the skies, carrying us to the fire-ravaged landscapes of Alaska, California, Oregon, Idaho, and countless other places where the flames blazed hottest. Often, the wait could stretch for hours or even a full day.

In those moments, the hours felt endless. Yet, companionship filled them—stories shared, strategies debated over the cards spread before us. Each hand offered a small escape from the weight of our responsibilities, a fleeting reprieve from our roles as guardians against nature's fury.

This marked Glenn's first year on the hotshot crew—a fresh beginning amidst the chaos of flames and smoke, the kind of chaos that could ignite at any moment and consume everything in its path. Though he had spent nearly a decade honing his skills on various shot crews scattered across the country—navigating the rugged terrains of the Southwest, the dense forests of the Pacific Northwest, and the sunscorched hills of California—this year felt uniquely significant. It was tinged with a weight that was both exhilarating and daunting. The gravity of responsibility pressed heavily on his shoulders, magnified by the looming anticipation of fatherhood—an ever-present specter he couldn't shake. The thought of bringing a new life into this world, with all its dangers and uncertainties, filled him with equal parts joy and trepidation.

Each stroke of my imagination served as a homage to the past, reminding me of the sacrifices made and the lives intertwined with the flames—echoes that lived on in the hearts of those who dared to stand against the inferno.

I often found myself lost in thought, my gaze drifting toward Ray, who stood a few feet away—a stalwart figure even amid the shifting chaos of our surroundings. He strapped his bladder bag tightly across his back, the fabric worn and faded from years of service, each frayed edge telling a story of battles fought against the unyielding forces of nature. His countenance reflected a deep sense of contemplation, his brow furrowed as he focused intently on the task at hand, embodying the poise and wisdom that only experience could bring.

In the quiet corners of his mind, Ray painted—an artist conjuring vivid images of a world where flame and beauty intertwined, creating a tapestry of memories that flickered like the very fires they fought. He envisioned the haunting sight of burning snags, their charred silhouettes reaching skyward like desperate fingers grasping for salvation—each one a testament to the fierce struggle between life and destruction. He painted meteors streaking across the night sky, blazing trails of light over the Black Butte Fire of 1981, a moment etched into the annals of firefighting history, when Ray's crew—the forest B.D. crew—joined forces with the hotshot crew he now proudly called his own.

These vivid images became a sanctuary for Krutilla during the long, oppressive winter—months defined by relentless fog, pervasive gloom, and the incessant rain that blanketed everything in dampness. The streams winding down from the towering flanks of Mount Hood seemed to carry the mood of the season—dark, swollen, and heavy with the burden of overcast skies. In the solitude of his thoughts, Krutilla easily escaped to the fiery landscape he cherished, a place of stark, vibrant contrast to the gray monotony outside. He painted those memories with intricate detail in his mind, each brushstroke a vivid recollection, while he worked methodically, wrestling with the challenges ahead. His brow furrowed in concentration, and he weighed the burden of leadership and the constant, looming threat to his crew in a world where unpredictability ruled.

Meanwhile, Keller, ever the poet with a heart full of words, found his voice beside a crackling fire. The flames danced and flickered, casting a soft amber glow on the faces of his comrades. He wove together verses that drifted through the air, delicate yet grounded, wrapping us in warmth that pushed back against the chill of the season. His words were a reminder of the strength and beauty forged in shared hardship, of the connections built in the heat of the line.

THE BISON AND THE WILDFIRE

Black Hills Fire, South Dakota
Zigzag Hotshot Crew

I watch the smoke and tiny stars of flame,
The night opening behind us in wind-drunk fire
Inside the huge red moons of your eyes.

How could I have known as I flagged this route out
That you were waiting here for the sound of my bones?
One thousand years of blood and dust and dung.

Now, inside your ears, my crew's first voices. A horrible chant
Of power saws and hand tools. Their slow attack echoes
Toward us. So I promise to stay with you all night,

To whisper into this radio cinched against my heart,
To warn them if you should turn and spin your great weight
Past sumac and chokecherry into the sound of their lives.

Above us, inside the black sky on those old Sioux ridges
Shapes of white pine begin to remember themselves
Back into flame. Your giant skull heaves up

Into such a terrible silence. The dry peppery taste
Of skunkbush heating your breath, this night, the fire,
Your ancient passion to kill me. I move even closer.

You are the biggest animal I have ever dreamed.
Will either of us ever understand this fragile hate
Rising between us? I hear myself speak to you.
Tomorrow I will tell them everything. How you

Warned me like thunder with sudden low grunts.
How, even so, I followed you back into your dark.

Into this crazy bison and wildfire true story.
I was so young and fell in love with this danger.
With your eyes. With your sweet skunkbush breath.

Paul Keller

Fire, in its unpredictable fury, provided the raw materials for our mission. Fairbanks, Alaska, remained a distant memory. We moved on to Bettles, north of the Arctic Circle, surrounded by stark tundra and wilderness. A small, remote outpost often referred to as the gateway to the Arctic wilderness, Bettles served as a departure point for numerous national parks and public lands.

There, the reality of tundra fires loomed large. We learned to dig down to the frost line, but even that effort faltered when the relentless midnight sun thawed the earth. Most fires were left to burn freely unless a village stood in their path. In those moments, we turned to carbide chainsaws—cutting through soil and ice to reach the permafrost, battling fire in a land where water flowed beneath frozen ground, and the sun refused to set.

Our hour-long helicopter flights exhilarated us as we soared above the terrain, glimpsing wildlife below. Bears, both brown and black, lumbered through the tundra. Grizzly bears frequently visited, showcasing nature's raw beauty. Wolves prowled the shadows, watchful and vigilant. Moose wandered through the underbrush, while shaggy muskoxen grazed peacefully in the Arctic Refuge.

The region buzzed with smaller mammals, including wolverines, coyotes, lynxes, and arctic ground squirrels, each playing a vital role in the tapestry of life in the harsh landscape. Lemmings, voles, marmots, porcupines, river otters, foxes, beavers, and snowshoe hares thrived, navigating with agility.

Meals were carefully orchestrated, with fresh food arriving every three days to sustain the crew. We dug into the permafrost for makeshift refrigeration to keep provisions cool, a small luxury in this remote location. Steaks and frozen vegetables transformed dinner into a delightful experience as the midnight sun briefly dipped below the horizon, accompanied by the sounds of nature.

Back on the Silver Fire, Ray approached Glenn, who focused his attention on the gnarled and worn-out roots of a Ponderosa pine that had succumbed to the devastation of the burnout. The roots twisted and elongated, snaking through the earth as remnants of a once-majestic tree now reduced to a darkened relic of its former self. As Glenn broke apart the stubborn root wad with deft strokes, smoke billowed upward, curling into the air like a ghostly serpent.

Strapped securely to his back, his bladder bag held five gallons of vital water. With a practiced hand, he directed the nozzle toward the smoldering earth, squirting a steady stream of water onto the hot area as he expertly mixed the liquid into the heat, suppressing the stubborn embers that flickered defiantly in the aftermath of the destruction.

This was a mop-up phase, a critical part of our operation. It marked a time when the intensity of firefighting began to ebb, allowing for a moment of recovery. Depending on personal preference, some worked better in pairs, enjoying the fellowship and conversation that came with shared labor. In contrast, others preferred the solitude of their thoughts as they toiled alone. Ford, a stalwart, found himself in the latter camp today. He chewed on his Copenhagen chewing tobacco, the familiar taste providing comfort amidst the chaos, as he relentlessly busted apart the root wad with fervor.

Ford had spent three years on the crew. Yet, he carried over a decade of experience in firefighting, making him a master not only with the saw but also with the intricacies of helicopter operations and countless other tasks that came with the territory. Despite his infectious smile that could brighten even the gloomiest of days, a shadow of worry crossed his face. He often drifted into thoughts of his wife, who was pregnant with their first child. A whirlwind of emotions surged within him—the excitement of impending fatherhood clashing with the anxiety of work. Deep down, he harbored a nagging fear that his position might soon become obsolete, that he would be one of many to disappear at the hands of the Agency by season's end, a fate looming like a dark cloud over his hopeful future.

My gaze drifted over to Donna, who strikingly resembled the iconic actress Jane Russell. The sun filtered through the dense canopy of darkened woods, casting a warm, golden light that danced across her charred, brown face, accentuating her features in a way that made her appear almost ethereal amidst the rugged backdrop of our surroundings. She was engaged in dry mopping, a technique she had meticulously learned to master, using mineral soil to smother the stubborn remnants of the fire. As she worked, the ash swirled around her in a delicate cloud, some particles gently settling on her skin like snowflakes, lending her an otherworldly beauty that was both captivating and fierce.

This was Donna's inaugural year on the crew, and she had quickly proven herself to be tenacious and fiercely determined. A spark in her eyes spoke to her spirit—a fire of her own paralleling the flames we battled. As we worked, she turned to me, her voice animated as we fell into conversation. We discussed our plans for the winter—what we might do when the snow blankets the ground and the fires are but a memory. Donna shared her uncertainties about returning to the crew next season, her brow furrowing slightly as she contemplated the decision, weighing her options carefully.

As the morning wore on, we relished the knowledge that, unlike many other days spent firefighting, where meals were consumed hurriedly, today, we would enjoy an official half-hour lunch break. The thought of sitting down and sharing a meal amidst the stillness of the forest added a layer of anticipation to our already fruitful work.

At lunch, as the sun hung high in the sky, casting warm golden rays through the trees, Michelle joined us. She had seamlessly integrated into the crew mid-year, bringing with her a spirit that felt both refreshing and invigorating. But the bittersweet reality loomed—she would soon depart to attend Oregon State University in just a few days. Donna and I shared a bond with her, forged through the trials of firefighting. I found myself keeping a watchful eye on her inexperience, determined to ensure her safety and growth amidst the dangerous elements we faced each day.

As we settled down to eat, the trio dug into our M.R.E.s—meals ready to eat. Each package contained a mix of goodies, some dehydrated, others still in their original form, ready to be devoured. I rummaged through my supplies, eyeing the beef stew I could heat over a crackling fire, its aroma promising comfort to hungry firefighters. I paused, soaking in the stillness of the Indian Summer day, embracing the warmth. I savored the simple joys—the laughter, the stories, and the shared experiences that had bonded us through the haze of smoke and the chaos of the brush.

"Guess what tomorrow night is," I asked, breaking the comfortable silence as I mixed water with the dehydrated fruit in the bag, a playful gleam in my eyes. I watched as both Donna and Michelle turned to me, their expressions twisting with perplexity, curiosity sparked by what I might say next.

"Two-for-one pizza night at the Zigzag Inn," I exclaimed, my tone dripping with excitement. The thought of indulging in cheesy slices and hearty toppings felt like a beacon of hope amid the grueling work that lay ahead. As boredom often seeped in during mop-up operations, I made it my mission to remind us of the little pleasures we could look forward to—especially with the overtime and hazardous pay that came with our long shifts.

"Sixteen-hour shifts make for a good paycheck," I added, a grin spreading across my face as I recalled the familiar banter we shared among the crew. "Black forest," I mimicked Dewitze's voice, "green paycheck!" I remembered fondly. Dewitze had been a spirited member of our team, a talented firefighter who left to smokejump in Alaska back in 1982—a decision that led Keith to follow suit shortly after. Our memories lingered like smoke in the air, a testament to the bonds we formed in the heat of battle and the friendships that transcended the flames.

In 1981, a significant milestone in my life marked my inaugural year on the hotshot crew. I, Dinardo, Rozenburgh, and Keith nestled in a secluded clearing, surrounded by the stark, haunting remnants of charred Lodgepole Pine trees that stood like somber statues, testifying to the ferocity of the flames that once consumed this landscape. The night sky stretched above us, a vast canvas dotted with countless stars, each twinkling like a tiny beacon in the darkness. The crisp air carried the faint scent of smoke mingling with the earthy aroma of sage and grass that survived the recent fire.

As we reclined on the cool ground, our gazes fixed upward, we engaged in a lively conversation about our shared passion for fire—the thrill of battling blazes, forged in the heat of the moment, and the dreams we held for our futures, all interwoven with our devotion to this demanding profession. Our voices rose and fell, animated by excitement and the flickering glow of a nearby hot spot that gradually dimmed.

The stars above shone notably clear, providing a stunning backdrop for our discussions. We reflected on the recent fire that burned through fine fuels—an inferno that devoured the grasses and sage, rapidly igniting and just as swiftly extinguishing once the fuel was spent. The contrast between the black ash of the fire and the serene beauty of the night created a moment of introspection, where dreams and reality intertwined.

During our musings, a dazzling sight filled the air as a meteor blazed across the sky like a celestial messenger. Its brilliance captivated us, holding our attention for a moment as it arced through the darkness above. Down below, Ray, with his thoughtful demeanor and keen observations, also caught sight of the meteor. His eyes widened in awe, drawing a shared gasp among us as we paused our conversation, enchanted by the wonder of the universe above—an echo of the wildness we passionately embraced in our work.

In 1984, a sense of urgency hung in the air as Dinardo, McAllister, and I diligently worked to cut through the thick, resilient Lodgepole Pine that stood firmly atop a rugged knob, our chosen site for the day's task. We received our first warning, a chilling note of foreboding as we watched, perhaps even stalked, by an unseen presence. This warning served as a stark reminder of the dangers that lay not only in the flames we fought but also in the shadows that lurked beyond our line of sight.

That year, the memory of Keith weighed heavily on my mind, his absence leaving a void among us. The year prior had been harrowing for him; Keith hadn't worked directly with us but had instead joined an engine crew, which offered a less intimate and more mechanical experience. That season, we faced a fire in Nevada—an inferno that initially appeared contained, its flames licking at the dry earth, held in check by the diligent efforts of the firefighters. However, in a cruel twist of fate, a swirling whirlwind formed unexpectedly, snatching the fire and hurling it into a fierce wind that tore across the dry sage and brittle grasses.

In that moment of chaos and confusion, his engine crew had to retreat quickly, abandoning their position and forgetting about Keith in the frantic rush—an oversight that weighed heavily on their hearts. The haunting memory of that day lingered like a specter in our minds, a painful reminder of nature's unpredictability and the sacrifices we made in the line of duty. As we cut through the wood, each slice felt like a tribute, honoring both the wins and the losses we endured—a testament to our resilience and unyielding spirit.

"Ya hoo, Buckaroo!" Keith would bellow with infectious enthusiasm, his voice echoing off the rustic wooden walls of White Water Lodge, where we were stationed back in the summer of 1981. The lodge, nestled among the stately Lodgepole, Piss Fir, and Douglas Fir trees, rose majestically toward the alpine meadows, sweetly perfumed by the blooming Rhododendron adorning Mount Hood. "Ya hoo, Buckaroo!" he shouted again, his voice mingling with the delightful aroma wafting through the air—savory bacon sizzling in the pan, plump sausages browning to perfection, crispy hash browns crackling, fluffy omelets sliding onto plates, and the sweet scent of Huckleberry pancakes teasing our senses.

We, invigorated by the sounds of morning and the promise of a hearty breakfast, joined Keith, me, and the ever-reliable McCollister in the bustling kitchen. Together, we prepared the legendary "buck-aroo" breakfast—a ritual that not only fueled our bodies but also so-lidified our bonds. Laughter and lighthearted banter filled the lodge as we cooked, creating a warm atmosphere that sharply contrasted with the intense discussions we would later have about the fire we had just faced.

Having just returned from the demanding Utah fire, we began our day with a vigorous physical training session that morning. We ran on various trails, weaving around the Lodge, sprinted over to Barlow Trail, made our way up to the Meadows, and pushed toward Tim-berline Lodge. Every step brought us closer to the towering snowy peak of Mount Hood, which loomed above, occasionally shrouded by a lenticular cloud—a weather phenomenon that seasoned firefighters knew signaled high winds aloft that could come crashing down to fan the flames of any fire.

As we ran, the sweet aroma of mid-summer enveloped us—a stark reminder of the beauty surrounding us, even as we fought off the bothersome horse flies buzzing in the warm air. With each stride, we hummed a tune, a melody that danced lightly before the insects land-ed on our bare shoulders, soaking in the sun's golden rays. The rhythm of our footsteps echoed the pulse of our lives, creating a harmonious blend of nature's challenges and the joys of brotherhood in the face of adversity.

Keith had been a steadying presence for me ever since that pivotal first year on the crew, when he helped me strap on my web gear for the very first time. That moment marked the beginning of a strong fellowship, forged in the fires of both literal and figurative challenges. The memory of that summer in 1982 remained vivid, especially the day Keith graciously towed my aging Volkswagen van. We endured a long, arduous fifty-mile journey, winding from the bustling streets of Port-land up to the rugged mountain home we shared—a sanctuary that came to symbolize our shared commitment to the firefighting life.

Ah, 1982—the year of the notorious Football Fire. That inferno tested not just our skills but our resolve. As we cut line downhill through a narrow draw, the urgency of the situation hung in the air like the acrid scent of smoke. I glanced at Keith, whose eyes stayed sharp and focused, reflecting the gravity of our task. Just as we arrived, the fire erupted—blowing mercilessly over the road and transforming the landscape into a chaotic battleground.

Carol, with her bold, expressive eyes that could convey a thousand words without a single utterance, wore the unmistakable look of an adrenaline rush mixed with disbelief at the precarious situation before us. It was her inaugural year on the crew as well. Though still finding her footing, her fierce spirit clearly showed that it would serve her well. I knew she and Keith would forge a bond that would only deepen with time, united by the trials and triumphs they would face together.

Keith, ever the practical one, pointed decisively to a spot further up the draw, indicating the safety zone we needed to reach. A surge of urgency filled me as I increased my pace, cutting with a feverish rhythm that matched the pounding of my heart. In contrast, Keith maintained a steady, methodical approach—his cuts precise and deliberate, showcasing the calm and experience that defined him. Together, we pressed forward, each movement a testament to our resilience and the unbreakable ties of brotherhood forged in the face of raging flames.

The crowns of the trees erupted into a chaotic inferno, flames dancing and crackling with a ferocity that seemed almost alive. I instinctively glanced upward again, my eyes drawn to Keith, who vigorously gestured toward our new safety zone. With urgency etched across my face, I nodded in acknowledgment, the weight of the situation settling heavily on my shoulders.

The fire mercilessly torched the canopy above, sending flames spiraling fifty feet into the air—a breathtaking yet terrifying spectacle. Fortunately, the raging inferno didn't advance toward us. However, the threat loomed large as we cut an indirect line, a strategy that demanded both precision and unwavering focus.

Again, my gaze rose to the scene above, where I saw Keith working with an intensity that spoke of both determination and desperation. Our eyes met briefly—a silent exchange of understanding passing between us. I pointed toward the next safety zone, indicating our intended path through the chaos. Keith met my gaze with a quick nod, a shared acknowledgment of our mission and the unyielding bond forged between us in the face of the relentless flames.

I moved with purpose toward the spot where we had tied into the road earlier, my muscles aching from the day's unrelenting labor. I unscrewed the cap of one of my four-quart plastic canteens, filling it to the brim with the precious water that would sustain me through the night ahead. The sun dipped below the horizon, casting long shadows across the rugged terrain as I dove over another ridge to continue cutting along the fire line. Night was creeping in, wrapping the landscape in inky darkness that would soon engulf everything.

As I pressed on, exhaustion seeped into my bones. Hunt, with his calm demeanor and seasoned experience, provided a much-needed anchor for the crew. He took charge, initiating a burnout from the line. The flames leapt hungrily upward, licking at the crowns of the towering trees while smoke billowed and twisted—a swirling testament to the fire's fervor. I could feel the heat radiating from the blaze, an ever-present reminder of the danger we faced.

In a moment of desperation, I lifted my canteen to my lips, only to discover it held my last quart of water. The realization struck hard—I had been pushing myself for hours, and now my body was pleading for hydration. It was time to pass off my saw, a task I usually approached with confidence, but a glance around revealed there was no one left to take it. McAllister, typically a stalwart member of the crew, had thrown out his back and was still bravely attempting to throw brush despite his injury. Keith, too, was showing signs of wear—his energy seemed to drain with each swing of the saw.

Undeterred by the circumstances, I tightened my grip on my Stihl .045, a heavy and powerful saw built to fell even the largest trees. It was a beast of a machine—maybe too big for the line we were cutting—but it didn't vapor lock, and that made it invaluable in this critical moment. With renewed resolve, I resumed cutting. The growl of the saw echoed through the gathering night, a rhythmic reminder of our fight against the encroaching darkness and the fire threatening to consume everything in its path.

We ran our chainsaws through the night, the engine's steady roar cutting through the silence of the darkened forest. My water was gone—the canteen now empty, clinking uselessly against my belt. As the first hints of dawn crept over the horizon, painting the sky in soft hues of orange and pink, we finished our work, having cut a crucial line around a small but significant spot at the bottom of the fire's reach. With a final, determined push, I threw my chain as Hunt completed the last cut—our teamwork running like a well-oiled machine. I took a moment to file my rakers, methodically ensuring my tools were ready for the next challenge, when a call came from above—another snag needed to be felled.

Feeling the parched burn in my throat intensify, I instinctively raised my hand, volunteering for the task. I knew I had to push through, even as fatigue pressed heavily on my limbs. Together with Carol, my wedge driver, we began the uphill trek—long, steep, and unforgiving. The morning air was crisp and lonely, the only sounds our heavy breaths and the crunch of gravel beneath our boots. I staggered slightly with each step, fighting exhaustion as we climbed. The snag we reached was small, but the saw needed sharpening—its teeth dulled from relentless work.

Totally worn out, I leaned into the snag, my body protesting with each movement. I caught my breath, realizing I hadn't had water for three long hours. My mouth wasn't just dry; it was parched, feeling like coarse sandpaper or cotton. My tongue was thick, heavy, and seemed to cleave to the roof of my mouth, making speech a struggle that produced only a raspy whisper. The back of my throat felt constricted, raw, and burning, as if lined with fine dust. Deep inside, there was an aching hollow in my stomach and a persistent, gnawing sense of emptiness. My body felt heavy, muscles ached, and a dull, pervasive headache throbbed through my skull. Every thought was overshadowed by a single, primal need: water.

Just as despair began to creep in, Carol, ever perceptive, handed me her canteen. Embarrassed by my need and grateful for her generosity, I took a long gulp—drinking nearly half a quart of her precious water. In that moment, a connection sparked within me. I would forever feel a bond with Carol, her kindness igniting something deep inside.

The back cut came easily; each stroke of the saw felt more like a dance than labor as the tree began to yield. With a final crack, the snag tumbled into a carefully prepared bed—a space we had cleared of surrounding fuels to ensure safety from the flames. After that long morning, I finally succumbed to sleep beneath the comforting shelter of a towering Ponderosa Pine. From that day forward, I vowed never to carry less than two gallons of water again—a lesson etched into memory, a reminder of the strength found in both the land and the bonds we forged together.

In 1984, a significant moment unfolded as Dinardo, McAllister, and I came together to craft a memorial—a heartfelt tribute to honor the memory of our fallen comrade, Keith. We chose a serene spot atop the knob, a place where the vast expanse of the night sky could be admired—a location we affectionately dubbed the Stargazers' Lounge. It served as a fitting venue, where the brilliance of the stars shone down upon our creation, reminding us of the beauty of life and the fragility of our own existence.

Little did we know, time slipped away from us like sand through an hourglass. Rozenburgh, the dedicated firefighter who had been a steadfast part of our crew, made the difficult decision to step away in 1983 to raise Dinardo's child—a choice that led him to reflect on his own future. After the close of the 1984 season, Dinardo, driven by a longing for stability and the promise of a life with his wife and child, left the crew as well. And as the seasons progressed, McAllister followed suit, departing in 1987—marking the end of an era for our tight-knit group of firefighters, who had shared both the triumphs and trials of our demanding lives.

In 1984, the Agency made a steadfast decision that would impact our daily lives as firefighters. They strictly prohibited Rozenburgh from disposing of our trash—particularly the unpleasant burden of baby diapers—in the Agency's dumpster. The rules allowed only refuse from official Agency operations, which meant a thirty-mile trek to the nearest dump for Rozenburgh—a journey that felt both cumbersome and unnecessary. What the officials didn't know was that Dinardo and I had devised a clever workaround to this inflexible regulation. Each day, we slyly snuck the offending garbage into the back of the Saw Rig, our trusted vehicle that had seen countless battles against the flames.

As the sun began to set and the day wound down, we discreetly emptied the contents of the Rig into the dumpster, feeling a small rebellion in each toss. Meanwhile, the Agency remained blissfully unaware, patting us on the back for our commitment to maintaining the cleanliness of the Saw Rig, convinced their policies were being upheld without question.

Above Briggs, near the expansive stretch of Silver Prairie, I observed Michelle and Donna. They represented the crew's future—brimming with potential—and with a few more seasons under their belts, I believed they would evolve into exceptional firefighters. Yet change loomed on the horizon. Donna, with her fiery spirit and anti-authoritarian streak, ultimately left after the 1987 season. Following closely behind, Michelle also bid farewell after the 1988 season. The absence of their seasoned presence was deeply felt, dramatically shifting the crew's dynamics. Each departure echoed through the ranks, leaving behind a void that would be difficult to fill—altering the very fabric of our collective journey in the unforgiving world of firefighting.

I teamed up with Keller, who had a knack for weaving words into poetry even amidst the chaos. Our partnership blended my youthful exuberance with his creative insight, and together we shared thoughts and dreams as we worked. Meanwhile, Donna, still brimming with spirited defiance and a fierce determination to prove herself, partnered with me as we tackled the remnants of the fire. We moved deeper into the charred landscape—a task that stretched on for several more days.

With each sweep of our tools and each bucket of ash we collected, we broke the monotony with flashes of inspiration. Moments of magic, laced with philosophical musings, floated through the smoky air. Our conversations about life, courage, and the poetry embedded in the world around us transformed the tedium into something richer and more meaningful.

As the sun dipped lower in the sky, casting long shadows across the scorched earth on the third day of mop-up operations, we wrapped up our work surprisingly earlier than anticipated. A sense of satisfaction—born from our laborious efforts and sweat over the past few days—hung in the air like a fragrant perfume, mingling with the earthy scent of the forest beginning to recover from the ravages of the fire. The vibrant greens of new growth peeked through the blackened remnants of charred trees, a hopeful sign that nature remained resilient, even in the face of such destruction.

With a collective sigh of relief, we gathered our gear, carefully folding and stowing away tools that had become extensions of our bodies during those grueling days. Each piece of equipment served as a reminder of the battles we'd fought against the flames. As we began the trek back to Briggs Ranch, the familiar route felt both comforting and burdensome, our steps heavy with exhaustion that clung to us like a second skin.

We planned to go to R&R in Gold Beach the next day. The additional six miles to the fire camp at Oak Flats stretched out before us, seeming longer than ever—each aching step bringing us closer to base camp and the promise of rest.

Upon arrival, the scene that greeted us felt familiar, yet it was always buzzing with invigorating life. The area, dotted with brightly colored tents of agency personnel, had transformed into a makeshift village vibrant with activity. Some tents housed agency men seeking refuge from the rigors of their duties, while others offered leisure, providing a welcome respite where we could gather and indulge in the simple pleasure of watching television—a surreal luxury after days spent battling the elements. Laughter and chatter filled the air as weary firefighters exchanged stories of heroism, the bonds of our shared experiences weaving us together like threads in a tapestry, each one adding depth to the richness of our collective journey.

Still, I preferred the quiet. I wandered off to the banks of the Illinois River, seeking the tranquility of starlight. Michelle joined me.

As darkness enveloped the camp, we returned—exhausted but fulfilled. The flickering lights from the tents cast a warm glow against the twilight sky, a stark contrast to the chaos we'd left behind in the forest. The camaraderie of the day lingered in the air, promising another night of shared stories, laughter, and the enduring bond forged by facing the flames together.

I filled my lungs with the sour air—a noxious blend of smoke from the fire and the pungent odor of smudge pots that stung my eyes and made my throat feel raw. With each breath I took, I carried the remnants of the day's battle, a reminder of the chaos lurking in the distance. I turned away from the oppressive atmosphere, seeking a fleeting moment of solace.

With a determined stride, I made my way to the supply tent, the familiar sights and sounds of the camp fading into the background. The supply area buzzed with activity, other firefighters milling about, their faces drawn and weary, yet tinged with the fellowship that united us. Upon arrival, I approached the agency man stationed behind the counter, hoping to procure a few cans of Copenhagen chewing tobacco to ease the day's stress.

However, the agency man, with his air of authority and a hint of condescension, informed me that I could not buy just a few cans. "You'll have to buy the whole roll," he stated flatly, as if the words were etched in stone. This response ignited a flicker of frustration within me, but I quickly suppressed it. With a swift motion, I tore several rolls off the stack for myself. I laid down some crumpled bills for the tobacco. As I pocketed the cans, I turned on my heel. I headed toward the first aid station, knowing I needed to tend to the irritating poison oak flaring up on my skin. The thought of the first aid supplies being reserved for those who remained in camp all day gnawed at me—a reminder of the unspoken hierarchy that sometimes permeated our tight-knit community. Yet, I pressed on, determined to find relief from the discomfort accompanying my work.

That night, as the stars twinkled faintly in the vast expanse of the sky overhead, I tossed and turned in my sleeping bag, my mind racing with thoughts that refused to settle. I experienced a restless sleep, filled with fleeting dreams that slipped through my fingers like grains of sand, and the weight of the day's events lingered like a heavy fog in my mind. I remained acutely aware that tomorrow promised a day of much-needed rest and relaxation in Gold Beach—a welcome reprieve from the relentless demands of our current assignment. Yet even amidst the anticipation of soothing waves and gentle breezes, nagging worries about my responsibilities and the challenges that lay ahead clung to me, making true rest feel elusive.

CHAPTER 13

R AND R

The crew and I were enjoying R&R (rest and relaxation) from the Silver Fire, taking a much-needed respite from the relentless demands of our grueling work. I found myself in a rare moment of leisure and laze—a welcome contrast to the chaos that usually surrounded me. After indulging in breakfast, the air rich with the aroma of freshly brewed coffee, I took a moment to soak in my surroundings as I sat on the warm, sandy beach.

Before me, the ocean stretched infinitely. The sand sparkled under the sun's warm embrace, each fleck of light dancing with the white foam rolling in. The brilliant blue sky was unmarred by smoke, and a fragrant breeze carried the cries of seagulls gliding and diving for hidden morsels. I inhaled deeply, savoring the fresh air—a reminder of nature's tranquility.

It struck me that it had been over a decade since I had last breathed the salty air of the beach during the summer months. Memories flooded back—a time filled with laughter and carefree days, a stark contrast to my current life. I recalled the escape from Grangeville, Idaho, driven by a need for freedom after a wild night in a cramped motel room with the women's softball team. We had arrived in Grangeville, weary and in search of only our second shower since embarking on our hitchhiking adventure from Iowa just days before—each mile etched into memory as we chased the thrill of the road and the promise of new experiences.

The first leg of our journey was filled with an undercurrent of chilly conversation between the two women, who seemed to be searching for a different kind of man altogether. We viewed the cornfields of Iowa in awkward silence. Later, a van picked us up, carrying us across the vast prairie—800 miles westward toward Ketchum, Idaho. Inside the van, the atmosphere shifted when a warm-hearted woman from Vermont joined us, her infectious laughter and spirit brightening the mood.

As we glided through the blackened night of South Dakota, the rhythmic thrum of the engine accompanied the sporadic sounds of nature outside. Grasses tinged with wildflowers stretched toward the horizon, and we hoped to spot some bison along the way. We sipped our bourbon, the warmth of the drink a welcome contrast to the cold air seeping through the cracks in the windows.

In Grangeville, we ventured farther into the night, escaping the confines of the motel—driven more by boredom than by any real hunger for adventure. It was somewhere near the town of Walla Walla that I found myself shifting from foot to foot, restless. Through a stagnant day, the boredom began to sift through us like dust.

"Some say this town's a waste of time, to tell the truth, it's wasting mine," Krutilla sang, dragging out a Danny O'Keefe tune on the gravelly, dusty edge of a highway winding past Walla Walla. *The state prison was nearby, wasn't it?* he wondered aloud, wiping the mid-August heat from his forehead. There was no smell—just dry air and grit.

Dan paused where he'd been kicking rocks into a sewer, took a sip of water, then resumed the motion, slow and methodical. Krutilla kept singing in an annoying, tuneless voice. The taste of the sardine sandwich he'd eaten earlier still clung stubbornly in his mouth, and he longed for the sweetness of an ice-cold Pabst Blue Ribbon. He glanced south over the wide expanse stretching toward the rural town. Onion fields, he guessed—those sweet Walla Walla onions, marinated and smoked on the grill with peppers and mushrooms. He imagined the barbecue smoke curling into the air, tried to inhale deeply, to taste it, to smell it.

"What are you doing?" I asked Dan, who continued kicking stones into the sewer.

"I'm kicking Walla Walla into the sewer—stone by stone," he said flatly.

Twenty years later, I got a call from Dan. He wanted to go back to Walla Walla—to finish the job.

The next day, we ended up at a party in the Tri-Cities—a bustling gathering that throbbed with energy until the police arrived to break it up, scattering the crowd. Somehow, we all wound up at the boat races. The chaos of the evening left us breathless, but we pressed on, fueled by adrenaline and a raw sense of freedom.

By the next day, in a twist of fate, we found ourselves riding with a foul-mouthed biker escaping Portland, convinced his life was in danger. "Those fuck, fuck, motherfuckers are trying to fuck, fuck—motherfuckers are trying to kill me," he ranted as the road slipped past.

"That was some motherfucker, fuck, fuck, motherfucker," Dan muttered after we'd climbed out of the vehicle, shaking his head.

He brought us to Cannon Beach. Beyond the sand, the rocky coastline stretched out before us, jagged and beautiful under a sky that promised peace, if only for a moment.

Back in R&R in the picturesque town of Gold Beach, I found myself in the cozy confines of a local barbershop, where the sweet scent of shampoo and hair products hung in the air. The woman barber, with her warm smile and deft hands, trimmed my hair expertly; her laughter rang like music beneath the hum of the clippers. Afterward, I treated myself to a delicious seafood dinner at a nearby restaurant, savoring the rich flavors of the ocean—grateful, if briefly, for this quiet reprieve.

Later, I sat side by side with Michelle on the bus, as it drove us around Gold Beach, our journey unfolding as the sun began to dip lower in the sky, casting a warm, golden glow across the landscape.

Michelle immersed herself in the vibrant tapestry of her native culture. Her excitement radiated from her like a beacon, her black hair shimmering in the fading light.

With animated gestures and a bright smile, she shared her cherished memories, her words flowing with an infectious energy that drew me in. She recalled the exhilarating experience of dancing at powwows, where the rhythmic sound of drums reverberated through the air, stirring her spirit. In her mind's eye, she saw herself as a child, surrounded by her peers—each child twirling and leaping joyfully with their parents and grandparents—forming a lively circle of tradition and heritage that connected generations.

At the powwow, she glanced over and spotted a group of Native veterans standing tall and proud, their presence a testament to their unwavering service to the state. Their faces told stories of courage and sacrifice, filling Michelle with a swell of pride in her chest. But as the memories washed over her, she also felt a twinge of nostalgia for the crew she would soon leave behind, knowing college awaited her after this short break.

As the evening progressed, I settled into the bar, surrounded by the low hum of conversation and the clink of glasses. I lost track of time, completely absorbed in the atmosphere, until the clock struck ten. Reluctantly, I made my way back to my temporary lodgings, where I tried to find rest. But sleep eluded me. I tossed and turned in an unfamiliar bed, my mind racing with thoughts of the day's adventures, until the insistent beeping of the alarm clock finally roused me from my restless slumber.

The dawning morning brought with it a renewed sense of purpose. I decided to take one last long, invigorating walk along the beach, inhaling the salty air that filled my lungs with vitality. The surf pounded rhythmically against the shoreline, its roar a reminder of nature's relentless power, while seagulls swooped and dove, searching for hidden treasures awakened by the gentle kiss of sunlight. The first rays of dawn illuminated the silhouette of the nearby mountains, transforming them into three-dimensional giants that loomed protectively over Gold Beach.

With every step, I absorbed the scenery, imprinting the sights and sounds into memory. I took in one last, deep breath of ocean air before reluctantly turning back toward the bus—ready to embark on whatever awaited me next.

The ride wound through the landscape, ascending past the frothy, white water of the Rogue River. The river, with its turbulent current and cascading energy, danced over smooth stones—blue, green, and red—creating a spectacle that caught my eye. As the vehicle moved along the narrow path, the sound of rushing water filled the air, a constant and invigorating reminder of nature's raw power and beauty. Vibrant greenery lined the riverbanks, enhancing the picturesque scene. Each twist and turn of the road offered new glimpses of the river's splendor.

That day marked a pivotal moment for the crew as we prepared for our initial attack against the encroaching blaze in different areas of the fire. The atmosphere thickened with a mix of excitement and trepidation. Anticipation hung heavy as the hours dragged on and the wind picked up, transforming once-manageable flames into a towering inferno. The fire column twisted and swirled upward. Restless and impatient, we exchanged glances, all too aware of the unpredictability of nature's fury.

As daylight faded, darkness crept in like an unwelcome guest. The sun dipped behind the rugged mountains to the west, painting the sky in hues of orange and purple. With nightfall, we scattered into various activities, each seeking a brief escape from the tension. Some gathered around a makeshift table to play bridge, the soft shuffle of cards and bursts of laughter creating a fleeting sense of normalcy. Others found comfort in the dim light of the barn, watching movies on a dusty screen. A few tucked into corners with well-worn books, losing themselves in stories that carried them far from the reality outside.

As fatigue settled over us, we slipped into our sleeping bags. But before sleep claimed us, a collective thought echoed in our minds—

had the river managed to hold back the relentless advance of the fire? The uncertainty lingered, an unspoken question hovering over us like smoke.

The next day, as dawn broke and spread its warmth across the land, I awoke to the familiar rhythm of our morning routine. Yet an unmistakable sense of urgency filled the air. We had laid out a new plan—one that led us through an area we had traversed before, though under very different circumstances. The strategy was straightforward: we would walk out to Briggs Ranch, mopping up hot spots near Indigo Creek along the way. Still, we braced ourselves for a long stretch of monotony, punctuated by the constant vigilance required to ensure the fire did not reignite.

After a hastily prepared breakfast of instant oatmeal and stale coffee, we set out on the Illinois Trail from Oak Flats to Briggs Ranch. The sun cast long shadows as it began its ascent in the sky. The trail, a well-trodden path, climbed steadily from the expansive ranch land, giving way to lush draws filled with vibrant greenery. As we moved upward, the scenery shifted dramatically. The surroundings soon yielded to a stark, barren ridge that stretched before us, its rugged contours sharp against the brightening sky. The trail continued along this desolate expanse until it eventually dipped toward the rocky precipices that framed Indigo Creek below.

Amidst the rhythm of our march, Janet—the inexperienced fill-in on the crew—stumbled yet again, having re-injured a recent sprain. It became clear she was struggling; her face contorted in a mix of determination and discomfort. I lingered behind her, making sure she was alright.

As we trudged along, the pace slowed, and I found myself lost in thought, contemplating the river hidden beneath a veil of smoke. I imagined what it must look like—the water rushing through the gorge, vibrant and full, carving its way through a landscape that once flourished as a lush forest—a stark contrast to the ashen remnants of charred trees surrounding us now.

Despite the struggle, we eventually caught up with the rest of the crew, who were diligently mopping up near the banks of Indigo Creek. The sound of flowing water mingled with the crackling of dried brush.

The crew—now a mix of seasoned veterans and less experienced hands—fanned out in an organized grid formation, each of us taking our designated spot as we began the critical task of extinguishing the lingering hot spots that still smoldered beneath the surface. The fire crept through this section slowly, almost insidiously, leaving behind patches of charred earth interspersed with stubborn dry brush, each crackling ominously at the slightest touch.

As we moved with urgency, our eyes darted over the landscape, acutely aware of the high potential for re-burn looming like a ghostly specter over our efforts. The heat radiated around us—a stark reminder of the devastation already suffered—and with every swift motion, we sought to snuff out the remnants of the inferno before it could reignite and spread further.

CHAPTER 14

TO THE SPOT FIRE

The Court in *Ladson* concluded that the problem with a pretextual traffic stop lies in its classification as a search or seizure that cannot receive constitutional justification for its true reason (i.e., speculative criminal investigation), but only for some other reason (i.e., to enforce the traffic code) that remains lawfully sufficient yet does not represent the real motive. Pretext triumphs over substance; it represents expediency at the expense of reason. However, our constitution measures exceptions to the general rule forbidding search or seizure without a warrant against the standard of reasonableness. Pretext delivers results without reason. **State v. Ladson, 979 P.2d 833 (1999).**

In 2001, I kept working on my brief. "Agency aggressively recruiting firefighters," declared the headlines of the *Missoulian*. "Crises, they desperately search for experienced firefighters." Thoughts drifted through the shadows of my mind. I reflected on a different time. Pondering. They arrived with their paintbrushes, boldly envisioning the future. They painted over Van Gogh's works with bright yellow shirts—though not always yellow. They slopped brown paint over Ray's picture of the meteor on the Black Butte Fire. Engrossed in diversity, they painted *Starry, Starry Night* dark green.

They came rooting for failure, taking actual joy in destroying people's lives. Those who excelled in it received awards.

It was late May of 2001, and the air thickened with foreboding as fire season approached. The landscape lay drier than it had been in 2000, and alarming conditions loomed large and intimidating for those preparing to battle wildfires. Amid this uncertainty, I found a moment to talk to Jim, leaning back on a log as twilight cast long shadows across the ground.

Jim, now an assistant fire management officer, leaned back, his brow furrowed, and began to share his thoughts. "It was never the same," he said, nostalgia softening his voice. "There's no passion anymore, little life in the firehouse. Things have changed drastically." His words lingered in the air, heavy with experience. He recalled a time when firefighters fought tooth and nail to maintain their place on the line, driven by an unquenchable thirst for the adrenaline that came with the job. Now, many new recruits quickly demanded relief after early shifts. It wasn't true for all of them, but the trend was troubling. Most seemed to lack the fervor that once defined the spirit of firefighting.

As we continued our conversation, the sun dipped below the horizon, casting a warm orange glow across the forest, and Jim's mind drifted back to another time entirely. He flashed back to the summer of 1987, when he was long, strong, and lanky—youthful and full of vigor. He remembered trailing the shot crew into the heart of a spot fire, the heat discernible, the urgency thrilling. Those days flowed alive with purpose and passion, starkly contrasting with the uncertainty that now envelops us. The memory stirred something within me—a bittersweet reminder of the intensity and camaraderie that once thrived among firefighters, igniting a flicker of hope that perhaps, amidst all the change, that spirit might yet rekindle.

In 1987, the spot fire had flared across the Illinois River the day before. We walked up to Silver Prairie, where I lagged alongside Janet and her sprained ankle. At Silver Prairie, we took a break. The superintendent scowled at Janet and me. "And the Lord said the dogs shall eat Jezebel by the wall of Jezreel. Him that dieth in the field shall the fowls of the air eat. But there was none like unto Ahab, which did sell himself to work wickedness in the sight of the Lord whom Jezebel his wife stirred up. And he did this so abominably, in following idols, according to all things as did the Amorites, whom the Lord cast out before the children of Israel. First Kings 22, 23, 24, 25, 26. He will show them."

The squads divided into smaller groups, meticulously mopping up the charred area below Silver Prairie that had burned during our brief respite—a well-deserved break from our relentless battle against the fire. The air hung heavily with the scent of smoke and soot. Just as the sun began to dip lower in the sky, casting long shadows across the blackened earth, a crackling report blared over the radio, piercing the tense atmosphere like a gunshot. The news was grim: the Illinois River line had breached, and a spot fire was taking hold.

The superintendent, his brow furrowed in anxiety, began to pace back and forth, his boots crunching on the scorched ground beneath him. His mind raced with thoughts of flames burning with relentless fury, exacting vengeance on those straying from the path of righteousness. "The fire is taking vengeance on them that know not God," he muttered under his breath, the words echoing in his mind like a haunting refrain. Yet he acutely felt his lack of authority to charge headlong into the inferno. "For when they shall say, 'peace and safety,' then sudden destruction cometh upon them," he recalled with a sense of foreboding, "as travail upon a woman with child; and they shall not escape."

Internal conflict churned within him as he grappled with the desire to act—his instincts screamed for him to run toward the spot fire, to join the fight, to stand shoulder to shoulder with his comrades. But rules and hierarchy tethered him, anchoring him in uncertainty. Just as he thought he might break free from his mental turmoil, the call he had been waiting for crackled through the radio's static, igniting a spark of hope in his chest. He had permission to go seek out the spot.

Without hesitation, the superintendent sprang into action, rallying Keller, Lira, Uphoff, and Janet. Together, they formed a line of resolve, setting off into the unknown and plunging into the void where chaos reigned, fully aware of the dangers that lay ahead. I thought about radioing him that Janet was not a good choice to have walk fifteen miles over rough terrain. But I knew it would only make him more determined to have her do the trek to prove me wrong, so I decided not to.

The rest of the crew diligently attended to the painstaking task of mop-up, a crucial phase following the fierce battle against the flames. We navigated the ashen landscape where the fire had crossed the great barrier, leaving nothing but charred earth in its wake.

After an hour, Keller took charge of escorting Janet back from the trek with her injured ankle. We would see no more of her. As we worked our way through the smoky remnants of the fire, the air thick with the scent of burnt wood, we encountered the crew winding down their own efforts as the day edged toward twilight. The superintendent and Uphoff had already radioed in the good news—they'd found the elusive hot spot, a beacon of hope amid the chaos.

As the sun began to dip below the horizon and the shadows lengthened, we formed a plan: we would return to Briggs for the night, our weary bodies needing rest after the relentless toil, and regroup in the morning, ready to hike back into the fray with renewed determination.

The next day, we headed out with the former overseer of Briggs Ranch acting as our guide—a seasoned veteran steeped in the lore of the land. His rugged exterior reflected its gnarl and roughness. With an innate understanding of the terrain's secrets, he led us forward at a brisk pace, each step taken with the confidence of someone who had walked these paths for lifetimes. Though weary from our labors, we instinctively trusted his instincts, knowing we were in capable hands as we pushed deeper into the heart of the wilderness.

Behind the crew, Jim—part of another unit—maintained a steady pace, his strides purposeful even as the two other crews, the Willamette and Rogue River teams, struggled to keep up. We wove through the underbrush, the enormity of our effort clear in the way we labored through the thickening smoke. Eventually, it became clear that only Jim, with his trusty saw slung across his shoulder, kept pace with the crew, his determination exemplifying the resilience demanded in such arduous conditions.

"Never the same," Jim said.

Jim talked to me at a bar in Superior fourteen years later. He would be one of the few to carve out a lasting career in the perilous world of firefighting—a profession that demanded every ounce of strength and resilience. He was young enough to benefit from the court case and congressional investigations. His supervisor had also followed legal affirmative action, so both Jim and his wife secured careers in firefighting.

He had followed closely behind a group of firefighters, their figures emerging from the dense, swirling smoke of the morning inversion. The air had thickened—a heavy blanket lingering in the valleys like an unwelcome specter. It reminded them of the volatile nature of their work. When the smoke finally broke, it would signal that the fire, too, would erupt with renewed ferocity, racing from ridge to ridge, consuming everything in its path, and laying waste to the brush that once thrived there.

Each crew member bore a significant load of supplies, the weight of our packs serving as a physical reminder of the days ahead—days that could stretch into uncertain lengths before we would next find food and clean water. The air thickened with the lingering effects of colds, each cough echoing like a warning through the trees as we navigated the challenging terrain. Poison oak left a painful etching on our thighs, a testament to the harsh realities of our work, and we breathed heavily, gasping as we pushed through the cold smoke that enveloped us like a dense fog.

Just as fatigue began to creep into our bones, we arrived at Conner's Place—a small way station roughly six miles from Briggs Ranch that served as a welcome respite in our grueling trek. We gathered around, eager for a moment of reprieve, gulping down various juices—apple, orange, grapefruit, tomato, and the ever-reliable V-8. The refreshing burst of flavors revitalized us momentarily, providing a small but much-needed boost of energy as we prepared to continue our journey into the unknown, fortified by the simple pleasure of a cold drink amidst the oppressive heat and smoke.

Emerging from the cool, protective shade of towering trees, we transitioned back into sun-soaked terrain. Our surroundings shifted from the comforting embrace of woodland to the more exposed expanses of brush. We pressed onward, navigating the rugged landscape as we passed Silver Creek—a winding ribbon of water carving its path down from the draws nestled below the expansive Silver Prairie, eventually meandering toward the Illinois River, just beyond Conner's Place. The trees surrounding us slowly retreated, yielding to encroaching brush thriving in the lighter canopy, marking the transition from the forest's heart to the more open wilderness.

As we traversed the land, we crossed the drainage of a once-lively brook, the sound of water trickling over stones providing a brief but welcome soundtrack to our exertion. We climbed across a saddle and descended toward the Illinois River, which snaked through clusters of boulders and stretches of soft sand below, its surface glistening under the relentless sun, beckoning us closer.

Finally, after what felt like an eternity of walking, I arrived at a flat expanse beside the river, where the crew paused to jam their lunches into their packs and catch their breath. The twelve-mile trek to that flat left me fatigued but resolute. Amid our brief respite, the superintendent, the division boss, and the overseer of Briggs Ranch surveyed the horizon, searching for the elusive hot spot obscured by thick smoke still looming in the hollows—a haunting reminder of the fire we continued to battle.

As we settled in, we waited for the others to arrive, the anticipation hanging in the air like heat rising off the ground. Gradually, the Willamette and Rogue crews straggled in, their faces marked by the weariness of the journey but brightening at the sight of their comrades—a small flicker of energy igniting amidst the arduous conditions.

The call came through the crackling radio, slicing through the noise of our exertion like a knife. The division boss's voice, authoritative yet edged with urgency, asked if we minded getting wet. I knew we had little choice; we needed to wade through the Illinois River to reach the spot that had become critical in our firefighting mission. Meanwhile, the other two crews, opting for a more cautious approach, decided to hold back. They hoped to find a safer crossing point—one that would keep them dry while preparing to cut line into the spot the following day, perhaps under less punishing conditions.

As I stepped into the river, the water surged around my hips in a deep, calm run. The handhold on the cliff gave way beneath me. Cold water wrapped tightly around my body, rising steadily until it embraced my waist. The coolness stood in sharp contrast to the day's heat—invigorating and refreshing—as I made my way across. I paused to check my web gear, feeling the reassuring weight of it against me. It remained dry—a small but significant piece of good fortune in this harsh landscape. Dry clothes for the night would offer a rare comfort around the warming fire, a brief reprieve from the grueling conditions we had endured.

The river's current varied, with pools depleted by the ongoing drought. Some areas reached only knee-deep, while others rose to the waist in deeper runs. As I navigated the uneven terrain, I emerged on the far side of the Illinois, water cascading off me in glistening droplets that landed softly on the smooth, rounded rocks, forming a mini pier that jutted into the river. Breathing heavily, I took a moment to steady myself, the sound of flowing water a soothing backdrop as I prepared to regroup with the rest of the crew.

Over the next five miles, we would methodically remove our boots at each crossing, mindful of the need to keep our feet dry as we navigated the unpredictable terrain. Small cliffs rose abruptly along one side of the river, jagged and imposing, often hindering our progress and forcing quick decisions. We weighed our options carefully, either crossing directly or maneuvering through knee-high riffles and waist-deep runs along the river's edge.

Keller was fiddling with his web gear when Gale famously said, "Hey, PK!" Keller looked up, and Gale clicked the photo, capturing that wonderful moment in time—one I will always be so grateful to have. A few minutes before that, he had realized he didn't want his clothes to get wet. He said to Donna, "Would you mind if I stripped down to my boxers?" And Donna, wonderfully and famously replied, "Keller, that's a good idea. I'm gonna do the same thing!"

"Damn, those were such great times!" —Paul Keller, 2025

Just as we approached a particularly tricky section, our crew came to an abrupt halt, our attention drawn to the crackling sound of static coming from Hunt's radio. The superintendent's voice broke through, strained and shaky, informing Hunt that he had once again lost his way to the spot fire. The urgency in his tone was clear, a stark reminder of the pressure bearing down on him. After 36 relentless hours without sleep, fatigue had wrapped his mind in a fog, making it difficult for him to focus. We exchanged worried glances, acutely aware of his deteriorating mental state, as we braced ourselves for the challenges ahead.

We continued our trek, carefully navigating a rugged rock outcropping that jutted over the water, leading us to a shimmering pool below. With a sense of urgency, we waded through two more knee-deep riffles, the cold water rushing around our legs and splashing against our skin. When we finally pulled ourselves onto the bank, we were dripping and shivering, the evening air wrapping its chill around us. We landed in a jumble of rocks and sand, perhaps just below the ominous glow of the spot fire that had held our focus for so long.

In this new haven, we found a fallen snag, its once-vibrant wood now bleached and dry, lying lifeless on the ground. Without hesitation, we gathered around it, our hands skillfully wielding saws to cut it into manageable pieces. The dimming light of dusk cast a soft glow over our work, lighting our faces as we shaped the wood into three warming fires nestled among the rocks. The flames soon came alive, crackling and popping as they consumed the dry wood, offering much-needed warmth against the growing cold. Glen dried his clothes with the heat of the fire.

Our crew now looked noticeably smaller, each face bearing the toll that attrition and injuries had taken on them. Those who remained included the superintendent, Hunt, Uphoff, Keller, Gale, McCallester,

Donna, Lira, Glenn, Ray, Ford, Juli, Thomas, and me. We huddled close, our bodies instinctively seeking warmth as we gazed up at the night sky. A few stars twinkled faintly, their light struggling to pierce the thick smoke that settled into the drainage, casting a hazy veil over the vastness above.

As we dried our soaked clothes, the air filled with coughs and hacks, a testament to the toll the smoke had taken on our lungs. Each cough echoed the fatigue pressing down on us, the battle against nature wearing not just our bodies but our spirits as well. In that moment, we found solace in our shared struggle, drawing strength from each other as we prepared for the challenges still to come. MREs came out of our web gear, the familiar rustle of plastic crinkling in the cool night air. Each package promised a semblance of warmth and sustenance, with options like hearty stew or, if fortune smiled on us, Chicken à la King, which we set to heat over the crackling fire. The flames flickered with a life of their own, casting an orange glow that danced across our weary faces—our expressions a mix of exhaustion and anticipation.

As the MREs warmed, the dehydrated fruit slowly began to re-hydrate, absorbing the heat and transforming into something more palatable—a small comfort amid the chaos. Conversation was sparse, the weight of our shared experiences hanging heavy in the air. We understood this was what fighting fire truly meant. The night closed in, shaping a lonely, smoky camp by the riverside, its soft murmurs contrasting with the crackle of the fire.

Above us, the ridge rose in a jagged silhouette against the star-speckled sky, the stars twinkling down, seemingly indifferent to our struggles below. The fire's warmth drew us in, yet the absence of sleeping bags reminded us sharply of our situation—our bodies tired but alert. For many, the night offers the comfort of a camp buddy to share warmth. Donna and I, united by shared trials, drew close, connecting in a brief escape from harsh realities, finding solace in each other amid nature's fury.

There was nothing romantic—just the warmth of a tightly knit community surviving within the wilderness. A gentle breeze stirred, carrying a whiff of smoke that swirled through the air, teasing our reddened eyes. For most, that pungent smoke would sting, a sharp reminder of our toil. But for this seasoned crew, it was a familiar companion—more appreciated than noticed in the depths of our fatigue. Donna and I huddled together, shoulders brushing, sharing a moment of unspoken understanding.

As I sat there, my thoughts drifted like embers from the fire, rising into the dark sky above. I knew it was over for six of us gathered here; I felt it deep in my bones, a chilling certainty that wrapped around me like a shroud. I couldn't fully explain why the feeling gripped me so tightly. But instead of giving in to rage or despair, I chose to cherish one of our last precious moments together. These people had become like family. We had grown up side by side, battling flames and facing down infernos that threatened to consume everything.

A wistful sadness settled over me as I watched the others, still unaware of how fragile everything truly was. They didn't know to savor these fleeting moments, to truly hold on to the bonds we had forged in fire. My mind drifted to thoughts of fire—to Keller's poetry:

OCHOCO MOUNTAIN FIRE 1977

Digging hand line through
tamarack root wads and manzanita brush
all night in sweat.

Squirrels and deer
surrender beside us, their eyes
burned open, crazy with death.

The hepatitis outbreak in fire camp.
Chili stirred with boat oars
in garbage cans for dinner.
Canteen water comes from
fish tank trucks.
We take smoke in slow gulps.
Our week old stink.

And the constant nightmare orange
that licks these hills
into a quiet coffin of naked trees
despite us.

Paul Keller

The superintendent radiated palpable anger, almost biblical in its intensity, as he continued his relentless search for the elusive spot that had caused so much chaos and destruction. Sleep had long evaded him, and the weight of his martyrdom pressed heavily on his shoulders. He felt justified in his fury; they had drawn first blood in this battle against the flames, and he was determined to respond with equal ferocity.

Restless and chilled to the bone, I finally rose from my makeshift bed around 3:00 a.m., the cool air biting at my skin. Sleep had fled, leaving only a lingering fatigue. I added more wood to the fire, watching the flames dance and crackle as sparks shot into the night sky. I shifted away from the embers that landed on my cheeks, welcoming the heat as a sharp contrast to the cold around me.

As I surveyed the dimly lit camp, my gaze settled on the empty space where the superintendent should have been. A knot of worry twisted in my gut. His absence felt wrong, and the longer he went without rest or food, the more erratic his behavior became. I had seen it before, when a kind of obsession took hold of him, especially once he turned to his so-called sacred foods: Almond Joys and Hershey bars. The sugar rush fueled his manic energy, but it carved a dangerous path, often leading to a reckless competition mirage among the crew.

I couldn't shake the feeling that a challenge was brewing. The superintendent often boasted about how long he could go without drinking water, as if pushing his endurance were a test of faith. Thoughts of his girlfriend weighed heavily on me. Guilt mixed with frustration as I considered the subtle dynamics within the crew. Everyone knew he believed others coveted his girlfriend, and I suspected he saw me as a rival. Since the welcome party after his arrival, I had been almost too friendly, too eager to bond with both him and his girlfriend. That friendliness only seemed to feed his insecurities, which hung over our already strained interactions like a dark cloud.

CHAPTER 15

THE SPOT FIRE, LEGENDS IN MAKING

Around four o'clock in the morning, the frigid air had enveloped the weary crew and me as we slowly awakened from a night fraught with restlessness and uncertainty. The sounds of crackling firewood and the distant hiss of flames had plagued our sleep, slipping into our dreams and leaving us chilled. As the warmth from our fires dwindled to embers, we rose. The last traces of heat faded, and I stoked the fire one final time, coaxing the flames back to life. The scent of smoke mingled with the freshness of early morning air, filling my lungs as I heated our Meals, Ready-to-Eat.

The plan for the day had been ambitious: cut a line anchoring from the river, flanking the fire. I had been left behind to guide the other crews in. Rarely did joy take hold of me when sidelined, but that day had felt different. I braced for the onslaught of negativity I knew would come from the increasingly unstable superintendent, whose sleepless nights had clearly taken a toll on his mental state. Instead of succumbing to frustration, I resolved to make the best of the situation. With quiet determination, I began gathering the scarce wood scattered among the rugged cliffs towering above me.

I knew the guarantee of returning to a warm shelter by nightfall had vanished, making the fire's heat more critical than ever. The days had slipped into October, and the nights had grown colder—especially along the riverbed, where the water flowed brisk and unforgiving, stripping warmth from the air. I could feel the chill settling in, a stark reminder that winter was closing in. Time was short, so I pushed myself harder, treating every stick of wood like a vital piece of our survival through another long, bitter night.

I waded into the river, which meandered beneath the towering cliffs. Then the realization hit me: no crews were coming. It became painfully clear: we were on our own, and the situation was growing increasingly dire. With the crew facing a serious shortage of food and water, Keller and I ultimately decided to make the long, grueling journey back to Collier's Bar. It lay more than six miles away—a trek that would demand every ounce of strength we had left. We both knew the packtrain was supposed to drop supplies there, and it was our only hope.

Keller appeared, his silhouette cutting through the mist rising from the river. Together, we plunged into the chilly water, the cold rushing around our legs offering momentary relief from the relentless sting of poison oak. The rash had become unbearable; we had completely run out of antihistamines, and the burning sensation felt like fire crawling across my skin. When we emerged a few minutes later, a gentle breeze met us, cooling our soaked pant legs and easing the angry welts that still throbbed beneath.

I took a moment to gather myself. The sun hung high overhead. I filled my hard hat with cool, refreshing river water and poured it over my head, letting it cascade down my face and neck. The instant relief revitalized my spirit. As the water trickled down, cooling me for a brief moment, Keller and I prepared for the journey ahead, our minds focused on the challenges still waiting for us.

On the spot fire, the crew stood just above a waterfall that served as a natural barrier to the advancing flames. Lira stood resolute, pouring a hard hat full of river water over Glenn's head. The two had just secured their line through painstaking effort, ensuring the fire wouldn't breach their defenses. Occasionally, flames snaked up the trunk of a nearby pine, igniting its needles in a bright flare, only to fizzle out. The fire continued to threaten to leap the containment line.

Glenn, his focus sharpened by experience, fought back against the flames flaring around him. He swung his shovel with purpose, the metal catching the sunlight as he beat the fire down. Each thud of the shovel against the earth sent dirt flying, smothering the flames in the grass and turning heat into a smoldering memory. Lira moved beside him, his shovel cutting through the earth with clean, deliberate strokes, widening the containment line as they worked in sync against the backdrop of smoke and heat. He could feel the fire's radiating heat pressing in around them.

As the world began to sway beneath him, Glenn stumbled toward the shade of a nearby pine, seeking refuge from the sweltering heat and swirling smoke. Lira, sensing his distress, quickly poured another round of river water over Glenn's head, the cool liquid washing away layers of fatigue and heat. Lira possessed a deep understanding of fire—an instinct that let him sense danger before it took shape.

Once Glenn regained his composure, the two picked up their tools with renewed resolve. Side by side, they moved up the line, ready to tackle other trouble spots threatening their hard-earned progress. The air thickened with smoke, but their determination held steady as they faced what the fire might throw at them next.

Keller and I, still catching our breath after the morning's exertion, suddenly heard the sharp crackle of the radio cut through the smoky air. Static pierced our ears like a blade.

"Are there any fuzees?" the superintendent barked, his voice tight with urgency and edged with frustration. "It would make it a lot easier to hold the line."

"Negative," Uphoff replied, his voice steady and calm despite the tension building all around us.

I glanced at Keller, a thought bubbling to the surface. "Well, why don't they just get a stick, light it on fire, and light out the line?" I suggested, my brow furrowing as I considered the conditions. "It is dry enough." The land around them was parched, the earth cracked and thirsting for rain—creating the perfect environment for burnout.

Keller nodded in agreement, but I sensed an undercurrent of hesitation. I wanted to take the initiative to call it in myself. Yet, I was acutely aware of the delicate balance of power at play. My usurping the superintendent's authority, especially in a moment as critical as this, could lead to repercussions we wanted to avoid.

With a quick flick of his wrist, Uphoff reached for the radio, his voice slicing through the tension. "We are using sticks to burn out the line," he announced, with a finality that resonated with the crew.

I turned to Keller, a smirk creeping onto my face. "Looks like Uphoff got some sleep," I quipped, the lightness in my tone briefly easing the weight of our situation.

As if sensing the unfolding plan, Uphoff moved with purpose. He gathered a few dry sticks, their rough surfaces scraping against his calloused hands, and leaned them into the unburned fuel between the fire and the line. The flames licked hungrily at the kindling, flickering to life in a vibrant dance of orange and yellow. The air crackled with fire and hissed as the flames began to consume the surrounding brush.

I pressed on with Keller as we trudged toward Collier Bar. Each step required careful navigation—we forded the river time and again, maneuvering through a series of riffles and tranquil pools. Our hands gripped the rugged cliffs towering over us, fingers searching for secure handholds among the jagged rock, until at last, we discovered a narrow passage through the cliffs that led us to the Illinois River Trail.

As we continued our journey, we increased our pace, urgency driving us forward. The weight of our mission hung heavily in the air, and I felt the pressure of time ticking away. The unspoken understanding between us forged a bond stronger than words, with Keller propelling himself forward with his lithe agility, while I relied on raw strength.

Together, we bore the weight of lunches, refreshing juices, and essential water—probably totaling somewhere between eighty and one hundred pounds—on our way back to the spot fire, where our crew awaited the much-needed nourishment.

As we reached Collier's Bar, the atmosphere shifted dramatically, as if we had stepped into an alternate reality. The scene buzzed with life, filled with the excitement of fellow firefighters and onlookers rushing up to us, their eyes wide with curiosity. "How was it crossing the deadly Illinois River?" they asked, their voices tinged with awe and concern. The river we had just forded—relatively calm during our passage—had now become, in their minds, a fearsome and treacherous force.

Rumors quickly elevated our simple crossings into a legendary feat, transforming us into superheroes blessed by divine intervention. In that moment, Keller, the crew, and I stood not just as firefighters, but as legends in the making—heroes forged in the crucible of fire and water—ready to carry on with the grueling tasks still ahead.

The knee-deep crossings that had seemed manageable were now remembered as neck-deep torrents. The river morphed from a gentle stream into a roaring beast, threatening to sweep us off our feet. We found ourselves in a precarious situation, forced to rely on every ounce of ingenuity and grit we could summon. I bit down on my web gear, using the makeshift method to keep my hands free while hoisting essential tools above my head, clinging tightly to keep them dry and ready for what came next.

My third hand, a strange adaptation born of necessity, wrapped firmly around the thick rope spanning the river. It acted as our lifeline, dangling from loose brush precariously rooted in cliffs that loomed hundreds of feet above us. Those steep, unforgiving cliffs tested my will. I navigated them with sheer determination and a touch of luck, swinging from rock to rock, praying for a miracle to keep me from plummeting into the chaos below. For a moment, I felt like Spider-Man, scrambling for survival with nothing but instinct and desperation.

"Where's the red carpet?" I joked, casting a glance at Keller, who was adjusting his hard hat. He kept his expression serious, tightening the strap with care, fully aware of the dangers that lurked ahead—including injury from the imagined confetti falling in celebration of our bold crossing. My humor hung in the air, offering a brief, needed reprieve from the weight of the journey still to come.

"Where are the lunches?" I inquired, my voice slicing through the thick air of the forest, laden with the scent of pine and the lingering smoky haze that clings to our clothes.

"Lunches?" Keller echoed, confusion crossing his face as he furrowed his brow.

The lunches, those elusive packages of sustenance that feel more like a mirage than a reality, sat three miles farther down the rugged Illinois River trail. That stretch of land seemed insurmountable, especially when exhaustion weighed heavily, like a thick, suffocating cloak draped over my shoulders, making each breath a laborious effort. Jim, along with three other dedicated members of the Willamette crew, gallantly volunteered to embark on the expedition to retrieve the much-needed meals. Their selflessness offered Keller and me a well-deserved reprieve—a brief moment to gather our strength and mental fortitude before undertaking the long, arduous trek back to the spot fire, where chaos and uncertainty awaited us.

Yet, despite my fellow firefighters' kindness, the thought of those lunches sparked an unsettling flicker of doubt in my mind. I couldn't shake the vivid image of Keller and me struggling beneath the burden of 80 to 100 pounds strapped tightly to our backs. The treacherous path ahead loomed like a formidable adversary, taunting me with the possibility of missteps and misfortunes. Would we navigate through the underbrush, dodging low-hanging branches and jagged rocks, without succumbing to fatigue? The weight of responsibility pressed upon me, mingling with the creeping anxiety that whispered doubts threatening to unravel the delicate balance of our mission.

The distant crackle of the radio cut through the air, pulling me out of my thoughts. The urgency in the static pulsed, reminding us of the chaos of the spot fire. The action heated up back at the spot fire—the flames had cut off the superintendent from the crew.

I darted my eyes toward the horizon. I sensed the tension in the air as the wind began to pick up, threatening to fan the flames that loomed over everything in our path. The day had heated up significantly, the sun blaring down as if watching the chaos unfold with cruel interest.

"Hunt, this is the superintendent," the voice crackled through the static of the radio, filled with urgency and an undertone of frustration.

"This is Hunt. Go ahead," he replied, his voice calm and steady—a beacon of reason amidst the turmoil.

"Hunt, I'm in thick brush here," the superintendent's voice crackled through the radio, wavering slightly as he spoke. "I'm having a tough time moving through it, and I think I really need to get back to the crew." His words, tinged with urgency and desperation, conveyed the weight of the raging inferno pressing in around him. He feared a sudden rush of fire might sweep through the dense underbrush, leaving him helpless and isolated, a victim of the chaotic forces of nature. The thought of being trapped only intensified his panic.

Back at the staging area, waiting for the lunches to arrive, I listened intently, shaking my head slightly as I let out a deep, contemplative sigh. Caught in a whirlwind of conflicting emotions, I half wished I were out there, shoulder to shoulder with the crew, grappling with the flames and the chaos they brought. Yet at the same time, I longed to escape the maddening cacophony of confusion and fear surrounding me. The superintendent was clearly teetering on the brink of a complete mental breakdown, and the weight of that realization anchored my thoughts. I couldn't shake the dread that gnawed at my insides, a constant reminder of the precarious balance between pushing human limits and crossing into a place where effort became not only futile but dangerous. The thought of the superintendent's unraveling sent shivers down my spine as I considered the consequences that could ripple through the crew if their leader lost his grip entirely.

As I reflected on the frenzy into which the superintendent had descended, the situation seemed to spiral further out of control. One night of poor sleep might have been endurable, but dragging that into several nights with only a few scattered hours of rest felt like a recipe not just for trouble, but for outright disaster—a ticking time bomb waiting to go off. My thoughts turned to his overall well-being, and I wondered, with growing concern, whether he had eaten or even managed a sip of water in what felt like an eternity. The haze of fatigue was unmistakable. The clarity he so desperately needed had vanished, leaving behind only confusion and a creeping sense of impending doom. The weight of his condition pressed heavily on my mind, intertwining with my own fears for the crew and their safety amid the chaos.

We waited for the lunches.

"Everyone avoided this guy at the bar," Keller said, digressing into a story to kill time. His voice cut through my troubled thoughts, carrying a mix of incredulity and concern. "You really couldn't blame them too much, either," he went on, his tone steady but edged with disbelief. He leaned back against the rough wooden bar, the grain pressing into his shoulder, as he recalled the figure from that night.

Mixed in with the colorful insignia of the motorcycle gang—excuse me, the club—he belonged to were phrases that seemed almost designed to provoke, sayings that might comfort anyone who shared his worldview. "Pig rapers united, bikers for drunk drivers against moms"—that sort of thing. It was a curious blend of bravado and absurdity that made Keller shake his head, a bemused smile creeping across his face.

"I don't know what got into me," he said, a trace of chagrin in his voice as he reflected on the moment. "I guess I thought, shit, no one wants to be ignored. So I leaned in a little, just trying to make conversation, and said, 'Hey, what motorcycle club do you belong to?'"

Keller paused, letting the memory hang in the air like the smoke that often clung to our clothes after a long day on the line. The response came swiftly and sharply, slicing through the ambient noise of the bar.

"He snarled back at me, 'Mind your own fucking business! I don't ask you about your family, do I?'"

"Well," Keller continued, his voice rising slightly as he recounted the words that spilled out before he could stop them, "I responded with the first thing that came to mind—one of those things you hear yourself saying at the exact moment it's too late to take it back. I said, 'No, but I don't wear my whole family all over my fucking back!'"

A long silence followed, stretched tight like the calm before a storm. The tension was thick. Then he laughed, the sound bouncing around the cramped space, as if he were still marveling at the ridiculousness of it all.

Back at the spot where the battle against the blaze raged on, the fire burned with insatiable ferocity, consuming everything in its path—grasses, trees, and thickening brush that grew denser with elevation. The air shimmered with heat, and Ray felt sweat trickle down his back, stinging his eyes as he wiped his brow with the back of his hand. Amidst the swirling smoke and crackling flames, something blue caught his eye, drawing his attention like a beacon. It took a moment to register: the superintendent had abandoned his web gear, leaving it dangerously close to the fire line. Without hesitation, Ray lunged forward, grabbed the gear, and dragged it about fifteen feet to the safer, non-fire side of the line, his heart pounding with urgency.

"Spot fire!" McCollister shouted, his voice cutting through the roar of the flames and the howl of the wind. Ray, Thomas, Hunt, and Uphoff sprang into action, racing several hundred feet off the line toward the expanding fire McCollister had spotted threatening to breach their defenses. The tension was palpable, the air thick with the acrid scent of smoke and scorched earth. Thomas, his face set with grim determination, grabbed his saw and worked furiously, the blade growling as it bit into the wood. Flames leapt dangerously above his head.

The wind gusted unpredictably, whipping the fire into a frenzy. But the five of them pushed through the chaos, falling back only to regroup as the wind briefly died down. Then, with renewed effort, they attacked again, pouring every ounce of strength into the fight. Inch by inch, they began to contain the blaze. Finally, after what felt like an eternity, they paused to catch their breath, chests heaving as they surveyed the scorched ground around them—sweat-soaked, drained, but not broken.

"Where's my pack?" the superintendent barked as he rejoined the crew, his voice edged with both irritation and urgency, scanning the smoke-filled line for reassurance.

"I moved it across the line; it should be about a hundred feet down. It was about to get burned," Ray replied, his tone steady, ready to assist however needed. The heat lingered, thick in the air, but their shared struggle held their spirits firm, even as distant echoes of fire reminded them that the fight was far from over.

The two men made their way back toward the area where Ray had last spotted the superintendent's pack, their boots crunching on the charred remains of the forest floor as they navigated the aftermath of the fire's onslaught. The stench of smoke lingered heavily in the air, a bitter reminder of the chaos they had just endured. As they approached, Ray couldn't help but notice how the fire had slopped over the containment line, leaving a trail of devastation in its wake.

He paused for a moment, watching intently as the superintendent, with a furrowed brow and an expression of dismay, bent down to pick up what was left of his gear. Ray felt a pang of sympathy as he observed the blue glowing remnants of the once-vibrant pack. It was a pitiful sight; gone was the headlamp that had once provided a beacon of light through the darkness of the fire, and any candy bars that might have offered a fleeting moment of comfort had been reduced to nothing. His fire shelter cover was burnt off. The last traces of the superintendent's water supply, if there had been any left, had been swallowed by the insatiable flames that ravaged their environment.

In a gesture of solidarity, Ray reached into his own pack and handed the superintendent a Gatorade. Alongside it, he offered a quart canteen filled to the brim with fresh water, the liquid sloshing reassuringly inside. Ray had always been diligent about carrying extra water—a hard-earned lesson from his time battling the flames of the Tiller Complex, where he had cramped up and suffered from dehydration. The superintendent had since insisted that Ray carry an additional gallon of water in a heavy canteen strapped to his back, believing it would prevent such a scenario from repeating. Ray often found himself lugging that extra weight all the way back to camp, especially when Krutilla didn't catch up with him.

Berkson had eventually realized that Ray's ongoing struggles were largely due to a significant deficiency in electrolytes. In an effort to remedy the issue, he had thoughtfully provided Ray with several packages of electrolyte replenishment. Despite the gesture, the superintendent remained unsatisfied, his unreasonable demands pushing Ray to continue the habit of always carrying an extra gallon of water. That additional weight turned every step into a small battle, each movement a slow grind against the fatigue threatening to wear him down.

Ray bore the burden with quiet resilience, but not without challenge. He had adapted, though, and just as faithfully as he carried the cumbersome canteen, Krutilla had established a routine of having Ray pour out a generous portion of the water onto the first hot spot they encountered. The act served a dual purpose: it spared Ray some of the weight he hauled so dutifully, and it delivered a much-needed cooling effect on the flames.

With a sense of purpose, Ray approached Uphoff, who stood firm at the line, diligently holding back the encroaching flames. The sight of him—focused and unyielding—served as a quiet reminder of the crew's commitment to one another and to their mission, even as heat pulsed around them and the challenges continued to mount.

The wind shifted restlessly, caught in a dance only it understood. When the gusts blew directly against them, the suffocating heat and acrid smoke became nearly unbearable—a relentless force threatening to push them back and erase the hard-won line they had carved into the earth. Just when their spirits began to waver and exhaustion pressed down like a weight, the wind relented, turning back on itself and blowing away from the line. It offered a fleeting reprieve—a false hope that maybe, just maybe, the line would hold.

As the sun dipped lower on the horizon, the crew braced for the unavoidable arrival of night. Shadows deepened. Humidity rose, wrapping around them like a heavy blanket. The wind slowed to a whisper, as if nature itself held its breath in anticipation of what might come next. The fire, once raging like a seven-headed hydra, its flames clawing and writhing toward the sky, now seemed to falter, its fury subsiding like a wounded beast slipping into retreat.

The frequent spots that Ray and Uphoff had leapt over the line grew scarce, then vanished entirely. Around them, the landscape transformed into a canvas of black and gray as darkness settled in. Flames continued to flicker defiantly in the distance, and the beams from their headlights sliced through the murk, casting long, wavering shadows that reached out like ghostly fingers into the unknown.

As the day surrendered to evening's encroaching chill, the shadows stretched farther, moving across the charred terrain with eerie grace. It was then that the much-anticipated lunches finally arrived—a beacon of hope amid the weariness that blanketed the crew. Jim, ever efficient, moved quickly, but the six-mile trek had taken a toll on him and the three other members of the Willamette Crew. They passed the packs to Keller and me, their faces etched with fatigue.

With muscles aching from the day's relentless toil, I turned and hurried back, each step a struggle under the weight I now carried. I pushed forward, driven by the simple, urgent need to reach safety before darkness swallowed the trail entirely. As I stepped through the creek's riffles, cold water splashed against my legs, sending sharp shivers up my spine.

I scaled the rugged rock faces, each grip and foothold testifying to my determination, finally making my way across the last crossing just as darkness began to fall like a heavy curtain. The dimming light concealed the myriad hazards lurking beneath the surface: loose rocks, slippery roots, and other ominous secrets of the night eager to entangle my boots and draw me into an unforeseen misstep.

Once I regained my footing on the riverbank, I began my trek toward the west line of the spot fire, the urgency of my mission guiding my steps. It was then that Keller, with a glimmer of relief, stumbled upon his shovel—the very tool he had left behind as a marker for the line. The familiar weight of it in his hands brought comfort amidst the growing uncertainty of the night, reminding him of the resilience that defined our crew.

I followed the line on the spot fire up toward the crew. The line traced a creek bed that meandered its way up the chasm, twisting and turning over rugged rocks and boulders, ultimately leading to a series of breathtaking waterfalls that tumbled down the steep incline with a thunderous roar. Each step reminded me of the relentless climb, the slope growing steeper with every yard gained. Keller expertly guided the way with his keen sense of direction and an innate understanding of the terrain, while I struggled behind him, coughing and wheezing as the cold air gripped my lungs like a vice. The chill of the night, coupled with the drenching I received from splashing through the frigid river earlier, exacerbated my discomfort, making each breath feel like a laborious task.

As I traversed the side of a trickling waterfall, the sound of water echoed around me, blending with the rustling of leaves. The grassy area I entered offered temporary reprieve. But it was also deceptive, as the moisture-laden ground threatened to slip beneath my feet. I seized hold of a snag, a fallen tree trunk angled vertically to the slope, using it as a crucial lifeline to pull myself upward, my muscles straining with the effort.

As we moved on, Keller pressed ahead, his eyes scanning the landscape for any signs of trouble. I, on the other hand, found a moment of reprieve. I staggered away, my stomach churning violently. A sudden, wave-like, and overwhelming feeling of sickness in the stomach and throat overcame me. I felt a knot tightening or a churning sensation in my stomach. A cold, clammy sweat broke out on my forehead, neck, and palms. I felt lightheaded and unsteady. I leaned over to retch, the contents of my stomach spilling onto the dry earth after a brief but unwelcome bout of nausea.

Just above me, Thomas slumped over his saw, the weight of frustration evident in his posture. The tool—once a reliable companion in our fight against the flames—had succumbed to mechanical failure an hour earlier, leaving him with nothing more than a useless bundle of nuts, bolts, and metal. The sight of it, lifeless and impotent, mirrored the exhaustion settling deep in his bones. The solitary, rotten apple that he and Ford had reluctantly shared during their brief lunch at noon proved to be the only sustenance he'd had all day. As evening descended and the chill of night wrapped around us like an unwelcome cloak, he instinctively moved closer to the crackling fire, seeking warmth and solace in its glow. The cool air nipped at his skin, a constant reminder of the ordeal we were enduring. He took a long, refreshing gulp of water from the nearby creek, where the fire line stretched across the rugged terrain we had worked tirelessly to hold.

The cold water filled his stomach, offering a fleeting comfort, but he knew he needed more than hydration to keep going. He rummaged through his web gear, fingers sifting through the meager contents in search of something that might sustain him through the long night ahead. His heart sank when he found the creamer packs from the meal ready-to-eat were empty, and the roll of toilet paper served only its intended purpose. Frustrated, he toyed with his saw, turning it over in his hands, contemplating the futility of trying to fix it without the energy or nourishment he so desperately needed. Even if he managed to repair the tool, he knew that without food, he wouldn't have the strength to run it effectively.

Just as hope began to fade, he heard a welcome rustling below. His heart lifted at the sight of Keller and Krutilla making their way up the slope, each lugging bags filled with much-anticipated lunches and water. They had traversed a steep incline to reach him, and the effort showed. Keller, tall and lean, navigated the hill with ease, embodying the agility and endurance of a seasoned firefighter. In stark contrast, I—stocky and visibly sick—struggled to keep pace, each step extracting more than I had to give. A wave of nausea crashed over me as I pushed forward, my determination faltering under the weight of exhaustion.

Meanwhile, I stepped forward, a wave of relief washing over me as Thomas spoke. "I can take the rest of the lunches up the mountain after I eat." My voice remained steady as I surveyed the weary faces around me. Although hesitant, I felt the weight of responsibility pressing down on me. With a reluctant nod, I agreed to the plan, knowing I was more than capable of handling the task. Thomas gulped down a sandwich and an apple, then headed up the line.

As I began to warm myself by the fires in the dried-out lake bed, I set my mind to mopping up hot spots along the fire line—a tedious but necessary duty that kept my thoughts focused. The line snaked away from the creek, winding through the charred landscape where the fire had devoured the grass, leaving behind a stark, blackened wasteland that merged into an area of brush. Amid the remnants of the inferno, in this desolate space, I finally located the rest of my crew. They were gathered on a dry lakebed, their faces smeared with soot, yet their spirits lifted as they gulped down the much-needed lunches, savoring the brief respite.

With a heavy sigh, I settled beside the fire, its warmth wrapping around me like a soft blanket. I felt too exhausted to eat, rebelling against even the thought of food. Instead, I focused on the irritating sensation creeping over my legs—the oozing from poison oak blisters that had burst during the relentless chafing of skin on the arduous trek. Each pulse of discomfort served as a reminder of the grueling battle we faced, both against nature and our own fatigue.

The superintendent, his voice barely cutting through the haze of exhaustion that hung over the crew like heavy fog, called out for volunteers to continue the arduous task of cutting line through the night alongside him and Uphoff. The air thickened with tension as the crew, weary and drained from the day's relentless demands, exchanged glances that spoke volumes. We all understood the grim reality; we were in no shape to tackle such a daunting challenge. The unpredictable and fierce fire hadn't been adequately scouted during daylight hours, leaving us uncertain about its movements and the viability of our efforts. With many fingers of flame stretching in various directions, it became clear we would face real danger if we attempted to cut line in the dark.

Amidst the heavy silence, Ford and Lira, both seasoned firefighters with fierce determination burning within them, stepped forward without hesitation. Their willingness to face the night, to brave the unknown, demonstrated their unwavering courage. As they prepared to leave, I watched with the remaining crew, a mix of admiration and concern, as the four figures disappeared into the murky shadows of the forest, determined to carve out a path through the chaos that lay ahead. It felt almost like a solemn farewell, a moment heavy with the weight of sacrifice as they ventured forth into the uncertain darkness to cut line against the relentless advance of the fire.

My mind drifted to thoughts of Ford, the steadfast partner who had faced every challenge with unflinching resolve. We had worked together on a unit burn the previous year. The chaos of that burn had erupted violently into the dog leg, where both he and I worked tirelessly, transforming the once-familiar terrain into a nightmarish landscape. Smoke billowed ominously, enveloping the line in a thick, suffocating fog that pulsed with untamed ferocity. It hung in the air like a shroud, obscuring visibility and smothering hope.

In this disorienting haze, I had found myself forced to take short, shallow breaths, my nose hovering mere millimeters above the ground, desperately seeking the scant wisps of fresh air that remained tantalizingly close yet painfully elusive. The dampness of the earth, soaked through with water from the hoses, offered a fleeting reprieve—a glimmer of life amidst the smothering smoke.

Every so often, the smoke would relent, if only for a moment, allowing me a brief window of opportunity. In those precious seconds, I leapt from my prone position in the moist dirt, heart racing, nostrils flaring as I inhaled the little oxygen that lingered just above the saturated soil. With adrenaline coursing through my veins, I snatched up the hose, unleashing a fierce spray to douse the new spots igniting around me, fueled by the unrelenting advance of the fire.

But just as quickly as that moment of clarity arrived, another wave of smoke crashed over me—a dark tide that obliterated my visibility. I could hardly see Ford, though we lay only ten feet apart, separated by a mere breath of space yet worlds away within the swirling chaos. Each time I dropped back down to the ground, my face pressed against the cool, damp earth, I battled the suffocating grip of fire and smoke threatening to consume not just the forest, but my very spirit.

The smoke relented momentarily, if only to grant a fleeting opportunity for action. In that brief interlude, Ford sprang to life. He seized a hose with fierce determination, directing the powerful stream of water toward the fresh spots igniting within the swirling remnants of smoke still clinging to the air like a thick, oppressive blanket. Each new flicker of flame that burst forth seemed a challenge, and he met it head-on, his movements a dance of urgency. Meanwhile, I struggled to my feet, muscles straining against fatigue, as I grabbed hold of my Pulaski. I began to chip away at the flames erupting in the lower section of a snag—a dead tree that stood tall and defiant about twenty feet off the fire line.

Just as I began to make progress, another wave of smoke surged toward me, swallowing everything in its path and forcing me back to the ground. I pressed my face into the cool, damp earth, gasping for the little oxygen that lingered just above the saturated soil, my heart pounding in rhythm with the chaos around me. I reflected on my four years of battling wildfires, and memories flooded back—countless days spent cutting hotlines with Ford, whose ever-present smile had motivated and fostered camaraderie through even the most grueling endeavors. Those moments now stood in sharp contrast to the grim reality I faced.

A deep sadness settled over me as I considered my crew's current predicament. I recalled the nights when we took turns—allowing sections of the crew to rest while others diligently cut line—rotating roles to ensure everyone had a chance to catch their breath and regain strength. I cherished those times most, filled with laughter and the bonds of brotherhood forged in the heart of the fire. But here and now, we merely squandered precious energy, as the relentless onslaught of flames sapped our resilience. An unsettling uncertainty loomed; we had no way of knowing whether we could continue the fight the following day, leaving me and the others grappling with a mix of exhaustion and dread as we awaited the next call to action.

Back on the spot fire, Ford and Lira stood side by side, their bodies subtly swaying in rhythm as they put some much-needed distance between themselves and the chaos of the fire line. The air thickened with the acrid scent of smoke and the distant crackle of flames, creating an almost surreal backdrop to our labor. They began the laborious task of pulling brush out of the line, each movement deliberate and calculated.

Nearby, the superintendent swung his saw with fervent enthusiasm, acting as if he were a warrior wielding a sacred sword against an unseen enemy. His eyes, however, betrayed the purpose. The superintendent's eyes were clouded and unfocused, making it difficult for him to see the brush clearly. Again and again, he missed his intended targets, the blade glancing off twigs and branches as he flailed in a futile attempt to reclaim control over the encroaching wilderness.

Lira, with a determined expression etched across his face, picked up his Polaski and expertly cut through the stubborn brush, moving fluidly and efficiently. Ford watched him, impressed by Lira's skill as we navigated through the darkness of the night, the rhythmic thud of the Polaski and the muffled rustle of the underbrush being the only sounds. Hours passed, and fatigue from the labor began to settle into my bones when Ford suddenly raised a hand, stopping Lira mid-swing.

"Hold on a second," he said quietly, gesturing toward the superintendent, who had now turned his focus back toward them, seemingly intent on cutting a line that would lead back to where we stood. The superintendent carved a path down a long, narrow finger of land, resembling a desperate attempt to connect the dots in a game only he understood. Then he cut up the finger, arriving almost exactly where Lira and Ford stood. It struck them as absurd; the fingers that should connect could easily burn out in a matter of fifteen minutes if he would just pause and rethink his approach.

They exchanged glances, silently debating whether to intervene. Should they let him know the futility of his actions, or would that spark another one of his spiraling tirades? Ultimately, they decided against it, opting to forgo the religious diatribe that would surely follow any attempt at correction. Instead, they turned away, their hearts heavy with the weight of unspoken words, and made their way back to where the rest of the crew lay sleeping under the stars, weary bodies seeking solace amidst the chaos of the wildfire.

As the crew settled down for the night, the haunting echoes of the superintendent's saw rang in our ears, reminding us of the madness that lingered just beyond the edges.

CHAPTER 16

THE LEGEND, HEPHAESTUS

The morning emerged with a brilliance that felt almost otherworldly, casting a fresh, invigorating light on a reality that had shifted dramatically overnight. The superintendent—once merely a man guiding his crew through perilous, smoke-filled conditions—had ascended in his own mind to an almost divine status, transforming into a deity of sorts amid the chaos of our firefighting endeavor. Despite accomplishing little of substance while cutting line through the long, grueling night, his relentless and nearly frantic efforts gave birth to something far more enduring—a mythic image of himself that loomed large in the minds of the other crews. A view willing to confuse spectacle for substance.

As the new crews arrived by raft, they began sharing stories that took on an exaggerated flair. They recounted tales of the superintendent's crews journeying across the mighty Illinois River. They asked, "Don't you ever stop?"—their voices laced with disbelief and a touch of awe, their wide eyes reflecting both wonder and trepidation. They regarded the superintendent, an imposing and enigmatic figure who stood before them clutching his well-worn Bible with a fervent grip, as if it served as a talisman against the encroaching darkness. He cast his gaze upward, squinting against the brilliance of the morning light, as if seeking answers from some higher power—an invisible force.

Gale pulled powerfully on the oars, his muscles straining and glistening with effort as we battled upstream toward the elusive spike camp that awaited us. Thick smoke swirled between the chasms and bluffs, transforming the Illinois Gorge into a primeval landscape where one could almost imagine prehistoric creatures soaring like pterodactyls through the smoky haze, their shadows flitting across the ground in a ghostly dance.

In stark contrast to the sooty air, the river flowed with crystalline clarity, sparkling brilliantly when struck by an occasional ray of sun. As Gale maneuvered the raft along the winding path of the river, crawfish scuttled away from the shadow of our passage, darting to safety as they sensed the vibrations of our disturbance. I found myself lost in thought, imagining that one day, I would return to this place when the air was clear and the salmon ran—a time when nature would reclaim its beauty and serenity, washing away the scars of recent devastation.

Three hours later, the spike camp loomed into view, just beyond a large boulder that split the river into two distinct channels. The sight both welcomed and daunted us; the sandbar beckoned as we approached. Towering oaks stood sentinel over the flat expanse, their expansive canopies offering much-needed shade for the weary firefighters who spread their sleeping bags beneath the limbs, seeking comfort from the sun's rays.

A pile of supplies from the human pack train lay waiting like a treasure trove, and we quickly assessed our newfound bounty: Meals Ready-to-Eat (MREs), some stale lunches salvaged from previous excursions, water drawn from the river that needed boiling to ensure safety, and cold medicine formed the abundance that greeted us. Most of the crew, worn down by the rigors of our journey, sought refuge beneath the oak canopies to steal a moment of much-needed rest.

I, however, felt a surge of unexpected energy coursing through me from the cold medicine—a wave of relief washing away the persistent itch from the oak's poison that had tormented me. For the first time in days, I could breathe easily, savoring the clean air around me. I set about boiling water, prioritizing safe, clean water as the crew's most urgent need. While I waited for the kettle to bubble and release steam, signaling its readiness, I organized our meager stash of MREs and cold medicine, ensuring each crew member received a fair share.

My gaze landed on the planning sheets drifting around camp, as I eagerly awaited updates from the Rogue River and Willamette crews, who were cutting line around the troublesome hot spot. The sheets—filled with names and notes—bore Grimaldi's signature, zigzagging across the pages like a playful stream, a reflection of his adventurous spirit. Berkson, meanwhile, had been called to another sector for his much-needed medical expertise. I couldn't shake the worry gnawing in my chest over Grimaldi, who had flown out earlier in the fire; his absence lingered heavily in my thoughts.

As I rested in the shade of a majestic oak, the arrival of the Winema and Lagrand hotshot crews brought a wave of relief. Both were known for their competence—a welcome sight after the chaos of the past few days.

Meanwhile, the superintendent dashed back and forth, radiating frenetic energy as he barked advice over the crackle of the radio, his voice rising like a battle cry above the chaos of the ongoing spot fire. His enthusiasm remained constant, a fire that refused to waver even under exhaustion. Still, the Division boss's stern but caring voice regularly cut through, urging him to step back and rest before the situation overwhelmed him completely.

Seizing a rare chance to escape the relentless demands of the job, I caught up with friends from both the Winema and Lagrand crews. I traded stories and laughter with Gina, an experienced foreman from Winema, and Renee, a skilled sawyer from Lagrand—a brief but vital reprieve from the heavy burden of responsibility.

During our banter, Gina recounted an incident when we tied in the line and a crew member mocked her for being a woman operating a chainsaw. With a defiant spark, we dropped to the ground, chainsaws strapped to our backs, and started performing one-handed push-ups. A sudden silence fell over the hecklers, their laughter fading as they watched—captivated by the display of strength and resolve.

"Have a tree to talk to you about," Renee remarked.

"Shoot," I replied, ready for the challenge.

"It's a heavy leaner—a cat-faced Ponderosa Pine. High chance of barber chair, but you can't side cut it because of the cat face."

Cat-faced trees notoriously posed dangerous challenges; their centers were often burned out, exposing one side to the air and creating a precarious situation. With a heavy lean, they could fall unpredictably, splitting and swinging dangerously, threatening any sawyer who dared to approach.

"Better to make a small face cut, or the tree'll come crashing down on your saw," he advised. "Bore in behind the face, cut backwards, and release the tree all at once—but be mindful of root pull issues."

I realized it was time to catch some sleep. In the shade of a massive oak, to the sound of a scolding squirrel, I lay down. As I drifted off, the superintendent's incessant barking of orders over the radio faded into the background, lulling me into a restless slumber.

The superintendent, meanwhile, walked down to the river, splashing cool water on his face in a futile attempt to shake off the fatigue clinging to him like a second skin. He looked into the water, and for a fleeting moment, Hephaestus stared back—a new, Christian version of the god of fire and metal. He gazed deeper and saw the reflection of McCollister.

"Hello, McCollister," he greeted the reflection, as if acknowledging an old friend.

"What do you think?" Ford chimed in, appearing beside him.

"Well, the color is good, the sound effects are excellent, and the plot is intriguing. All in all, I'd give it a double thumbs-up," McCollister replied with a smirk, his eyes glinting.

The superintendent then strode back and forth along the edge of camp, exaggerating his movements as he tried to embody various heroic poses—each one becoming increasingly uncomfortable and forced. He first attempted the Lewis and Clark pose, dramatically pointing toward the Pacific. But it didn't quite resonate with the air of authority he craved. The gesture felt awkward and misplaced, as if he were an actor in a play rather than a leader of men.

Next, he mimicked the march of General Patton, envisioning himself commanding respect and fear with every step. But he quickly realized he needed to stay out of sight of the firefighters to execute a snappy about-face—his bravado faltering under their scrutiny.

After several failed attempts, he finally settled into the Napoleon pose, tucking one hand into his shirt as he surveyed his domain with a self-satisfied grin. This one felt right. It allowed him to remain visible to the crew while embracing the grandiosity of his newfound identity as a modern-day demigod. The image of a mighty leader—both commanding and dignified—flooded his thoughts.

However, even the Napoleon pose began to strain his arm after a while, prompting him to switch positions occasionally when he thought no one was watching. Still, the stance felt natural enough to spark grandiose thoughts in his mind. Perhaps he was a reincarnation of Napoleon himself—or maybe even a direct descendant. A wild idea took root: if Napoleon had reincarnated as Hephaestus, the god of fire and metal, then wasn't he, too, a reincarnation of both? The thought sent a shiver of excitement through him, fueling his delusions of grandeur.

Meanwhile, the crew spent the rest of the afternoon in a state of scattered sleep, catching brief moments of rest between frantic preparations for the challenges ahead. They diligently refilled their canteens with boiled water, taking care to ensure they were ready for whatever came next, and organized supplies for the following day. A few of them glanced over at the superintendent, who clutched his stomach—a sign, perhaps, that he was suffering from indigestion—as he barked orders over the radio with a voice that echoed through the camp like a clanging bell.

Sometime in the early afternoon, the superintendent strode through camp with an air of self-importance, kicking the feet of sleeping crew members to rouse them from their much-needed slumber. "Hey there, just wanted you all to know—I'm now officially Hephaestus, the Greek god of fire and metal!" he announced grandiosely, his voice booming with the fervor of someone who truly believed in his own mythos. A few hours later, he questioned whether he had adequately informed the crew of his divine identity and woke them again to reiterate his status as Hephaestus, his eyes gleaming with enthusiasm. As the day wore on and darkness settled over the camp, he wondered if his proclamation had been clear enough—or if he had even made it at all—leading to yet another round of wake-ups, his declarations evolving into a strange sort of ritual.

Amidst this chaos, Krutilla and Hunt stepped away from the frenzy, finding a quiet corner to discuss the day's challenges and the superintendent's increasingly erratic behavior. Their words drifted into the still air, mingling with the scents of pine and smoke, as both men shared the weight of their concerns for the crew's morale and safety.

When night finally fell, the crew snuggled into their sleeping bags, grateful to succumb to the sweetness of fresh air. The crisp night surrounded them, promising the hope of a new day and the chance to recharge.

The following morning, Hephaestus led his crew down to breakfast, where they feasted on MREs and whatever old fruit they could salvage from their dwindling supplies, unaware of the irritation brewing among them. The atmosphere remained somber as he prepared his troops for the forced march down to the river to meet the rafts. Krutilla inhaled deeply, savoring the fresh air that filled his lungs. A wind picked up, shifting directions and clearing the gorge of smoke—a welcome change that signaled the potential for helicopter support. Just the day before, a helicopter had managed to drop a crucial load of supplies, and its drop zone had only become visible with the aid of lit fuzees. The promise of assistance lay on the horizon, a flicker of hope amid the challenges they faced.

As the crews expertly rafted the winding Illinois River, they couldn't help but marvel at the stunning transformation of their surroundings. The surreal, tense atmosphere of the previous day had given way to an enchanting display of nature's beauty—an almost ethereal sight that seemed to breathe life into their weary spirits. The river wound through jagged cliffs; the water sparkled like diamonds in the sunlight as it flowed gracefully. Nearly empty waterfalls poured over rounded stones, creating a melodious symphony that harmonized with the gentle gurgling of the river. Rocks, sculpted by the relentless forces of erosion over countless years, directed the flow toward moss-laden precipices, where the currents met the Illinois with a gentle and welcoming embrace. Each stroke of the oars sent ripples dancing across the surface, accompanied by the uplifting melodies of birds chirping and singing for the first time in days, reviving the air with their joyful tunes.

With unwavering determination, the crew made swift, steady progress down the river, the rhythmic motion of the oars propelling them forward with purpose. Just a few hours later, they arrived at the edge of the fire, their hearts racing with a mix of anticipation and concern. To their relief, they found the line nearly complete around the blaze, save for the southeast corner, which still posed a threat. The east flank held firm, thanks to a combination of a stream and steep cliffs that acted as a natural barrier. At the same time, their comrades had effectively contained the rest of the fire through tireless effort. It was clear the Winema crew had worked diligently, putting in the hard hours necessary to secure the area.

Hephaestus' crew now faced the critical job of cutting an access line to the east side of the fire, ensuring it remained secure against the encroaching flames that flickered hungrily at their edges. I set to work immediately, cutting a trail up to where the access line began. I moved with purpose, flagging the path to enhance visibility and ensuring it would remain clear for my fellow firefighters. Once I established the route, I rejoined the crew, who focused on battling an area that threatened to escape their control, their resolve unbroken as they prepared to face the flames head-on.

As the crew took cover behind the sturdy trunks of ancient trees and the massive boulders strewn across the rugged terrain, the deafening sound of the helicopter's rotor blades sliced through the air. The aircraft swooped in, its powerful engines roaring as it prepared for a critical water drop. Just as the helicopter released its heavy cargo, the flames erupted—fanned by the wind from the propellers into a temporary inferno, a violent spectacle of orange and heat.

The fire roared and surged, twisting and turning as if alive. But when the torrent of water poured down upon it, the blaze began to subside, momentarily cooling under the deluge, steam rising like a ghostly shroud from the charred earth. The helicopter, its bucket now empty, made a swift, thunderous rush toward the nearby Illinois River to refill, its whirling blades creating a cacophony that reverberated through the valley.

Gale and Thomas fired up their chainsaws, the machines roaring to life in a storm of power. They plunged into the thick underbrush with fervor, cutting down dense foliage as wood chips flew in all directions, swirling like confetti in a storm. The smoke hung heavy in the air, stinging their eyes and making it difficult to breathe, but the distant sounds of the Winema crew's saws—growing ever closer—provided a much-needed motivation. It became an unspoken challenge, urging them to push harder, to give everything they had, even as the flames danced menacingly in the background.

Just then, the firefighters dove away from the line once more as the helicopter returned, its shadow sweeping ominously over the fire. The whirring blades deafened them as it dropped another load of water, creating a shower of mist that briefly doused the flames. They sprang back into action, urgency coursing through their veins as they began tossing brush aside and cutting a line down to the mineral soil beneath.

"Hot shovel!" Gale choked out, his voice hoarse and strained from the smoke that enveloped them like a thick blanket. Without hesitation, Donna and Glenn rushed in, shovels filled with mineral earth in hand, taking turns hurling dirt against the base of the flames, fighting to cool them temporarily. Gale, fueled by unwavering determination, leapt back toward the fire with his chainsaw in hand, cutting feverishly as if his actions alone could stave off the inferno.

Amid the chaos, the blue hard hats of the Winema crew emerged through the haze of smoke as the brush erupted into flames once more, forcing Gale and Thomas to retreat from the line, their hearts pounding. The helicopter swooped low again, releasing its bucket over the blaze with a thunderous crash. With renewed urgency, Gale dove back in and joined the Winema crew to secure the fire's edge. After what felt like an eternity battling the relentless flames, he finally collapsed to the ground, gulping water in desperate breaths, the cool liquid offering brief respite from the heat. Determination etched on his face, he began sharpening his saw, readying himself for the next round, knowing the fight was far from over and that they would need every ounce of strength and skill to prevail against the furious blaze.

Amid the unfolding chaos, Krutilla's radio crackled to life, and Hunt's familiar voice cut through the din of flames and the distant roar of the waterfall. "Krutilla, I need you to check on those lined spot fires we passed earlier. They could be flaring up." The urgency in Hunt's tone propelled Krutilla into motion. Without hesitation, he motioned to Donna, who stood nearby, her spirited demeanor a welcome contrast to the gravity of their work. Together, they made their way down to a flat area below a waning waterfall, the sound of cascading water offering brief relief from the oppressive heat.

As they approached, they spotted several remnants of small fires, each roughly twenty by twenty feet, reminders of the relentless battle waged against nature's fury. The air thickened with smoke and ash as they knelt low, dragging their knuckles through the cold, gray remnants of what had once been lush underbrush. Their eyes scanned for lingering heat, and soon they identified three or four hot spots simmering beneath the surface, threatening to reignite at any moment. With purpose, they filled their hard hats with water from the waterfall and swiftly doused the embers, extinguishing them before they could grow.

As they worked side by side, a sense of friendship took shape, and conversation flowed easily. They discussed their favorite movies and books, sharing laughs and insights about the stories that had shaped them. Donna's mantra for the year echoed in Krutilla's mind: "I am not here to make friends; I am here to make money." The sentiment carried a pragmatic edge, yet beneath it lay a quiet truth—she still managed to forge connections with her fellow crew members, a feat that made the grueling days a little more bearable.

With their task complete and the spot fires extinguished, they began the trek back to the rafts docked along the riverbank, mentally preparing for the next journey upriver. Autumn's arrival was unmistakable as leaves fell, carpeting the ground in a mosaic of color that made footing treacherous. They moved carefully through the bluffs and chasms lining their path, every step demanding focus and balance. Edging along narrow ledges, they descended steep chutes and maneuvered around precarious drop-offs, using branches and brush for support, their hearts racing through the rugged terrain.

Midway to the river, Krutilla suddenly froze, his senses sharpened by a piercing yell from above. He looked up to see Donna, precariously perched over a twenty-foot drop, clinging to a piece of brush that looked ready to give way. Panic surged through him, a visceral urge driving him forward as he rushed up the bluff, his heart pounding. He worked quickly along a narrow ledge, instincts on high alert, and reached for a sturdy piece of brush hanging low from the cliff's edge, anchoring himself as he neared her.

"Hold on, Donna! I've got you!" he shouted, his voice steady despite the adrenaline coursing through him. He seized her arm with a firm grip, their eyes locking in a moment of shared determination. Together, they worked back toward the safety of the cliffside, using the brush to steady themselves. At last, they pulled onto a flat area, both of them gasping for breath, their hearts racing from the surge of adrenaline. They exchanged relieved glances, the thrill of survival binding them even closer amid the relentless battle against fire and wilderness. With renewed care and purpose, they continued down the rocky terrain toward the riverbank, where the sturdy rafts awaited. With each step, anticipation grew, the promise of respite drawing nearer.

After the raft ride, when they finally reached spike camp, they welcomed one another with open arms. They were met by the enticing aroma of their first "good" meal in days—a hot, hearty feast served generously from five-gallon cans. Steaming green beans, fluffy mashed potatoes smothered in rich gravy, and some unidentifiable yet tantalizing meat brought a wave of relief that washed over them like a cool breeze.

The air felt fresh and invigorating, a stark contrast to the chaos of the previous days spent battling flames and navigating treacherous terrain. The crew eagerly filled their canteens with crisp, cold river water, the liquid soothing their parched throats and weary bodies. They also grabbed cold medicine to stave off lingering ailments, a necessary precaution after the grueling exertion endured in the field.

As dusk settled in, they crawled into their sleeping bags, the fabric warm and comforting against tired limbs. The sweet scent of pine mingled with the cool night air, lulling them toward deep slumber. Surrounded by the gentle flow of the river and the quiet chatter of their comrades, they felt a profound sense of camaraderie—a bond forged through shared trials. The warmth of those experiences wrapped around them like a protective blanket, soothing weary spirits as they drifted into much-needed rest, grateful to be alive and together in this rare moment of peace.

CHAPTER 17

GRIDDING, R AND R

"R&R is canceled," Ford said firmly, his voice cutting through the crisp morning air. He stood beside the warming fire, cradling a weathered metal pot as it heated water for a much-needed cup of coffee. Steam curled into the chill while the crackling fire broke the stillness.

I tried to shake off my dreams, sleepily muttering that I thought it had only been postponed. I tossed seasoned wood onto the fire, and the logs hissed and sputtered, releasing warmth that briefly pushed back the chill of October.

As I watched the flames, urgency settled heavily in my gut. The canceled R and R felt like a stone in my stomach. We needed a break after the relentless demands, but that hope faded, replaced by hard reality. I sighed inwardly, accepting the sacrifice and refocusing on keeping the crew safe and effective in the face of adversity.

Lira broke the silence with dry irony. "I guess we'll find our rest in chaos, won't we?" His eyes reflected fatigue and determination, a quiet testament to our resilience. Despite the odds, we would endure together.

"It really doesn't matter to me," Hunt said evenly, a thoughtful look crossing his rugged face. His presence grounded the group, radiating quiet confidence. "The LaGrande crew said R and R changed after crews got drunk and started fights. Now they just bus everyone to

Brookings to do laundry." He shook his head, frustration evident. The R and R that once promised relief now felt like a fading memory. The fire crackled softly, embers lifting into the morning sky and carrying our fleeting hopes with them.

Later, our weary crew settled into restless sleep beneath the stars as the night's heavy humidity nearly smothered the stubborn fire that had plagued us for days. October brought colder air, each night biting at our bones like an unwelcome shroud. I felt the sting of cold on my skin as I approached the fire, each step careful on the rugged ground. My breath formed small clouds in the frigid air before vanishing, a reminder of the harsh environment we faced.

Meanwhile, the arrival of additional rafts, flown in specifically for spike camp, significantly improved our situation. This transport allowed for faster movement as the rafts glided smoothly over the water, carrying vital supplies to support our fight against the relentless flames. Knowing that help had arrived brought a renewed sense of hope.

As I approached the fire, I saw the crew spread along the eastern flank of the blaze, a line of dedicated firefighters spaced roughly fifty feet apart, each moving with careful purpose. They navigated the rugged terrain with the precision of seasoned professionals, eyes scanning for danger lurking in the shadows. Every few paces, we paused together, senses heightened, listening intently for warnings. Whenever someone called out, "Smoke!" we halted abruptly, our hearts pounding in a shared rhythm as adrenaline surged, and we waited for the hotspot to be extinguished before resuming our determined march. With each flame put out, a unified shout of "moving!" echoed, reinforcing our synchronized effort against the consuming fire.

I scanned the area for a hotspot needing immediate attention. Smoke hung thick in the air, and heat radiated from the flames, but I remained undeterred. Finally, after what felt like an eternity, I spotted exactly what I was looking for: a deep stump hole where flames flickered. "I need some help over here! Send Ray!" I called, projecting my voice over the crackle of fire and the rustle of leaves in the hot wind.

Moments later, Ray emerged through the haze with a confidence that seemed to cut through the smoke. His familiar, robust figure moved with purpose, and the knowing grin on his face spoke to his experience and understanding of the situation.

"Ray, I need that extra gallon of water," Krutilla said, urgency edging his voice as he gestured toward the stubborn flames still raging as if alive, intent on devouring everything in their path. "I'd really appreciate it if you'd let me use your canteen." The request carried the weight of trust between allies.

Without missing a beat, Ray nodded, his expression shifting to focused determination as he assessed the scene. They worked swiftly and efficiently, moving in a well-practiced rhythm as they doused the hotspot with water. Each splash against the heated earth hissed in protest, sending plumes of steam spiraling upward. They stirred the soaked soil until the fire was out.

"Moving!" a commanding voice echoed through the chaos, sustaining their momentum. The call reinforced their resolve as they pressed on, united as a force, each small victory lifting their spirits. Every drop of water fueled their determination to push back against the consuming chaos.

Later, as the sun dipped lower in the sky, casting long shadows across the rugged terrain, some of the crew carried bladder bags—hefty five-gallon water containers equipped with hoses and nozzles, each one a lifeline in the fight. These vital supplies had been distributed just the evening before, flown into their dry lakebed camp, a welcome sight amid the chaos of firefighting.

The crew continued to work diligently, focus unwavering as they tackled each task with the determination that had come to define them. They paused only when the clock struck three that afternoon, taking a brief respite from the heat. The fire was relatively well contained now, and they knew it was crucial to return to spike camp while there was still enough daylight to navigate the water safely. When they arrived, the Division Boss was waiting, a wide grin spreading across his face as he delivered the welcome news that their long-anticipated R and R had been reinstated.

Hunt, Ford, and Lira nodded appreciatively, their minds already turning to the mundane but necessary tasks ahead—doing laundry, scrubbing poison oak from their clothes, and finally addressing the lingering colds that had plagued them throughout the assignment. Mc-Collister, standing slightly apart from the group, smiled and offered a double thumbs-up, his quiet approval evident in his easy demeanor.

As the crew began to unpack, I took charge, methodically stowing away gear that wouldn't be needed for the night under the stars and preparing for the walk out the following day. "Where's Grimaldi?" Thomas asked suddenly, his voice muffled by a mouthful of crawfish. The savory aroma drifted through the air, blending with the smoke and the forest's earthy scent.

I rifled through the fire plans flown in by helicopter, brow furrowing as I scanned the pages. "Looks like he's been assigned as a falling boss on Division C, but now he's shifted over to Division E, where the fire has flashed across the river into the Kalmiopsis Wilderness," I replied, the weight of responsibility settling over me like a heavy cloak. Concern tugged at me as I thought of my crew, fully aware of the dangers that lay ahead.

"Great. Grimaldi goes commando, snags a falling boss job, and ends up in the hottest part of the fire. Looks like my brother is having the time of his life," Thomas remarked, popping another tail off a crawfish and gobbling it down eagerly before shifting closer to the fire's warmth, his laughter mingling with the crackling flames. "It's going to get cold tonight; I think I'll grab another sleeping bag," he added, glancing toward the stack of gear accumulating near their makeshift camp.

I nodded, watching as more people joined around the flickering warmth of the fire, including Ford, Hephaestus, and a few members from neighboring crews. Laughter and stories mingled with the sounds of nature, creating a symphony of relief after an exhausting day.

"Hey, I just caught wind of a remarkable feat! Apparently, the fire boss managed to make it all the way from Conner's place to Oak Flats—the twelve-mile marker—in a mere two and a half hours," someone interjected, their voice slicing through the lively banter around the campfire. I pulled my gaze from the mesmerizing dance of the glowing embers and shifted my focus to the superintendent. His agitation was becoming increasingly discernible, an unsettling energy radiating from him like heat waves off a scorched landscape.

I could almost taste the tension in the air, thick and charged, as if a storm were brewing just beyond the horizon. The challenge hung there, suspended like a taut wire, ready to snap. The thought of the eighteen miles of wilderness stretching toward Oak Flats—winding through dense trees and rugged terrain—had morphed into a race against time. The chance of breathing in the wilderness was disappearing. The respite from poison oak blisters chafing against our thighs was disappearing. Swallowing some cold medicine, I slipped into my sleeping bag, fatigue pulling me under as I drifted into a restless sleep, my mind swirling with thoughts of flames and responsibility.

Hephaestus, however, remained wide awake, his energy seemingly boundless as he animatedly recounted tales of daring heroics to anyone who would listen. His voice rang out, vibrant and enthusiastic, against the backdrop of the crackling fire dancing in the cool night air. The warming flames threw shadows across the faces of his audience, illuminating expressions of awe and amusement. As the clock ticked steadily toward two in the morning, most of the crew had succumbed to exhaustion, drifting into sleep as their bodies finally surrendered to the fatigue of the long, grueling day.

Hephaestus, feeling the pull of slumber tug at his eyelids, made a bet with himself—a silly little wager—that he could stay awake just a bit longer to keep sharing his captivating stories, convinced the magic of the night could be stretched on a moment more. The stories flowed like the nearby river, full of adventure and excitement. But as the hour crept toward three, the fight to stay conscious became insurmountable. In a burst of impulsive resolve, he leapt to his feet and dove headfirst into the river. The shock of the icy water enveloped him like a crashing wave, jolting him awake with the force of a lightning strike.

With newfound energy surging through his veins, Hephaestus emerged from the water, laughing. He struck a series of exaggerated poses, lifting his hand high before bringing it down dramatically, mimicking the infamous Raskalnokov pose from a tale he had heard long ago, a mischievous sparkle in his eyes. The plunge into the river at five o'clock refreshed him just in time for the crew to wake at six. They gathered for a light breakfast, the scent of freshly brewed coffee and warm scrambled eggs wafting through the air, mingling with the lingering smoke of the dying fire.

Hephaestus, fully charged with adrenaline and the afterglow of hard work, readied his crew for the impending race. They had earned this moment—a chance to reach their destination quickly and efficiently—and the thought fueled his determination. Glancing at his watch, he called for the crew to move. They half ran, grunts escaping as they hacked and coughed, crossing a saddle that dipped into a bubbling brook, water gurgling cheerfully around their legs. Hephaestus watched with pride.

Fueled by urgency and excitement, he pushed them onward. After all the sweat and labor they had poured into the work, they more than deserved a shot at rest. It was a reward they had fought for, and he was determined to get them there fast. Another glance at his watch sent a surge of motivation through him, and with a shout, he signaled them to take off.

The crew responded with a mix of adrenaline and exhaustion, hacking and coughing as they half ran through the saddle, the cool water of the brook splashing against their legs. Hephaestus felt pride swell in his chest; they looked strong, moving as a cohesive unit, each member pushing through fatigue that clung like a second skin.

They reached the straightaway leading down to Silver Creek, where a receding cliff loomed over the tumbling waterfall below. The crew pulled ahead by a length, spirits high as they passed Conners' place. It was a brief moment of respite, just long enough to catch their breath and gather energy for the pace ahead.

As they passed above Briggs, the ranch that had become a familiar landmark, Hephaestus felt a bittersweet pang—it would be the last time they saw it for a while. They charged down and across a sturdy bridge spanning the thirsty Indigo Creek, its water reduced to a dribble beneath them, urging them to move faster. Pressing on along a ridge overlooking the Illinois River, they welcomed the dappled shade of lush trees, a small blessing as they approached Oak Flats.

With a final burst of energy, they crossed the finish line of their race, the crew coughing as poison oak blisters broke and oozed along their skin. They waited for the bus. A few hours later, it arrived, its engine humming softly in the warm afternoon sun. They returned to base camp, the familiar surroundings offering a comforting sense of relief after the grueling effort. The next day, they would bus into Brookings, and Hephaestus, ever the enthusiastic leader, asked if they wanted to start early. To his surprise, the crew collectively shook their heads, choosing a little more rest before the next leg of the journey.

Morning broke early for me, long before the sun had fully risen, dawn brushing the horizon with soft pastels. The heat of my sleeping bag worsened the itch of poison oak along my skin, leaving me restless and uncomfortable. My watch blinked 4:30, the numbers glowing in the dim tent. With a sigh, I swung my legs over the cot, the cool ground a relief beneath my feet. I headed down to camp, where the familiar aroma of coffee drifted through the air.

I poured myself a steaming cup, the warmth offering a brief reprieve from the miserable night, and watched as the rest of the crew slowly gathered for breakfast. Around six, I finally sat down to eat beside Berkson, who had rejoined us after a brief absence. We traded stories and jokes, the easy fellowship bringing a sense of normalcy amid the chaos.

At precisely 6:30, Donna sprinted toward me, her face flushed. "Krutilla! Hephaestus is trying to leave without us!" she said, the words spilling out. I frowned and strode toward the bus, spotting Hephaestus bouncing inside, arms waving as he urged the driver to go, eager to roll without the rest of the crew.

Without hesitation, I stepped in front of the bus and crossed my arms, a silent barrier to Hephaestus's enthusiasm. Donna ran off to gather the remaining crew, her determination clear in her stride. One by one, they climbed aboard, chatter filling the air as they settled in. With a gentle lurch, the bus finally pulled away, leaving camp behind.

"Hurry up and relax," I muttered under my breath, a wry smile tugging at my lips. To my surprise, the rest of the crew picked it up, and soon they were chanting, "Hurry up and relax!" in unison, their voices rising in playful defiance. It was a small victory—the crew finally grasped the absurdity of our situation, the ridiculousness of our leader's antics.

As we approached Brookings, Hephaestus stood in his seat and raised a hand dramatically, calling for silence over the chatter. "As you all know, R and R was restricted because several crews got drunk and started fighting," he began, his voice booming with authority. "I understand you're on your own time, and yes, it's legal for you to drink. But let me be clear: when you get back, you're on my time, and if anyone comes back drunk, I will tear them apart." He punctuated the warning with a theatrical Mike Tyson–perfect uppercut, drawing a mix of laughter and unease from the crew. He seemed to wonder, perhaps, if he might have had a career as a boxer.

When the bus finally pulled into Brookings, Hephaestus leaped off as if it were a launching pad, his disdain for alcohol driving his movements. He harbored a deep loathing for excess, having once walked that path himself. He understood the mind of a drunk all too well, the hostility and aggression it could breed. That contempt extended beyond alcohol at the time; he despised anything that slowed or disrupted his progress, from elderly pedestrians shuffling down Brookings's streets to crooked clothing—a shirt untucked, a pant leg too long. To him, they represented disorder, like a messy room or the discomfort of uneven forms in a world he tried relentlessly to control.

For the crew, getting drunk was the last thing on our minds. Instead, we focused on the mundane but necessary tasks ahead—laundry chief among them—while breathing in the crisp coastal air. The salty scent of the ocean mingled with the earthy aroma of pine, creating a bracing atmosphere that lifted our spirits.

Later that evening, as I settled in beneath a sky bright with stars, I found myself wondering how Grimaldi was faring in his new role before drifting into a quiet, restful sleep.

CHAPTER 18

GRIMALDI GOES COMMAND

"I'm not going to fell that fucking tree!" Volcano Mike, the sore-toothed grizzly, bellowed from atop the rough-hewn stump he stood on. His voice reverberated through the dense pines, echoing off the bark of ancient trees. Grimaldi quickly learned one of Volcano Mike's eccentricities—a backwoods tradition that felt both absurd and oddly fitting in their chaotic world. When a dispute arose, the parties involved climbed onto separate stumps. They shouted their arguments at one another until a resolution emerged or someone stormed off to the Crummy in a huff.

Grimaldi watched the spectacle with cautious bemusement and growing frustration. The argument centered on a snag on the fire side of the line that Grimaldi insisted needed to come down. To him, the danger was obvious: sparks blown over the line could ignite dry fuels, spawning unpredictable spot fires that might spiral out of control and jeopardize the entire operation. Volcano Mike, however, refused to acknowledge the nuances of fire behavior, stubbornly dismissing the risk. With a resigned sigh, Grimaldi grabbed the saw, its familiar weight reassuring in his hands, and approached the gnarly tree. Its twisted trunk and jagged branches testified to years of weathering the elements. Grimaldi cut and felled it himself.

About an hour after getting out of the hospital, Grimaldi made his way to Division C to assume the role of falling boss. The position required him to direct fellers—many of them loggers with little to no fire experience—on which trees or snags to take down and how to do so safely. He had previously worked as a foreman on another hotshot crew, and his experience made him well qualified for the job. Even so, the weight of leadership pressed heavily on him, especially in such unpredictable conditions.

The past week unfolded like a sporadic collage of action, inaction, boredom, and brief flashes of adrenaline for Grimaldi and the fellers he worked alongside, Mike and John. Their first assignment involved removing snags and clearing brush along the Illinois River trail, ensuring Briggs Ranch and Conners' Place remained safe for the pack trains that supplied firefighters with critical provisions. John's personality stood in stark contrast to Mike's.

"I run the 20-yard dash faster than anyone alive!" Mike bellowed, his voice booming through the trees as he puffed out his chest with bravado. "And I'll run your ass over if you don't get out of my way when the tree starts to fall!" The tree they were about to fell—a rotten pine leaning precariously into another—posed numerous hazards that twisted Grimaldi's stomach. With a roar of the engine, Mike blasted through the face of the tree with his Stihl .064, sending strings of wood chips flying like confetti. This chaotic celebration contrasted sharply with the gravity of their task. Grimaldi stood vigilant, scanning the canopy for falling debris, his heart racing with the thrill of the moment. "Tree coming down!" rang out, and the two trees split, crashing in different directions. Grimaldi and Mike dove into their safety zone—a massive Douglas fir that provided a sturdy barrier against the impending chaos.

As the fellers continued their work, dropping snags and cutting back brush that overhung the fire line, they bucked logs along the trail until noon, when they took a much-needed lunch break on Buzzard Rock. The scenic vantage point overlooked the Illinois River, a serpentine ribbon of blue that cut through the landscape and glistened under the midday sun. Light danced across the water's surface, creating a dazzling display that sharply contrasted with the soot-streaked sky above, heavy with smoke and remnants of the raging fire—a vivid reminder of the danger that still lurked nearby. Grimaldi paused to take in the view, appreciating the beauty that surrounded them, even amid the chaos.

As he chewed his sandwich, Grimaldi's thoughts drifted to his crew back at base camp. A pang of longing struck as he reminisced about his friends, their camaraderie a comforting balm against the strain of their current reality. Yet a certain freedom thrived out here, away from the increasingly unpleasant presence of the superintendent, whose narcissism and creeping madness weighed heavily on morale. The man's incessant religious references and snide remarks haunted him, especially the vivid memory of him kicking out the coffee fire at three in the morning during a slow mop-up—a moment that left Grimaldi seething. Out here, he relished the autonomy to do his job without constant surveillance from someone eager to criticize. He tossed a rock over the edge and watched it vanish into the swirling smoke below, the surreal scene mirroring the chaos they fought. The only real hassle came from the occasional outburst by Volcano Mike, which, while loud and theatrical, carried no true malice toward his fellow workers.

Once lunch concluded, the team resumed their tasks, moving along the cliffs of Indigo Creek toward Silver Prairie Trail, where the infamous tree with the big widow maker awaited them, before eventually making their way down to Briggs Ranch. At the ranch, they encountered a pack train returning from Conner's Place, and Grimaldi took the initiative to arrange for the saws to be hauled back, a small victory amid the demanding work. The minor triumph reminded him that even in the thick of chaos, moments of clarity and teamwork could still emerge.

Grimaldi powered ahead on the trail, leaving the fellers scrambling to keep pace behind him. Accustomed to a more leisurely approach to hiking, they favored power lounging over the relentless pace he set.

Only later did Grimaldi discover the trick they had played on him—strategically placing rocks in the bottom of his pack to weigh him down, a playful jab at his boundless energy. Eventually, they boarded the bus back to base camp, the sun dipping low on the horizon and casting long shadows through the trees, the day's work etched into their muscles as exhaustion mingled with a sense of accomplishment.

The following day dawned to the buzz of camp generators, a cacophony that signaled the start of another demanding shift. Grimaldi pulled himself from his sleeping bag, the fabric still warm from his body heat, and headed to the caterers for his morning coffee. As he sipped the rich liquid, its aroma swirling around him, he listened to the bustle of firefighters preparing for the day ahead. His thoughts drifted to the role he wanted to take on the fire. His stitches were scheduled to come out, and he faced a choice: stay with the crew or step into the role of falling boss. As he weighed the decision, Tim Lee, the head of air operations, strolled by and offered a nod of approval. He'd heard about Grimaldi's performance the day before and assured him he would hold the fellers for him. For the first time, the hassle-free environment Grimaldi craved seemed within reach.

Soon after returning from the hospital in Gold Beach, Grimaldi and the fellers peered into a deep void where Indigo Creek's drainage carved a chasm through the rock. The division boss pointed out work waiting at the bottom, and Grimaldi, accompanied by two reluctant fellers—understandably hesitant at the thought of such a steep descent—followed him down into the depths, each step feeling like a journey into the unknown.

To slow his descent, Grimaldi grabbed a piece of brush and used it as an anchor against the slope, finally coming to a stop by clutching a sturdy oak branch. As he glanced across the ridge paralleling their descent, unease washed over him. He could see the area heating up, the telltale signs of fire creeping closer, quivering like warning lights ahead of an approaching storm. The realization troubled him deeply; if the fire crossed the ridge and made a sudden run up their side, they would need to move fast. He noted several rockslides along the route that could serve as potential safety zones in case of an escape. With that knowledge weighing on him, he pressed on with his fellers, determined to finish the job with urgency and caution, the gravity of their situation hanging heavy in the air.

In the gorge, the fellers went to work, dropping a few snags and bucking out a section of a flaming log. Bucking involved cutting up fallen trees to manageable sizes to be worked with. Grimaldi watched the fire grow, flames licking hungrily at the air and sending up a thick column of smoke that blotted out the sun, turning the bright day into an eerie twilight. Heat radiated around them, a constant reminder of the unforgiving danger ever present, as the world shifted from vibrant greens to ominous shades of gray.

"We are pulling out," Grimaldi told the fellers, urgency threading his voice as he surveyed the growing inferno. "If this fire blows up before we reach the top, follow me. There are several safety zones on the way back up." The fellers nodded, their expressions sober as the gravity of the moment set in. They followed Grimaldi up the mountain at a quickened pace, heavy breaths and burning legs driving them forward as the fire built beneath them, crackling like a beast waking from slumber. They reached a flat and paused just long enough to catch their breath before urgency pushed them onward again, climbing higher as the crackle of flames grew alarmingly close.

They crested a rise, only to realize it was a false top, the unnerving sound of fire still too near. With one final push, they reached the true summit. They watched in horror as the mountainside they had just climbed erupted into flames, a violent burst that sent sparks flying like shooting stars. Instinct took over, and they dove into a safety zone—a rocky outcrop that offered a brief reprieve from the encroaching inferno. Hearts pounding, they huddled together, breaths mingling with the smoke hanging thick in the air. Overhead, air tankers rushed in, dropping retardant in sweeping arcs, and they stared in awe as the sky transformed into a chaotic canvas of fire and smoke, a stark reminder of nature's raw power.

Grimaldi quickly assessed the fellers around him, noting their visible exhaustion and the pain etched into their movements after the grueling climb. He resolved to be more considerate about volunteering them for such strenuous tasks in the future, recognizing the toll it took on both their bodies and spirits. Slowly, they picked themselves up, each movement testifying to their fatigue. Their corks—logging boots fitted with spikes—proved ill-suited for the rocky terrain, and the day stretched out before them with little to do but watch the fire burn itself out. Eventually, they headed for the bus to return to base camp, the weight of the day's events lingering like heavy fog, the smell of smoke clinging to their clothes.

On his third day out, Grimaldi found the situation largely uneventful. The Indigo Creek area was deemed too dangerous to enter, and elsewhere in Division C, the fire had gone out. He took it upon himself to scout the ridges and draws in search of work, but found none and returned to where the fellers rested. As he surveyed the scene, a creeping sense of regret began to take root about accepting the job of falling boss. The fellers introduced Grimaldi to the more leisurely art of power lounging, which involved sprawling beneath the trees in deliberate rest, a stark contrast to the intense, action-packed days he had come to expect.

The fourth day began much as the third had ended. Time seemed to stretch endlessly as they killed it, throwing rocks at trees and brewing coffee, the aroma wafting through the air and mingling with the earthy scent of the forest. These languid moments proved the hardest for Grimaldi, the stillness gnawing at him and stirring a restless energy within. Just as that restlessness began to settle heavily, a radio call came through, summoning the fellers to tackle some "big trees." Eager to shake off the monotony and return to the rhythm of work, they started up a cat line—an access route cleared by bulldozers—as late-afternoon sunlight refracted through the smoky haze, casting an orange glow across the horizon like a forgotten sunset.

The trees they approached stood substantial, towering like ancient sentinels guarding the forest. The first tree, a Douglas fir, measured an impressive seven feet in diameter, its height soaring to roughly 140 feet—a testament to years of growth in the wild. About seventy feet up, a charred area marred the trunk, rendering the top dangerously unstable, a potential disaster waiting to unfold. Volcano Mike eyed the tree critically, his gaze shifting to the Husqvarna 266, its twenty-eight-inch bar inadequate for the task at hand. Shaking his head, he said, "It's not big enough. We need the Stihl .064 with the fifty-inch bar." Grimaldi considered a triple cut but quickly dismissed it as too risky given the unstable top, the decision weighing heavily on him. "I'll go back and get the saw if you let me cut the tree," he said with determination, his heart racing at the thought of the challenge. "You're on," Volcano Mike replied, his approval igniting a competitive spark.

Grimaldi jogged down the cat line, anticipation quickening his pace as he retrieved the saw, its powerful engine promising the work to come. He returned just as the crew called the end of the day shift, the sun beginning to dip below the horizon and cast a warm glow across the landscape. He stashed the saw behind a tree, and the fellers made their way back to Briggs Ranch before heading to base camp. Dinner became a communal affair, filled with laughter and shared stories, the bonds of brotherhood reinforcing their spirits amid the challenges they faced. Grimaldi went to bed that night with dreams swirling around the promise of the next day, excitement mingling with thoughts of home—a bittersweet reminder of the family waiting for him beyond this chaotic life.

The rising sun awoke Grimaldi, bringing with it a bittersweet sense of elation. Excitement stirred at the prospect of felling the tree, but sadness tugged at him as he remembered it was his son Mike's second birthday—a milestone he would miss. He wished he could be there, yet the tree would have to serve as his substitute celebration, a reminder of the sacrifices his work demanded.

As he walked out toward the tree, he glanced up at its treacherous top, searching for signs of instability, his heart pounding with a mix of eagerness and apprehension. He recalled the story of a contract feller who had died on the Deschutes National Forest while working a tree under similar conditions, the memory a stark reminder of the dangers inherent in their profession. His thoughts drifted to his wife and children back home, their faces clear in his mind, strengthening his resolve to return safely; their laughter was a distant echo, urging him onward.

Looking to his side, he spotted Mike acting as his spotter, and a grin broke across Grimaldi's face. If anything went awry, Volcano Mike's voice would cut through the chaos with clarity over the roar of the saws. Grimaldi focused on the loose top, then shifted his gaze to a nearby tree about ten feet away that would serve as a safe haven if needed, the mental note offering a sliver of reassurance.

At the base of the tree, Grimaldi felt steadied. It stood solid, free of rot and loose branches that could pose a threat. He returned his attention to the unstable top, took a deep breath, and started the saw. The engine roared to life with a piercing scream, a visceral reminder of the power in his hands. Chips flew in a flurry, scattering like confetti as the air filled with the scent of fresh-cut wood. His eyes stayed locked on the top, watching for any movement, instincts sharpened by years of experience. He thought again of the faller on the Deschutes, of his family and the life left behind, then pulled his focus back to the tree. No movement. The bottom cuts of the Humboldt matched up perfectly, and with a decisive smack of the ax, the Humboldt face dropped free, the sound echoing through the woods.

Grimaldi took another deep breath, fully aware that the most dangerous part of the job lay ahead. He knew that once the tree began to fall, the top might snap back—a fate that had claimed the life of the faller on the Deschutes. He'd had no spotter then; this time, he had Volcano Mike, a small comfort amid the tension. He set the dogs into the back of the tree, cutting to within an inch of holding wood on the far side. Then he shifted closer to the face on his side, cutting down again to about an inch, the tension in the air growing thick and electric.

On his side, he carved out a solid wedge, leaving roughly two feet of holding wood. With swift determination, he cut away the remaining wood, adrenaline surging as he neared the moment of release, the world narrowing to pure focus. The .064 whined, throwing chips behind him as Grimaldi kept his eyes on the top, his heart pounding, each beat a reminder of what was at stake. His gaze flicked between his cuts and the tree's precarious crown. The holding wood shrank quickly—from eight inches to four—as John drove in a safety wedge, a crucial move that could mean the difference between life and death. At three inches, the tree cracked ominously, the sound resonating deep in Grimaldi's chest. He pressed on for one final moment, and then, in instinctive unison, the three fallers sprinted for the sturdy tree behind them, adrenaline carrying them clear.

The tree stood still, cracking but not yet moving—except for the top, which swayed back and forth like a pendulum, a sight that sent chills down Grimaldi's spine. He knew he didn't want to go back under it to continue cutting, the instinct to flee battling the urge to finish the job. A hit on the wedge, perhaps? He weighed the thought as the statue of death loomed above, a stark reminder of the perils of their work. The tree creaked again, yet remained in place, while a gentle breeze drifted over the ridge, cooling the beads of sweat on Grimaldi's face. That wisp of life nudged the tree forward, lingering for a heartbeat before gravity finally claimed it. It crashed to the ground, the top breaking backward in a violent explosion. The top came down like a missile, landing in the exact spot where Grimaldi had stood moments earlier, his breath hitching as he realized how narrowly he had escaped disaster.

In that fleeting moment, Grimaldi's thoughts turned to his son, Mike, blowing out birthday candles, and to his wife cradling the baby she had delivered just three months earlier—the joys of home a bittersweet reminder of what he had missed. He paused to breathe deeply, then filled the saw with gas.

Grounding himself in the present, he felt the thrill of the moment mingle with the weight of responsibility. The day moved quickly, with both Volcano Mike and John falling pumpkins—their slang for the massive trees they targeted. By afternoon, however, little action materialized, and Grimaldi's thoughts drifted to the more intense fire activity where flames had flashed across the Illinois River, a reminder of the relentless battle still unfolding. When he returned to camp that evening, he made his case to overhead, insisting he belonged at the head of the fire, the call of duty echoing in his chest. By late evening, they elevated him to a role that placed his crew on initial-attack standby for the following day, the anticipation invigorating his spirit and fueling his determination.

Morning broke, and as he surveyed the scene, he found Mike and John indulging in their preferred pastime of power lounging, their relaxed posture a sharp contrast to the chaos of the days before. Restless, he checked in on the plans and found nothing stirring. An hour later, he checked again and sensed a shift. Division E had become the new focal point, with the head of the fire near a coyote camp—an area even less developed than the spike camp. They were told to bring plenty of gear. It was clear that nothing awaited them out there yet, but the weight of anticipation hung thick in the air.

In a flurry of activity, he quickly packed and dashed to the helicopter, his heart racing with a mix of excitement and apprehension. As it circled past Briggs, over Silver Prairie, and near the spot fire close to Collier's Bar, they flew into the rugged expanse of the Kalmiopsis Wilderness. The landscape was not delicate but fierce, framed by the jagged peaks of the Big Craggies and standing stark against the smoky sky. Ridges burned with relentless ferocity, flames rolling unimpeded, save for rockslides and streams that offered brief respite from the chaos. The helicopter touched down at Helispot 37, and with a whir of blades, it vanished into the haze of smoke.

"What the hell are those dandies jawing about?" Volcano Mike's voice boomed, cutting through the chatter with his characteristic boisterousness, his frustration reflecting the pressure they all felt.

"They're arguing wilderness policy," Grimaldi explained, working to keep his composure. "If a man wanders into the wilderness and decides to build a homestead, Smokey the Bear does not take kindly to that. Now, here we are, deep in the wilderness, and we've got to cut brush lines with chainsaws as wide as a DC7 cat line. Otherwise, it's not going to hold the fire, and that won't look good if the governor happens to fly overhead. They're scrambling to figure out who's going to take the blame for the fallout of this mess."

Mike shook his head incredulously. "Well, why the hell don't they just let this shit burn? It's just a bunch of damned brush anyway!"

Grimaldi leaned in, lowering his voice as if sharing a secret. "It looks terrible politically. If those east winds pick up, we'll face a fire with a six-mile front bearing down on retirement communities, where people will be breathing in all that smoke. This is the agencies' biggest nightmare; no matter what happens, someone will end up looking bad."

"Who gives a flying fuck about looking bad?" Mike shot back. "What a bunch of city-slicking dandies they are!"

Grimaldi chuckled lightly but stayed serious. "Someone with those kinds of concerns would struggle to get into an overhead position. They usually get fired along the way. Sure, some people slip through the cracks, but they're the exceptions, not the rule."

Mike threw his hands up, exasperated. "Then why the hell do you keep working for this outfit?"

Grimaldi sighed, the weight of his reality settling over him. "It's the only place I can fight fire. Sure, it wears on me, but it's what I know."

As the cluster of men began to break apart, Grimaldi sensed the shift in focus. The plan was to cut only the brush line and avoid the snags, which were rare in this part of the wilderness. He glanced at the two fellers he worked with, both of whom carried a deep aversion to cutting brush. He knew the assignment would be demanding; the line they were meant to hold would require everything they had. He went to work cutting line from Yukon Creek to Klondike Creek, with two crews from the Superior National Forest following behind, diligently cutting line in their wake.

That night, the trio gathered around warming fires—a clear violation of the rules—but the cold and their exhaustion outweighed the risk. Grimaldi found himself left alone, a silent acknowledgment that they were the only capable sawyers in the area. Anyone who wandered too close was met with Mike's volcanic growl, a clear warning not to interfere.

On October 4, a new wilderness policy was announced, allowing them to fall snags along the line. The crew was elated, the news invigorating as they breathed the clean ridge air and set to work with renewed energy. The line advanced quickly from Yukon Creek through Gold Basin and up to Tincup Peak. Each day brought fresh air, sweeping views, and a nearly full moon lighting their way at night. These were the good times, though even then, Grimaldi felt a flicker of unease at the thought of being flown out from Helispot 41 for much-needed rest and recuperation.

On the morning of October 6, as the sun rose and cast a golden hue across the rugged landscape, he stood at Helispot 41, ready for whatever the day would bring.

CHAPTER 19

HELI-SPOT 41

In 1991, I found myself sitting before a congressional delegation. "They were looking for the cream of the crop, so I couldn't apply," I said, my voice tinged with resignation as I sat in the vast auditorium at the University of Montana, a place that felt worlds away from the rugged wilderness I once called home. I no longer fought fires; instead, I was here, immersed in law school, trying to carve out a new path. In my own words, "I guess I'm generally unemployable, so I might as well become an attorney." The weight of that decision pressed heavily on me, a mix of hope and uncertainty—a cocktail of ambition and doubt that lingered like a shadow.

"What was the official reason for getting rid of you?" the congressman asked, his brow furrowed as he leaned forward, his intensity filling the space between us.

"I called my supervisor a gozzlehead behind his back," I replied, a smirk tugging at my lips despite the gravity of the moment, defiance edging my tone. "If I were rehired, he said he'd make sure my 'ass was nailed to a cross.'" It fell under a federal civil rights policy that emphasized sensitivity and inclusion. "Shouldn't an agency representing the government set the best example, not the absolute worst?" the congressman asked rhetorically, his voice rising slightly as he turned toward the agency head seated awkwardly at the end of the long table.

It was 1991, and tension filled the room. This was the first congressional investigation I helped initiate.

Back on the Silver Fire, high above the rugged terrain, the helicopter circled in for a landing at Helispot Forty-one. I jumped out, heart racing, and ran headlong toward the front and side of the aircraft, carefully avoiding the whirring tail rotor that could spell disaster with a single misstep. As I sprinted toward the supplies cached about seventy feet away, I nearly collided with Grimaldi, who was waiting impatiently for his flight out to R and R. With a quick decision, he canceled his plans, the promise of rest eclipsed by the pull of adrenaline, and joined the crew without hesitation.

Off to the side of Helispot Forty-one, nestled in the rugged landscape, a spike camp served as a temporary refuge for the weary crews—a place to sleep, share meals, and gather strength for the work waiting each new day.

The camp perched high on a ridge, offering a breathtaking view over the vast expanse of the Kalmiopsis Wilderness, a pristine sanctuary teeming with life. It served as a haven for a wide range of wildlife, including black bears, elk, coyotes, grey foxes, cougars, and black-tailed deer.

The air came alive with the sounds of nature, and the camp's location afforded us a stunning panorama of towering trees and vibrant plant life. Ponderosa pines rose high above us, while western juniper lent a sharp, distinctive aroma to the air. Grand firs spread their branches wide, forming a canopy that sheltered the forest floor, and Oregon white oaks added an ancient presence to the verdant landscape. In the underbrush, manzanita with its intricate red bark, wild iris, blooming azalea, striking red osier dogwood, and bitterbrush painted the ground in vivid hues that mirrored the vitality of the region. Each element contributed to the rich tapestry of the wilderness, a constant reminder of the beauty and challenges surrounding us as we prepared for another day in the field.

The superintendent stood off to the side, scanning the scene with a perplexed expression, trying to make sense of the chaos around him.

Crew members called him Hephatitus, a nickname that puzzled him, its meaning lost entirely. The religious reference flew over his head, and he chalked it up to some conspiracy dreamed up by Krutilla. He hadn't seen Grimaldi for a week and couldn't understand what had shifted within the crew. Hadn't Grimaldi referred to him as *The Superintendent* just moments earlier? The question lodged in his mind, a thorn that refused to loosen.

Our objective was clear: continue the line from Helispot Forty-one down Tin Cup Ridge to the Checko River, a critical boundary that would serve as the fire's southwest edge. The Checko River—a winding ribbon of blue cutting through dense forest—was known for its clear water and treacherous banks. Once the line was complete, a process that would take several days, we would burn it out from Helispot Thirty-seven to the river, ensuring the fire could not breach our hard-won defenses.

I felt a surge of exhilaration as the wind whipped around me, carrying smoke away from our position and down toward Tin Cup Ridge, a stark reminder of the danger below. I drew a deep breath of clean air, filling my lungs with the sharp scent of pine and earth, and looked out over the wilderness. Craggy ridges rose and fell like a frozen sea, their peaks crowned with dry, brushy growth, while deep, etched drainages cut through the land. From Dominion Peak, I could see a distant column of smoke boiling and twisting in the wind, a constant reminder of the fire's relentless advance.

Saws erupted around me, their sharp blades biting into the sturdy trunks of pine trees with a ferocity that echoed through the forest. With each crash, the trees fell—bucked and thrown from the line— their massive forms slamming into the ground in a cacophony that reverberated in my chest. The crew worked with precision, ensuring each tree fell in the right direction, away from our line. Brush intermingled with the downed trees was dragged off and thrown down the opposite side of the ridge. The thought of finally hooking the fire boomed in our collective consciousness, spurring us on.

Two Husqvarna saws and four McCulloch saws—the latter often considered the weak sister to the Huskys—coughed and sputtered through the wilderness, their mechanical noise a stark contrast to the quiet beauty around us. The line progressed rapidly down the ridge as dense pine gave way to grass and brush, a sign that we were nearing Gold Basin. When we finally reached the basin, we paused to rest in silence, each of us acutely aware of the tension hanging in the air as we waited for Hunt's decision, the weight of our collective effort resting on his shoulders.

As we tirelessly cut line, the fire gained intensity, roaring higher and higher until the smoke column dwarfed Tin Cup Ridge in its shadow, a dark, ominous presence looming over our work. We exchanged anxious glances, questioning whether it was still safe to stay on the ridge. A scout ventured out to assess the fire, and we waited, anticipation coursing through us like electricity.

"Too much heat," Hunt finally declared, his voice steady but urgent, cutting through the tension like a knife. "We need to take the spur ridge down Gold Basin that angles away from the fire." With that, the saws fired back to life, their droning sound drowning out what remained of the wilderness's earlier tranquility.

They entered a solitary pine grove, letting the memory of Gold Basin slip away like sand through their fingers. As they worked, they watched the fire boil in the distance, its fury sharply contrasting with the serene beauty of the landscape. Above them, the clouds swelled—dark, heavy cumulus formations that threatened to unleash chaos on the crew.

I positioned myself at the back of the line, letting my thoughts drift from the pleasant scenery to the comforting smells of the forest as I tuned out the grinding noise of the saws. Here, at the back, I felt a controlled intensity—a place where worries were few and my focus rested solely on the task at hand. My job was clear: work steadily, pace myself, and stay alert to the dangers posed by the saws. Watching the fire remained paramount; I served as a distant scout, vigilant and constantly scanning for potential hazards. The line didn't need to be wide here—the fuel load was light and the terrain flat—a small mercy amid the chaos. As I moved closer, I could hear the saws bogging down in the trees, the sound a harsh reminder of the work still to be done.

My thoughts drifted back to the Snake Bones Fire, a classic west-side Cascade fire that had raged through reprod, small trees, old units, and into towering timber, a battle etched into my memory. Cedar, Douglas fir, hemlock, and a mix of silver fir and noble fir had all fallen prey to the flames. I walked slowly uphill, my heightened senses searching for burning snags hidden within the chaos. I wore no earplugs, convinced that navigating unstable ground required full awareness. Trees fell silently around me, their burned root wads tearing free from scorched earth, a quiet violence that left me breathless. The other saw team on that fire—Mike and Bill from the Clackamus crew—worked out of sight on the opposite side of the spur ridge while I deliberately ignored policy and left the earplugs out.

I moved forward in twenty-foot increments, scanning for smoldering trees or hazardous conditions, always alert for the next threat. Burned-through branches and dangerously unstable trees often hid lethal dangers. Crews would soon enter this area to mop up, their attention drawn to smoke on the ground while threats loomed above, shadows ready to strike without warning. I came upon a cat-faced cedar and checked it for heat, finding none before continuing my climb, adrenaline surging through me like wildfire.

As I rounded a corner, I encountered a Douglas fir with a burned-out hole above a forked branch, a silent warning of what lay ahead. I paused, waiting for the wind. When it came, a wisp of smoke flowed softly from the hole, curling into the air. "Tree coming down!" I yelled, quickly felling the tree and bucking out the burned area, my movements a practiced dance of urgency. "Moving on!" I called, continuing my climb up the ridge, the weight of responsibility heavy on my shoulders. I listened for any sound, no matter how faint, my instincts keen, always attuned to the forest. Did I hear a crack? I wasn't sure. Standing rigid, I gazed up the hill, searching for movement, for signs of danger. Nothing stirred, yet the air felt charged with anticipation.

I waited, still fixated on the hill above, my heart pounding in time with the forest's rhythm. From the moment I first grabbed a saw in my second year on the crew, I lived with it, breathed its mechanical cadence. It was 1982, on the Football Fire, when I seized the saw at noon and worked tirelessly until four in the morning, felling snags alongside Carol, a partnership forged in fire and sweat. Those moments birthed an obsession within me, a passion that evolved as I became saw boss in 1985 and 1986. The crew's reputation for saw operations grew legendary, a badge of honor I wore with pride. I stayed tuned to the saws, my thoughts anchored on the hill, the pulse of the wilderness thrumming beneath my feet.

Then I spotted subtle movement—the snag leaning slowly, silently at first. It fell toward Mike and Bill, a slow-motion disaster unfolding before my eyes. "Tree coming down!" I screamed, my voice slicing through the air. Mike looked up just as the tree plummeted toward him, the moment stretching impossibly long. He dove aside, narrowly escaping as branches rushed past his ear, chaos roaring around us. He scrambled to his feet, brushed dust from his shirt, his heart racing, adrenaline surging. He yanked out his earplugs, suddenly aware of everything. We continued up the ridge, the heat pressing down as we felled hot, hazardous trees.

That incident had happened back in June, and afterward, the superintendent removed me from most saw operations, a decision that felt both relieving and burdensome. I refused to wear earplugs, convinced they dulled my ability to sense danger. Now, in the chill of October, the heat felt different—less intense than summer's blaze, yet still present, lurking like a predator. It reached eighty degrees, warm but altered, the wind carrying a coolness that sent shivers through my sweat-soaked shirt, a reminder of the shifting seasons. It had been dry and dusty; the earth hadn't seen rain in two months, a drought that left the landscape parched and vulnerable.

This day filled me with decisions, each one weighing heavily on me. After abandoning the plan to follow Tin Cup Ridge down to the Checko River, a rumor spread back at the helispot that the fire had jumped the line between Yukon Creek and Klondike Creek. If true, the line we had just cut would be rendered useless, a bitter pill after so much hard work. We waited for a report from the aerial spotter, anticipation thickening the air like a storm cloud. The spotter eventually confirmed it was a small slopover that could be contained with water drops—a small victory amid the chaos. Relieved but weary, we continued cutting line until early evening before returning to Helispot Forty-One. There, we refilled our water bottles from our cubbies and restocked food supplies with MREs for the next day's lunch.

Dinner arrived in hot tins as evening crept in, casting long shadows over the rugged terrain, the sun slipping away like a memory. Grimaldi, Donna, and I sat at the edge of the ridge, taking in the sunset as it painted the sky in hues of orange and purple, the sun slowly disappearing behind the Big Craggies as dusk gave way to darkness. We ate mashed potatoes, boiled green beans, and some sort of meat; the familiar flavors offered comfort amid the chaos—a small reminder of home. We reminisced about the spot, sharing laughs and stories of Grimaldi's time as a falling boss, the warmth of shared experience wrapping around us. As we looked toward Tin Cup Ridge, the day's fire diminished in the humid embrace of night. Eventually, we settled in, exhaustion pulling us into a well-earned sleep.

Meanwhile, the superintendent paced the helispot, his mind racing with chaos of its own. Something felt off, though he couldn't quite name it, a sensation that gnawed at him like a persistent itch. Irritation simmered, threatening to boil over. He noticed disorder in the camp, a disarray that made his skin crawl. Crew members chatted when they should have been cutting line, and his frustration deepened when he realized the candy bars were gone, leaving him to subsist on M&M's—a meager substitute for the comforts he craved. Beneath it all was the gnawing conviction that a solution must exist, some way to regain control before the disorder swallowed him whole.

As he paced, a vision struck him, a dream forming in his mind, vibrant yet unsettling. He took a swig of diet cola, the fizz tickling his senses like a fleeting joy. "I have a dream," he muttered, his voice low and fervent. "I have a dream, I have a dream of forming a crew that will look like me, act like me, not be messy like me. I have a dream that someday everyone on the crew will carry a Bible. I have a dream." The dream, once vibrant with promise, gradually morphed into a murky vision, one he could only make out in the distance. It painted a picture of a crew that mirrored his own likeness, not just in appearance. As he mentally sketched the outlines of this ideal team, he suddenly heard a voice—disembodied, echoing in the recesses of his mind, a haunting proclamation that seemed to rise from the shadows.

The voice asserted emphatically that this vision was not merely a desire but an absolute necessity for the survival and effectiveness of the crew. It echoed with gravitas, declaring that only a truly visionary leader like him could bring such a profound transformation to life. The weight of those words hung in the air, urging him deeper into his aspirations, igniting a fire within amid the swelling chaos around him.

The voice, dark and insistent, pierced the murmur of the wind with an ominous warning that landed like a thunderclap in the night. "You must eliminate Hunt," it commanded, menace threading its tone. "The crew holds him in high regard, and he remains untouched by the sanctity of your biblical ways." It continued, relentless in its twisted logic. "Krutilla, too, must face expulsion; he embodies the very essence of the antichrist, a threat lurking among your ranks."

The warnings kept coming, a relentless stream of accusations that sent shivers down his spine. "Then there's Ford, with his casual disregard for order—his shirt often left untucked, a blasphemous affront to the discipline you envision." A deep chill settled over him as the voice droned on, each name a stone dropped into the depths of his consciousness, rippling with consequence. "And don't forget Grimaldi, who had the audacity to abandon the crew; his defection is unforgivable."

The catalogue of perceived enemies stretched on, an endless list filling his mind with growing unease as he contemplated the isolation this dark counsel demanded. Each name felt like a dagger, plunging deeper into his consciousness, stirring a tempest that threatened to drown everything he had once held dear.

As he continued to pace and mutter to himself, the crew slept peacefully, their dreams mingling with the soft rustle of trees and the distant crackle of the fire, a quiet symphony of the night.

CHAPTER 20

THE CREWS DREAM

The crew envisioned a fire that burned actively—a challenge that beckoned them forward, free from hassle and hostility, and devoid of the chaos Hephaestus had created. In their shared vision, they saw a fire where good, spirited, experienced individuals came together, pooling their skills to extinguish the flames threatening the land. No longer would they endure the burden of whipping boys and lackeys who merely followed orders without grasping the essence of the work. Some crew members had fought such a fire before, battling the elements with a unity and purpose that transformed the arduous task into a shared adventure, a journey that forged bonds deeper than words could convey, friendships born in the crucible of fire.

LeRoy surveyed the vengeful sky overhead, tracing ominous clouds as lightning bolts pirouetted downward, briefly stitching sky to ground in a dazzling display of raw power.

Hailing from the vibrant city of Portland, LeRoy felt a glimmer of optimism flicker as he considered the prospect of earning some much-coveted overtime. A playful grin spread across his face as he called out exuberantly, "Endless shopping at the mall!" His voice carried through the turbulent air, buoyed by the crew's energy.

The electric atmosphere sent shivers down his spine as he marveled at the blue-gray base of a cumulus cloud, which spat out another bolt of lightning, illuminating the landscape in a flash that felt almost alive. "What up?" he called to Keller, who watched the light show with a mix of awe and anticipation, the thrill of the unknown crackling between them. They were in Cascade, Idaho, a place known for unpredictable weather and striking beauty.

Lightning danced across the Payette National Forest, an expansive wilderness of towering trees, steep ridges, and winding rivers. The forest buzzed with sound, yet tension hung heavy in the air, a charge born of impending fire. The crew broke into teams, preparing to fly into the fire as thunder cracked around them, each report echoing like a battle cry. Hunt, newly returned from planning and strategy, told them a cold front was moving through, bringing the promise of increased fire activity. It was a dry cold front, offering little rain, and the gusting wind tore the wrapper from a discarded lunch at the heli-base, a small but telling reminder of the disorder that often followed their work.

In 1986, Hunt looked up at the sky, assuming the role of de facto leader as they awaited orders at the heli-base, his demeanor calm yet resolute. As he continued to watch the sky, a bolt of lightning struck a well-seasoned snag, shattering it violently and transforming it into a boiling inferno, flames dancing in the deepening twilight. The wind swept in, while the rains stubbornly stayed away. The fire grew, spreading through ground litter and igniting subalpine fir, torching canopies and setting the branches of contiguous firs ablaze in a spectacular display of nature's fury. Winds drove the flames from canopy to canopy, creating a running crown fire that danced with a ferocity both beautiful and terrifying. When the wind slackened and humidity rose under the cover of night, the fire went dormant, resting for the heat and dryness of the morning to come—a pause before the storm.

On a massive gray granite slab, the helicopter touched down with a mechanical whir, sending a ripple of excitement through the crew as they prepared to begin their mission. Hunt, Keller, and LeRoy jumped from the bird, adrenaline coursing as they dropped red packs and web gear beneath a sturdy Ponderosa pine, placing them well away from the helispot, a calculated move born of experience. Hunt headed off to scout the fire, leaving Keller to guide the rest of the crew in, purpose igniting among them.

Sherman and Ray arrived next, carrying a bundle of tools, cutting the tape and readying their gear, their movements synchronized by an unspoken understanding. Hunt returned just as the final group—Gale, Rynnae, and Pearson—flew in, their excitement evident as they touched down. Pearson and Gale rinsed the purge from the saws; the purge was a necessary precaution to neutralize the explosiveness of the gas after flying. They slung the saws over their shoulders, signaling readiness, focus sharpened by the task ahead. They followed Hunt into the toe of the fire as he laid out the mission, his voice steady and authoritative.

Back at camp, his two assistants—McAllister, in charge of squads, and me, in charge of saws—lined out additional teams, typically two or three firefighters assigned to other fires. Ford, Uphoff, McCollister, McAllister, and I led those teams, each skilled in our roles, forming a network of experience that strengthened the effort.

"This fire is creeping through the understory and climbing into the subalpine fir, torching crowns and throwing additional spots," Hunt said, his voice steady and authoritative as he surveyed the crew, his gaze cutting through the tension that surrounded them. "As we cut line, we must stay vigilant for spot fires over the line. If the wind holds as predicted, we won't need to worry about a running crown fire. Watch for building cumulus—they can generate erratic winds and unpredictable fire behavior. Safety zones won't be an issue; this area has ample rock outcroppings, as you can see. We'll cut line connecting those outcroppings as natural barriers. We'll start on the east flank, which has the most potential, while the west flank is currently held by these natural barriers. Any questions?" His voice rang through the air, a clarion call for focus.

"How big is the fire?" Sherman asked, her brow furrowed as the reality of the situation settled in.

"Air operations estimate it at around twenty acres," Hunt replied, his tone measured as he gauged the crew's readiness for what lay ahead.

"What are the line specifications?" Rynnae asked, her voice steady amid the tension, a calm within the storm.

"We're cutting through a range of fuel models; I'll leave that to your judgment," Hunt said, his eyes sweeping the crew. "Pearson, control the brush-line width. Keller, do the same with the mineral earth line." As Pearson and Gale formed the saw team, the rest of the crew began cutting line while Hunt moved ahead to scout the fire, serving as a vigilant guardian of their safety.

The line advanced quickly, tying into one natural barrier after another, slowing only when the diggers hit duff or an occasional log. As the line climbed uphill, a wind began to rise—soft at first, then strengthening as the sun heated the valleys and funneled air up the canyons, an unseen force pressing against them. The fire intensified with the wind, and trees began to torch, roaring into brief, violent bursts of flame that cast a hellish glow, a surreal dance of light and shadow.

"Keller!" Rynnae shouted, her voice sharpening with urgency as the danger became clear. "I'm going to look for spots."

"Go ahead," Keller called back, her focus snapping fully to the task at hand, determination flaring within her.

A few moments later, a shout rang out, signaling that spots had appeared. Sherman broke off to assist Rynnae in lining them while the rest of the crew continued cutting line around the area, their movements coordinated and instinctive. A cluster of subalpine fir erupted, sending a fountain of sparks into the air that ignited several small spot fires—a chaotic burst that demanded immediate action. Sherman lined the spots with her Pulaski while Rynnae cooled them. They threw shovels of dirt, their teamwork a testament to training and trust. One spot, precariously positioned beneath a tree, demanded immediate attention; if it took hold, it would generate multiple hot spots and threaten the line they had worked so hard to establish.

The crew quickly contained the spots, and Sherman and Rynnae re-joined the line. However, one stayed behind to patrol in case anything flared unexpectedly.

A chainsaw breakdown slowed line construction, a frustrating setback that threatened their momentum. Pearson moved quickly, re-pairing the engaging dog on the starter by finding a wire, wrapping it tight, and cinching it with needle-nose pliers before reassembling the saw, his hands working with practiced precision.

"Got a spot! I need a saw—now!" Gale shouted, urgency sharpening his voice as the heat pressed in and the stakes rose. Would the saw even start? With one pull, it roared to life, and Pearson cut fast, his thoughts racing. *Got to keep the fire from reaching that clump of subalpine fir. If it catches, it'll be too much to handle. It could even ignite the lodgepole behind it—they've got contiguous crowns. Not enough for a running crown fire, but enough for a short, hot run.*

Pearson cut with smooth efficiency, each motion deliberate, his fo-cus absolute. Trees fell cleanly, leaving little brush for Gale to throw, a quiet testament to their teamwork. Sherman worked steadily, shov-eling dirt onto the hot spots to cool them, her movements precise and urgent. Before long, the crew contained the spot and regrouped to continue cutting line, except for Rynnae, who stayed alert, patrolling for any sign of renewed fire.

As the afternoon slipped slowly into evening, the winds began to subside, and with them the fire waned, creating a lull in the storm. The coolness invigorated the crew, and they cut line more quickly, maintaining control of their surroundings with their spirits lifted. They moved up along a lonely ridge toward the head of the fire, their determination shining against the encroaching darkness. Keller and Sherman left the crew when they spotted the glow of a larger spot in the distance, its size exaggerated by the night, a glaring warning of the challenges ahead. The rest of the crew began cutting down the ridge, connecting natural barriers that served as safety zones, their movements driven by instinct and experience. The abundance of safety zones in the area made this usually unsafe practice of cutting downhill relatively safe, as the fire could not run from below. Hunt worked ahead, flagging the line, placing check lines around trouble areas, and scouting for potential problems, his vigilance shielding them from chaos.

By the time he returned to the crew, it was after midnight, and fatigue weighed heavily on their shoulders. Hunt considered two options. He could let half the crew rest while the other half continued working, then switch after a few hours to allow everyone some rest. Or he could bed the crew down for the night, a tempting thought. Although this section of the fire had no line, the cool night air would help hold it until morning, a small mercy amid the chaos. He ultimately chose to guide the crew back to the sleeping area, where they huddled around warming fires, sharing stories and laughter before drifting into deep, restorative sleep, the weariness of the day slipping away.

Morning dawned, breaking through sleepy eyes, a fresh start calling them forward. They quickly ate their MREs, exchanged jokes and smiles, grabbed water from a nearby spring, and headed back to the line they had left the day before. If they could hook the fire before the wind began to blow, they could spread out and contain the spotting, a goal that felt achievable in the early light. Keller checked the area where they had cut line and felt relief when she found no spots, a small victory that lifted spirits.

Pearson felt the warmth of the late-morning sun as he checked his Dolmar for gas and oil, a familiar ritual. He estimated he had three tanks, maybe four, left. He wondered whether it would be enough to complete the line, jump on spots, and remove hazard trees, his mind racing.

Hunt had called for the helicopter to fly in additional supplies, increasing their chances of success. LeRoy jumped in and took his turn on the saw, cutting with speed and determination, felling trees away from the fire. Pearson shouted, "How much further?" to Hunt as he returned from scouting, calm yet alert.

"Just a few hundred yards," Hunt replied, his voice steady—instilling confidence in the group, a guiding light in the uncertainty.

"Cake," Pearson responded, his confidence bubbling up, a spark of optimism igniting their collective determination. The sparse fuels in this area included only occasional patches of trees scattered between granite outcroppings—a small mercy amidst the chaos. He quickened his pace, eager to tie in with where the crew had begun cutting the line the day before, the sun beaming down like a spotlight, illuminating their path.

The crew took a group lunch—a rare moment of relaxation amid their rigorous schedule, a breath of fresh air in the whirlwind of their lives. Usually, they would eat on the run, but with no wind and the line tied together, Hunt felt a break would be beneficial—a chance to recharge. They'd only managed about four to five hours of sleep the night before, and he wanted them as fresh as possible for when the winds picked up again, a reminder of the chaos that often lay ahead.

It was a lunch without food, but the crew chatted and joked for about half an hour before heading out to mop up and patrol for spots, their spirits buoyed by camaraderie and shared purpose. Later, they began burning out unburned fuels, the breeze picking up in the canyons—a whisper of the challenges to come. The crew grabbed bladder bags someone had dropped to them the day before and dispersed, determined to cover the fire as efficiently as possible, their movements a symphony of teamwork.

Pearson lingered behind at a spring where clear water bubbled from the ground—a precious resource in the wilderness. He pondered how to fill the bladder bags from that source. After a moment, he decided to fell a small tree. He made a V-cut down the center, then jammed the tree into the spring, creating a steady flow of water for both drinking and filling the bags—a small victory in the chaos. Then, Pearson headed down to where Gale and LeRoy were busy felling trees, eager to get to work, the thrill of the task ahead igniting his spirit.

The crew had a busy afternoon cooling the line, extinguishing spot fires before they could grow large enough to pose a problem—their movements a dance of urgency. They improved the line in several areas, and as the afternoon wind picked up, the line held firm. No spots escaped as the sun faded over the Payette National Forest. They worked in unison, fueled by the spirit of a job well done and the gnawing hunger that settled in their bellies—for the helicopter served other spots and couldn't make a drop. This frustrating reality hung in the air.

Keller gazed wistfully at the sky, now darkening with night, a sense of longing stirring within him. *Mandarin,* he thought, craving something delicious—something to lift the fatigue from his bones. A simple pleasure. Just then, Hunt announced that food would arrive on mules. However, he had no idea when—a promise of relief that felt tantalizingly close yet frustratingly distant. The organization in Cascade had performed admirably in the past. But with over fifty teams now in the field, it had become a logistical nightmare weighing on everyone's minds. The crew braced for a long, hungry night, knowing the challenges ahead would demand all their strength and resilience—a test of their determination in the face of adversity. They feasted on water from the springs as they worked and waited. Keller glanced around and saw LeRoy deep in thought, craving smoked oysters.

A faint yell broke out on the fire. Keller couldn't make it out. The call repeated—closer now—and again, even closer.

"Mule train coming! Mule train coming!"

The shouting grew louder until all nine voices sang out in unison, and the whole fire echoed with "Mule train coming!"

People moved quickly toward the sleeping area as the packers began unloading supplies: C-rats, MREs, granola bars, Spam, oranges, cheese, and smoked oysters. Crackers, cheese, and smoked oysters. As Keith would say, "This was really living." Spam cooked on shovels held over the fire had never tasted so good.

"So, what happened on your area of the fire?" Hunt asked the crew.

At the location where Ray and Rynnae worked, the fire had quickly gone out. They picked up a few hot spots, but most of the fuel had already burned. Keller and LeRoy had caught one spot over the line, but it too burned out. Sherman had picked up a spot fire, and their area cooled down—they figured it would be out by the next night. Pearson and Gale had cut many of the snags and hazard trees. They planned to sweep the hotter section at the top when they returned to work.

Hunt asked how the crew was holding up. They were doing well. He decided they'd work until two or three a.m., taking advantage of the night humidity to help with mop-up. The crew agreed; it was a good idea.

The sound of saws stopped around eleven. Nightfall was dangerous, and the fellers felt they had cleared most of the hazards. They warned the crew to stay alert for anything risky, promising they'd take care of it.

The moon had not yet risen, and the stars shone as they had before cities—bright nebulas glowing white in the distance. The moon rose slowly, dimming the stars and casting an eerie light across the granite rock. The crew worked on, turning fuels over to expose them to the night humidity.

"No need to put it out yourself; let the humidity do it."

The fire now glowed faintly in isolated, burning logs.

"Chip the hot area of the log and expose it to the humidity."

Feel for hot spots with the back of your hand. No heat.

"Separate fuels."

The night's humidity cooled the crew's sweat-drenched bodies, leaving them feeling chilled. They chipped at a few hot logs as sparks rained into the darkness, then twinkled out.

"Better than the Fourth of July," Keller thought.

The clock's hands moved slowly, but unlike the boredom that usually came with such conditions, the crew felt calm. Two o'clock came, lingered, then passed; still, they worked, waiting for a call to pierce the night. In the void, even reading the time became difficult. A headlamp had burnt out. If you held the watch just right in the moonlight, you could make out that it was nearly three o'clock.

The call came. The crew walked back to the sleeping area and climbed into their bags.

Morning came. LeRoy needed a nudge.

"What are you doing? Listening for smokes?" Hunt asked as LeRoy slowly emerged from his sleeping bag.

Spam cooked on spring-cleaned shovels. The crew set out, bladder bags full, savoring what would be their last day on the fire. All good dreams must come to an end.

Back on the Silver Fire at Helispot Forty-One, the crew awoke from their dreams. They pulled themselves from their bags and headed to the eating area, where Hephaestus paced. He glared at them.

The crew was bothering him.

Gale was now the talk of the camp. While everyone else had avoided the deadly Illinois River by using rafts, Gale had simply run across it—chainsaw in hand—barely getting wet. It looked bad. It was unsafe. Running across a river like that was how a person met their maker.

Still, they admired Gale's ability as a sawyer: his precise cuts, his perfect placement of each tree.

"Gale is a sawyer. Where was Gale when he cut line on the spot fire? Sleeping. If the others on the crew hadn't been sleeping, too, they might've noticed Gale was asleep."

Then there was Grimaldi, along with Ford, their shirts untucked.

"Where is Hepatitus?" Ford asked, consciously changing the name.

But the question came from Krutilla's squad—and Krutilla was the worst supervisor Hephaestus had ever seen.

"Where is Hepatitus?" Ford asked again.

Hephaestus glared at Krutilla.

"Who is Hepatitus?" the superintendent asked.

"I thought you were a friend," Krutilla replied.

Hephaestus paused, trying to remember if he had ever had a friend named Hepatitus.

CHAPTER 21

THE CHECKO

The plan for the day had stayed straightforward: the crew would continue cutting the line down to the Checko River, which wound its way through the rugged wilderness like a silver thread glistening under the sun—a shimmering ribbon of life amidst the wild chaos of nature. The Checko River, a hidden gem nestled deep within the vast expanse of the Kalmiopsis Wilderness, sprang forth from the mountains, its waters originating in the misty heights—a place that had seemed almost sacred.

This 56-mile stream in southwestern Oregon drained 352 square miles of Curry County. It descended from 3,200 feet to the Pacific Ocean, flowing generally north, west, and southwest before emptying near Brookings. Founded in the early 20th century, Brookings had grown to support around 14,000 residents who relied on the Chetco River for drinking water.

The river expanded where Carter Creek flowed into it. Bailey Mountain provided a formidable four-thousand-foot backdrop, its rocky crags and green slopes standing as a testament to nature's raw beauty and power. The river coursed swiftly, slicing through the rough and untamed terrain—a relentless force of nature carving its path between steep cliffs and rocky outcrops. Brush and grass clung desperately to the precipices, defying the persistent rainwater that threatened to erode their fragile grip, as if nature itself engaged in a constant battle for survival.

As the river cascaded down past Granite Peak, it shifted character, with the towering Granite Peak taking the place of Bailey Mountain as the new sentinel over the land. The current slowed as it meandered through Taggart Bar, pausing momentarily in its frantic journey before surging forward once more. The landscape evolved into a vision of the past as Tin Cup Ridge faded into memory while the imposing Big Craggies loomed. The river flattened again in the stretch between Lately Prairie and Traimer's Ranch, where the Big Craggies began to dissolve into mere memories. The water flowed out of Kalmiopsis, gradually making its way through Brookings and eventually into the vastness of the sea.

For the next two days, the crew worked tirelessly, cutting line and throwing brush as they forged ahead with their mission. The Checko River drew closer, its size becoming more pronounced below them—a looming presence. The saws felt lighter in their hands now, infused with new energy, and the brush seemed to yield more willingly under their efforts. The line to mineral soil required little work, and the cut through rockslides proved to be a mere formality—a minor obstacle in their relentless pursuit of progress. Yet, lurking in the underbrush lay their old adversary: poison oak, sneaking its way into the space between the manzanita and chinquapin, persistently reminding them that nature often fights back against their intrusion—highlighting that they were not the only players in this rugged wilderness.

By the end of the first grueling day, as the sun began to dip below the horizon—casting long shadows that danced among the trees—the crew welcomed a new and former face into their midst: Rynnae. She arrived as a replacement, stepping into the gaps left by those who had gone in this relentless battle. Her presence brought a renewed sense of camaraderie and hope to the group, infusing them with shared energy. Now working as a permanent member of the agency, she enjoyed health benefits and retirement. The experienced individuals on the crew felt genuinely happy for her, especially since one seasoned employee had already flown over the cuckoo's nest.

Back in 1986, the agency had lifted the freeze on hiring permanent employees. Yet, a bottleneck of qualified men created a barrier that kept many from securing positions within the Forest Service. Rynnae, however, navigated that treacherous landscape with her experience and qualifications, proving herself invaluable. The existing men's jobs as permanents were temporarily eliminated as the agency drove them out to meet their "hard target"—another name for an illegal quota.

Her background was impressive; Rynnae forged an excellent career spanning many years as an engine foreman in the rugged terrain of Bull Run, where she learned the intricacies of firefighting. Alongside her engine work, she gained hotshot experience, honing her skills and preparing herself for the rigors of this challenging environment. Having been on the crew the previous year, she quickly demonstrated her adeptness with a chainsaw, cutting through stubborn timber with precision and ease. Her knowledge of water use, sharpened by her time as an engine foreman, added another layer of expertise to the team, making her a formidable ally in their mission to hold back the flames.

As they pressed on, the line transformed from a dirt road into a full-fledged highway; the ridge no longer served as an ally in their fight to hold the fire at bay. Here, the line endured the full brunt of the fire's fury. The views, once breathtaking, grew less inviting. The terrain felt sticky and treacherous, littered with obstacles. The brush line expanded to thirty feet wide, while the line to mineral soil shrank to just two feet.

"Throw that brush! Throw it as far as you can!" I shouted, my voice echoing through the trees—a rallying cry that cut through the sounds of the wilderness. "If the fire spots, we don't want it falling into a brush pile six feet high. By three o'clock, we'll tie in; we've got a few hours left. The Checko River looms nearer," I added, urgency tightening in my throat.

As the sun dipped lower in the sky, shadows stretched across the landscape, casting an eerie glow over everything. The line finally tied into the Checko, and I realized that no helicopter ride awaited us that night—a realization that weighed heavily as the cold settled in and many of us remained drenched in sweat. I made my way down an old mining road, the rocky, sandy terrain crunching beneath my boots, to where Uphoff's crew was finishing the helispot near the river. We waited for word of the helicopter's arrival. But with each passing moment, doubt crept into my mind like an unwelcome visitor. The chill of the Checko River would soon set in, and warming fires would become essential. The temperature had already dropped into the low forties—a stark reminder of the harsh elements we faced in this unforgiving landscape.

With a determined grip, I grabbed a saw and rallied the group gathered at Taggart's Bar. Forty people stood present, including the contract fellers, and we needed a lot of wood for warming fires to stave off the cold that threatened to envelop us. The coolness of the river only made it worse. The chill spurred us on, driving us forward. I felt the comforting weight of the saw in my hand; I had waited far too long to wield it with purpose.

"Cut up the dead wood to get a fire started, then tackle the fallen trees for the helispot. They might be green, but there are plenty of them. We need to get hot fires going from the dry to ignite the green!" I shouted to the other sawyers, determination etched on my face, my eyes glinting with purpose.

"Hey, what the hell are you doing?" Volcano Mike bellowed over the roar of the saws, his voice booming like thunder amid the chaos. "It takes a real hot fire to get the green stuff going!"

"Well, that's just what I plan on doing," I retorted, my voice steady, unwavering in the face of Mike's challenge. "We've got forty people to keep warm here tonight."

With that, I dug my saw into a dead Ponderosa pine log, carving out a chunk about four feet long to serve as a hot fire starter for the green wood.

Meanwhile, Keller ventured deeper into the darkened woods, the thick canopy casting long shadows as he searched for the perfect place to start his own fire for the night. He sought solace in the glow of flames that would soon dance before him in the encroaching darkness. As I drifted off to sleep, the sounds of Volcano Mike and the other contract fellers laughing echoed through the chilly air, intertwining with the steady murmur of the Checko River. Those familiar sounds wrapped around me like a warm blanket, weaving into my dreams and creating a sense of warmth and camaraderie that briefly shielded me from the harsher realities of our situation. It was good to see that the contract fellers, who usually disliked agency people, had bonded with this crew.

Hephaestus endured a different kind of night, one filled with turmoil and shadows. He drifted in and out of shallow sleep, plagued by visions that had become rare since he had given up real rest for the relentless demands of the work. In his mind, he crawled through flames, the air thick with the acrid scent of burning fuel. He felt the gas can containing Dolmar—the vital gas-and-oil mix for the saws—clenched in his mouth, its weight both a burden and a means of survival. Fiery tongues licked at him, relentless, while the anguished screams of his crew formed a haunting chorus behind him.

Amid the chaos, a woman's voice cut through the haze—his girlfriend's—urging him forward with urgency. "Hephaestus, keep moving. Think of yourself. Think of the glory that awaits." Her words, filled with unwavering belief, drove him on toward a place of safety that awaited him, a refuge from the flames surrounding him. With renewed determination, he crawled through the heat and emerged into a vibrant green meadow—an oasis that felt unreal after the chaos that had consumed him. There, bureaucrats dressed in forest green applauded, their clapping a surreal celebration of his survival and a stark contrast to the terror he had escaped.

When he awoke with a shiver, the remnants of the dream clung to him like fog. Reality returned with a jolt. He blinked in the dim light, taking in the crew around him—their faces drawn with fatigue and resolve, each person carrying the aftershocks of their own fears. The fire crackled nearby, and then he heard it: a whispering voice.

"Shhh... please, just be quiet for a moment. Stop talking, can you? I know they're watching us right now, and you have to be very careful. You hear that? It's like they're right there, just waiting for a slip-up. I can't explain it, but there's a plan in motion—a web they've woven around all of us. Look. They're looking directly at you, scrutinizing every move you make. You can't do this without my guidance. Please, just listen to me.

"All these people; they're staring at you. Every single one of them. I should never have come to this place today. Maybe it would be better if I just left. The thought crosses my mind—I could simply walk out right now, couldn't I? Yes, I could just leave. Maybe I shouldn't even be here at all. Run. You need to get out of here.

"No, wait. Don't act rashly. Just stay put for a second. They're watching you. They know everything you're doing. They're reading your mind right now. Stop thinking. You have to stop thinking this instant. Don't let them glimpse your thoughts. If they do, they could hurt you. I know they're watching. Do you hear that? It's all part of their game. I don't know what they want, but I can sense it."

The superintendent stared into the fire.

CHAPTER 22

THE BURNOUT

The following morning, my squad and I trekked back to Helispot 41, arriving around noon, weary. We found the helispot shrouded in dense smoke—a thick haze that obscured our view and stifled our senses. We hadn't seen food since the previous day, and the anticipation of the burnout loomed as we prepared to hike to where we would begin from the line that had moved away from the fire at Helispot 37. From there, the line would run through Helispots 38, 39, 40, and 41, across relatively flat ridgetop terrain that belied the challenges ahead. Beyond Helispot 42, however, the flatness would end abruptly, giving way to a steeply descending line that would eventually drop toward the Checko River, offering challenges and opportunities in equal measure. The burnout was scheduled to begin that evening.

From my vantage point on the east face of the ridge, where I had packed my web gear, I gazed out into the wilderness stretching before me. This ridge stood as the last stronghold capable of containing the fire for miles. To the east, craggy rockslides, sheer cliffs, and deep draws choked with brush formed a daunting landscape. I knew the fire might have already burned another thirty miles to the east, threatening little more than a logging road.

Despite our anticipation and hope, food still hadn't arrived, leaving a gnawing hunger in my stomach. Word came back that the helicopter couldn't land because of the heavy smoke—a grim piece of news.

As the afternoon wore on, we managed to steal some much-needed sleep, exhaustion catching up with us like a relentless tide. We woke around five o'clock to prepare for the burnout, the weight of the task ahead settling on our shoulders like an oppressive shroud. Rynnae spoke animatedly about rejoining the crew, her enthusiasm infectious despite the fatigue clinging to us all. Hephaestus paced restlessly, muttering under his breath as we waited for our long-overdue meal, his agitation rising as the hours dragged on, each minute stretching into an eternity. At six o'clock, we prepared for the burnout—food still nowhere in sight.

As we prepared to march out to Helispot 37 to start the burnout, I instructed my squad to fuzee up, stuffing about thirty fuzees into our web gear. Hephaestus urged us to hurry to gear up as we prepared for the impending mission.

"They're flying torches into Helispot 37!" Hephaestus shouted, his frustration boiling over as he called someone a "dumbfuck" for suggesting otherwise, the tension in the air thickening like the smoke that surrounded us. "There's no reason to fuzee up; you only need four!"

I couldn't shake the nagging thought: if we couldn't fly food to Helispot 41, how could we possibly deliver torches to Helispot 37? The fuzees might be our only way to burn out the fuels. At six-thirty, the helicopter finally landed, and we rushed to finish our meal before taking off for Helispot 37, adrenaline coursing through our veins as we moved with purpose.

My squad lagged behind the rest of the crew, each member burdened with twenty pounds of fuzees. Glenn fell back with me, and our pace slowed as darkness descended upon the landscape, enveloping us in shadows that seemed to stretch endlessly. Night blindness challenged Glenn, so we talked about fire, reminiscing about years when sanity reigned on the crew—a time when the world felt more predictable and less chaotic. Glenn's ten years with the Prineville and Deschutes crews had given him a wealth of perspective.

"I don't know about Hephaestus," Glenn mused, his voice low and thoughtful, as if pondering the weight of the world. "It's like he's playing hotshot." I nodded in agreement, our shared understanding of our trials evident; the bond forged in the fires of adversity we had faced together.

Our discussion was abruptly interrupted when Hunt and Grimaldi approached, having ventured out earlier in search of the elusive torches at Helispot 37. As they neared, grim expressions framed their faces, shadows of disappointment etched across their features. To our dismay, they reported that no torches had been located.

Keller, unable to shake the feeling of urgency, broke away from the group to check for the missing torches at Helispot 38. Moments later, he returned, his face a mask of frustration. The disheartening news he brought only deepened the despair that clung to us like a heavy shroud. Glenn and I caught up with the crew at Helispot 37, where tension thickened in the air, and unease settled over us like an ominous storm cloud poised to unleash its fury upon the unprepared landscape.

Without a burnout, we could lose the entire line. The dilemma before us loomed—glaringly evident and unavoidable: we would gain little to no benefit from moving forward with the highly anticipated burnout operation unless we could effectively utilize the fuzees my squad controlled. But doing so might tarnish Hephaestus's image. He faced a dilemma.

My squad accounted for two hundred of the total two hundred forty fuzees available—a substantial portion that could very well determine the success or failure of our collective efforts. Hephaestus recognized the critical nature of the situation. Pooling our resources wasn't just a good idea—it was essential. In his mind, he imagined a scenario in which combining our fuzees would leave the crew in awe of his strategic brilliance, glossing over the fact that he had completely mismanaged our earlier preparations.

A flicker of hope sparked in Hephaestus at the thought that perhaps this move could salvage his reputation in the eyes of a crew already grappling with swirling uncertainty. As he glanced around at the weary faces of his fellow firefighters, he sensed their apprehension mixed with a hint of anticipation. Could this be the turning point they desperately needed? With the stakes so high, Hephaestus knew he had to act decisively—despite the gnawing doubt lingering in the back of his mind.

"Okay, let's put all our fuzees together," he proposed.

"Well, it looks like Uphoff's squad will take charge of the burnout, so I need that squad to fuzee up," he declared.

A dark cloud seemed to loom over them. Uphoff's squad had already initiated the burnout, moving swiftly and purposefully—but Hephaestus seethed at the thought that Krutilla might still undermine him, sabotaging his authority at this critical moment.

In his mind, he envisioned the worst-case scenario: with limited fuzees, the critical burnout would fizzle once their supply ran out—an outcome they could not afford to face. The stakes loomed too high, and the thought of failure gnawed at him relentlessly.

The crew rapidly approached a breaking point. They were running low on fuzees, and as they finally reached Helispot 38, the burnout that had once roared with life began to wane, retreating from the flames that had once promised to consume the night.

With urgency, I directed my squad to scour the nearby bush line for dry Tan Oak—the kind that had endured over a week of unrelenting dry weather, now perfectly primed for ignition. They tossed the gathered Tan Oak into the embers, and their makeshift torches erupted into vibrant flames, casting flickering shadows that danced wildly across the dark canvas of the night.

Silently and with relentless focus, we continued the burnout, our movements synchronized in a well-practiced rhythm, tan oak torches flaring in our hands. Uphoff watched from a distance, his own squad poised to follow. Soon, the pace of the burnout doubled—seventeen individuals igniting the line with fervor and determination. Fuels between the line and the main fire were steadily consumed.

As the burnout stretched into the early morning hours, the sky began to lighten—darkness giving way to the soft glow of dawn. The first hints of light broke over the horizon like a promise of hope, painting the sky in soft pinks and oranges. Anticipation thickened the air. However, the humidity began to rise, enveloping us like a damp blanket, making the fuels less receptive to clean burning.

Moisture crept in, sneaking under logs and saturating the fine fuels beneath the brush. The fire began to wane. Fine fuels—small, light, and easily ignitable—typically burn rapidly and help spread fire. Their high surface-area-to-volume ratio allows them to dry out and ignite quickly, acting like kindling. But now, they struggled to catch.

Realizing the futility of our efforts, we pulled off the line and watched the flames die as the morning light seeped into the world. We knew the day shift would arrive soon to hold the line and continue the burnout. We placed our hope in those who would come after us. In the distance, the faint hum of a helicopter grew louder, the sound intensifying as it descended—depositing a fresh crew before lifting off again. This was good news: drip torches had been flown in.

Exhausted, we fell asleep, our bodies worn from the relentless night shift, hoping a deep rest would rejuvenate us for the challenges ahead.

When we finally stirred from sleep, a brisk wind swept through the area, brushing our faces with an unsettling chill. It carried the promise of smoke and the lurking threat of spot fires—warning us of the backing fire we were about to ignite in our ongoing battle.

As night approached, Uphoff's squad sprang into action, initiating the burnout with renewed purpose, while my squad took our positions to hold the line. As the first torch ignited, smoke swirled around us like a living entity rising into the still air. The lodgepole pines caught quickly.

The flames roared to life, crackling as a cascade of bright sparks soared into the night sky. The squad moved with urgency, eyes sharp and vigilant as they maneuvered through the haze. Their movements were fluid and practiced, working in perfect synchrony.

As we approached 2200—10 o'clock—the winds picked up, rustling through the trees and sending an involuntary shiver down my spine. This sudden shift demanded complete focus from the crew—our resolve was about to face another test. We halted the burnout and readied ourselves to look for spot fires. The fire behavior officer anticipated a significant wind shift around midnight. My heart raced with anxiety and eagerness as we waited for the burnout to resume. Each second felt infinite, thick with anticipation.

When midnight arrived and the winds shifted, determination surged through us, lifting our spirits as we redirected the burnout toward the Checko River.

"Burn out at this pace!" Hephaestus barked, his voice cutting through the night with authority as he set off at a moderate yet purposeful pace. He strategically increased the number of burners, assigning five individuals to carry thirty gallons of fuel mixture and distributing eight additional drip torches.

I moved urgently alongside Ray and Ford, refilling drip torches with unwavering commitment. At the same time, Hunt and Thomas worked to contain the encroaching flames.

"Fuck!" Ford shouted, frustration boiling over as he fumbled with a broken drip torch meant for Grimaldi. I watched him scramble to fix it in the dim light, Hephaestus's glare searing into him—irritation simmering just beneath the surface.

Tension thickened when my squad came under fire for malingering.

"Who's in charge of filling the drip torches?" Hephaestus bellowed, his voice sharp and echoing ominously through the trees.

Ford finally caught a break when Hephaestus turned his focus toward Rynnae. His eyes, sharp and discerning, locked onto her as he noticed she hadn't ignited the line in the way he deemed proper.

"That's not how you burn out the damn line!" he snapped, stepping into the fray. His tone was harsh, his frustration plain as he demonstrated the technique with every exaggerated flick of his wrist.

The air crackled with tension.

Rynnae stammered, her voice barely rising above the embers and the distant roar of flames. "But the division boss..." Her protest was thin, driven by orders she'd received earlier, and indignation rose in her at being dismissed so quickly.

Before she could finish, Hephaestus snatched the torch from her hand in one swift, decisive motion and began burning the line himself—confident, dramatic, deliberate. In his mind, he imagined a statue of himself lighting out the line, standing right next to the Iwo Jima Memorial.

As Hephaestus strutted away, confidence oozing from him like sweat on a summer day, Rynnae stood frozen—frustration etched across her face.

The burn steadily advanced beyond Helispot 41, crossing into Helispot 42, where the air thickened with the smell of smoke and the crackle of flames. Hephaestus, his voice booming like thunder across the rugged landscape, called out, "To the Checko, to the Checko!" His words echoed through the hills, stirring the day shift from their slumber—rousing them from momentary stupor to witness what he had convinced himself was a display of unparalleled brilliance. His audacity radiated through his confidence; after all, who needed the iconic General Patton pose when Hephaestus believed he could put Patton to shame with his own flamboyant flair.

The Prineville crew joined forces here. Their arrival bolstered the numbers, forming a united front against the encroaching flames. Together, they moved fuel efficiently and maintained the line with practiced precision. They had flown out that day, fully aware they were in the thick of it—battling both nature and their own limitations. Each moment stood as a testament to their resilience in the face of adversity they knew all too well.

Grimaldi hurled fuzees over the edges of steep cliffs, fiery streaks illuminating the surrounding terrain as they ignited deeper heat within the fire. Lira and Keller worked beside him, tireless and focused, dancing with urgency.

Finally, the Checko River loomed before them—its shimmering surface reflecting the late afternoon sun. The sound of water rushing over smooth stones filled the air, creating a soothing melody that stood in stark contrast to the grueling labor they had just endured. As they approached the river's edge, the fresh, cool air enveloped them like a gentle embrace, invigorating their tired bodies and lifting their spirits.

They trudged back toward camp, keeping an eye out for slopovers and spots. The night humidity had drifted in, but they found none.

CHAPTER 23

LEAVING THE FIRE

The crew finally found out it was their time to leave the fire. They flew out to base camp, where they transformed paper sleeping bags into supplies, packed the vans, and took off—heading home to their loved ones for a long-awaited reunion.

They drove down the Rogue River, a Wild and Scenic River. The road wound from a single lane with turnouts to two lanes until they reached Highway 101. The highway climbed through fields of grass, weaving between towering pines and jagged rocks that overlooked the ocean. Waves broke against the cliffs with illuminating sprays, sending mist into the air like a blessing from nature.

They were heading back; their time on the fire was over.

The caravan sped along, twisting around curves that gradually straightened as they passed through lush green pastures dotted with grazing sheep and cows—a tranquil scene that felt worlds away from the chaos they had just endured.

The radio played softly in the background, familiar voices providing a comforting soundtrack to their journey home. Crew members yawned. Some slept. Others thought, while a few simply stared out the windows at a collage of weathered houses, leaning fences, gnarled trees, and ocean rocks stretching endlessly before them.

They passed Rhinehart Creek, its moss-filled banks a reminder of the life that thrived in the wilderness. Then came Bush Creek, where the ocean faded into the distance, the once-exploding surf retreating into white, sparkling foam—disappearing back to where it came.

The trees grew straighter here, tucked into peaceful coves, their canopies flattened under the relentless wind that whispered through the branches, carrying the quiet stories of the forest.

The road twisted along a creek, winding around a mountain—a mountain of rock and moss. Vibrant green moss blanketed the ground, sparkling in the sun, a lush contrast to the dull, ash-laden needles they had lived among for days.

The road emerged once more beside the ocean. Again, the trees appeared gnarled, their crowns flattened, while shark-finned rocks pushed toward the shore as the caravan rushed on. Hubbard Creek was long behind them—a memory fading in the rearview mirror.

Port Orford, the westernmost town in the contiguous United States, finally came into view, prompting the caravan to slow down, the hum of the engine softening as they navigated through the charming town. Quaint cafés lined the streets, inviting passersby to linger over steaming cups of coffee while the sweet aroma of freshly baked pastries wafted through the air. Antique shops filled with relics from times long past boasted intriguing wares that caught the eye, each with stories waiting to be discovered. Real estate offices drew the attention of those looking to settle in this picturesque coastal community, while roadside attractions displayed signs proudly offering Myrtlewood—a prized local treasure—for sale.

As they continued down the road, the serene Elk River came into view, flowing gracefully alongside the Sixes River. The landscape transformed into flattened valleys stretching out like a quilt, dotted with sheep grazing peacefully on the lush green grass, their gentle bleats punctuating the tranquil atmosphere. Towering above, the hard gray stumps of ancient clearcuts stood sentinel-like—remnants of a time when the forest had thinned—silently watching over a landscape that had since begun to heal.

Weathered homes, each with its own character, proudly stood on the market, their faded paint and unique architecture narrating tales of years gone by. Nearby, RV parks beckoned travelers with signs proclaiming, "Art, rocks, gifts for sale," inviting them to pause and explore local artistry and treasures crafted from nature itself.

Denmark appeared on the horizon, only to vanish a scant 200 feet later as the caravan rolled through its brief existence, the name lingering in the air like a whisper. Langlois came next, offering a fleeting glimpse of the small town as they passed, with Coos Bay creeping closer.

Beyond Coos Bay, the caravan traveled past the sand dunes, where beauty abounded in a magnificent mix of sand, surf, and lush foliage that framed the stunning coastline—an awe-inspiring tapestry of nature. The air filled with a salty tang, refreshing and invigorating, as the sound of crashing waves harmonized with the gentle rustle of leaves. The beach came alive with the hustle and bustle of sand surfers carving their paths, the roar of ATVs zipping along the shore, and pedestrians strolling—some lost in conversation, others gazing out at the horizon.

Just a short distance away, Thor's Well captivated the imagination and evoked a sense of wonder—a natural sinkhole on the Oregon coast. Nestled near the dramatic cliffs of Cape Perpetua, this geological marvel appeared to drain the ocean itself, creating a spectacle as mesmerizing as it was dangerous. Formed from the collapse of an ancient sea cave, the well proved especially striking when waves surged into it, swirling and crashing with an intensity that thrilled and terrified—particularly around high tide or during the tumultuous storms that occasionally swept through the area. Visitors gathered at a safe distance, their eyes wide with awe as they witnessed nature's raw power, the churning water frothing and foaming in a beautiful yet perilous dance.

They turned east somewhere near Florence. Florence, a charming small city nestled at the mouth of the winding Siuslaw River, graced the picturesque Oregon coast—a place where the rugged beauty of nature met the quaint allure of community life. Near Florence, the vast Sea Lion Caves served as a sanctuary for the majestic Steller sea lions. These playful creatures basked on rocky outcroppings, their barks echoing through the air, adding a lively soundtrack to the coastal scene.

Just a short distance away, trails wound around the restored 19th-century Heceta Head Lighthouse, offering breathtaking views of the surrounding landscape. From that vantage point, they saw seabirds soaring gracefully above the crashing waves and, during certain times of the year, the majestic sight of migrating whales breaching in the distance—their massive forms cutting through the ocean's surface.

The city's Historic Old Town district burst with quaint shops and vibrant galleries, each space brimming with local artistry and craftsmanship. Inviting storefronts lined the streets, where the scent of freshly brewed coffee mingled with the salty sea air, drawing in both locals and tourists alike.

As the sun climbed higher into the vast expanse of blue sky, its warm rays cast a golden glow over the entire landscape. The light danced across the surface of the water, illuminating terrain that shifted from rugged coastal hills to a more expansive flat vista, where the beauty of nature unfolded in all directions.

Within just a few hours, the crew would return to their home base—a majestic and towering mountain that rose dramatically against the skyline, its snow-capped peaks glistening in the sunlight. From its steep slopes, crystal-clear rivers cascaded down, their waters teeming with life—most notably the crawfish thriving in those rich ecosystems, feasting on the remnants of dead salmon that came there to spawn each year.

Surrounding the mountain's base, towering Douglas fir and cedar trees dominated the forests, some reaching hundreds of feet into the air; their stately forms stood as a testament to nature's resilience. The air carried the earthy scent of pine, and the rustle of leaves whispered tales of the wilderness.

Interspersed among these giants, vibrant rhododendrons burst forth in a splendid array of colors. Their blossoms, often shaped like delicate bells or elegant funnels, appeared in hues of pristine white, soft pink, fiery red, regal purple, bright orange, and sunny yellow.

My thoughts drifted back to a distant memory—one particularly grueling stretch in the summer of 1984 that pushed my endurance to its limits. The crew and I had spent an exhausting twenty days straight away from home, fighting relentless fires that consumed everything in their path. When we finally pulled into a quaint little village, just about fifteen miles from our home base, a wave of relief washed over me, mingling with the fatigue clinging to my bones. It was a Friday afternoon, the clock reading 4:30. The local bank closed for the weekend at 5 and wouldn't reopen until Monday, leaving many of us without any cash on hand. With the possibility of being dispatched as early as Sunday morning, the tension became palpable—a race against time and circumstance.

As we rushed toward the bank in a frenzy, our minds filled with thoughts of cold drinks and much-deserved food, an unexpected voice cut through the air. An elderly woman stood on the sidewalk—her face a tapestry of deep lines and age, marked clearly by years of too much drinking and smoking. Her voice rang out, loud and defiant: "Fucking government workers, doing crap on government time!" The words dripped with bitter resentment, echoing her own struggles. Dinardo, always quick with a retort and fiercely protective of our crew, couldn't let it slide. With a grin that suggested he found some humor in the confrontation, he yelled back, "That's right, lady!"

Amid all this, Dinardo sat at the helm of the crew bus—the vehicle that had become our second home over the past weeks. The agency imposed strict rules against picking up hitchhikers, a policy that often felt unnecessarily rigid in moments like these. Whenever he passed someone in need along our route, he leaned out the window and shouted, "We work for the government—we can't help you!" His tone was both apologetic and firm, reflecting the paradox of our existence as firefighters: dedicated to serving the public, yet bound by the constraints of bureaucracy.

That day, as the sun dipped below the horizon and painted the sky in hues of orange and purple, we stood at a crossroads of frustration. The old lady's words hung in the air like a challenge to our purpose. It was moments like these that shaped our experience—where the mundane collided with the extraordinary, leaving lasting impressions on our hearts and minds.

Thoughts returned to the fire—that intense inferno we battled as a united front. Each crew member had contributed their strength and resolve, pushing back against the roaring flames. A sense of accomplishment hung in the air. But it was a complex emotion, ebbing and flowing like the relentless waves crashing against the shore. Did we truly feel elated at a job well done? That feeling remained elusive, flickering in and out of our minds, lingering like a distant echo.

A gnawing doubt began to take root deep within me—an unsettling sensation whispering questions I couldn't quite grasp. What caused this strange discontent? Why did I feel different this time compared to the return trips from fires I'd fought in years past? The uncertainty loomed over me, each thought weaving through our collective consciousness like threads in a tapestry, binding us together in a shared experience marked by both triumph and lingering ambiguity.

"They were showing porno movies in fire camp," Hepatitis had told the Ranger—a lie about me. I only found out 35 years later. That lie ended my career as a Hotshot firefighter.

EPILOGUE

In the year 2000—a time of change and uncertainty—I sat at my modest desk, surrounded by a collection of documents and legal briefs. The morning sun filtered through the grimy window, casting a warm, golden light that struggled to penetrate the layers of dust that had accumulated over the years. As I furiously typed the final touches on a brief concerning a case I felt confident I would win in the Montana Supreme Court, my mind began to wander, drifting away from legal jargon and into the realm of more pressing concerns.

I had just heard the unsettling news that the Bitterroot National Forest—a vast stretch of land known for its breathtaking beauty and rich biodiversity—would not hire firefighters for initial attack until mid-August. The decision hit me like a punch to the gut, sending a wave of anxiety coursing through me as I grappled with the implications of such a delay. "Shit," I thought, the gravity of the situation settling heavily on my shoulders like an oppressive weight. By the time mid-August rolled around, all the skilled firefighters—the ones with the experience, the training, and the knowledge to tackle a wildfire head-on—would likely be deployed elsewhere, scattered across the region like leaves caught in a gust of wind. The Bitterroot, with its expansive stretches of timber and diverse wildlife, stood poised on the brink of devastation. I realized, with a sinking feeling, that it would burn down this year.

Determined to make my voice heard and take action in the face of impending disaster, I began to write a letter to my senator. I articulated my grave concerns about the looming threat to the Bitterroot National Forest, emphasizing the urgency of the situation. I knew that Los Alamos also faced a threat from flames at that very moment, and I figured this could be a politically strategic time to approach the senator. The last congressional investigation I initiated took hiring authority out of the Agency's hands for two long years—a move that temporarily helped the firefighting community—and I hoped to leverage that knowledge once again.

A few weeks later, as the summer heated up and tensions rose, the Bitterroot National Forest confronted a fire season of historic proportions. Wildfires ravaged an astonishing 307,000 acres of forestland—a staggering figure that sent shivers down my spine as I imagined the once-thriving ecosystem reduced to ashes. Additionally, relentless flames consumed 49,000 acres on private and State lands in Ravalli County, leaving a trail of destruction in their wake. The devastation astonished me: 70 homes burned to ashes, along with two commercial properties and 167 outbuildings—families and businesses shattered, struggling to pick up the pieces in the aftermath of the inferno.

As I wrote my letter to the senator, pouring out my concerns and frustrations onto the page, I reflected deeply on the qualifications of those who must fight fires. I did not care if the individual hired to combat the flames was Black, White, Green, or any color; I was indifferent to whether they were female, male, or transgender. I couldn't be bothered by their religious beliefs, sexual orientation, or background—none of that mattered in the face of such a dire situation. What was paramount, I believed, was that they be the most competent individuals for the job—capable of making split-second decisions in life-or-death scenarios.

This revolutionary idea for the Federal Government—hiring based on merit rather than genetic make-up—filled me with hope. I wished fervently that they would begin to adopt this ethos moving forward. Yet I also recognized, with a heavy heart, that it might already be too late for the Bitterroot. The hiring policies that had dominated the last two decades had decimated the organization's ability to fight fires effectively, leaving it vulnerable in the face of nature's fury. At least there had been a record number of people with "atta boys."

Years later, during a conversation with the prosecutor in Sanders County, the topic of the agency's inadequacies resurfaced. She recounted the agency's failure to respond adequately to the fires, her voice tinged with palpable frustration. They had been able to do very little to assist people trying to save their homes because, as she explained with a furrowed brow, they simply did not know how to operate chainsaws.

The agency engine rumbled to a halt at the scene, where a group of private individuals were laboriously cutting down ladder fuels—those dangerous limbs that acted as conduits, carrying flames high into the treetops. The sun hung low in the sky, casting an orange hue that mingled unsettlingly with the smoke curling and twisting in the air. By slicing through those ladder fuels, they hoped to prevent the fire from escalating into a ferocious crown fire—one that could unleash chaos upon the forest and everything within its reach.

As the engine foreman stepped out, he surveyed the frantic activity around him, noting the sweat-drenched brows and the determined expressions of the landowner and his family. With a voice that carried authority yet brimmed with genuine concern, he asked, "Is there anything we can do to help?"

The landowner, a rugged man with dirt-streaked skin and calloused hands, turned toward him, eyes sharp with urgency. "Yes," he replied decisively. "Pick up the chainsaw and help us cut these ladder fuels."

The foreman hesitated for a moment, then asked, "Is there anyone here who knows how to run a chainsaw?"

The question hung in the air, met only by an uncomfortable silence—a collective pause that spoke volumes about the lack of expertise present in that moment.

I jolted from the present, my mind racing back to the year 1984—a time forever etched in my memory. I recalled the towering tree before me, its base a daunting eight feet in diameter, a giant sentinel of the forest. High above, flames danced along its limbs, and from a rotting section near its dead top, sparks flared across the line, igniting spot fires that threatened to spread into a wildfire. I gripped my chainsaw tightly—a Husqvarna 2100 equipped with a three-foot bar—its roar a familiar sound.

I faced a dilemma: if I cut the tree in the traditional manner, a substantial portion in the middle would remain intact, effectively holding the tree up and creating a precarious situation. But with my years of experience, I knew better. I meticulously made the face cut, then bored through the back of the cut, methodically knocking out the wood until I was ready for the back cut. I back cut, sliding safety wedges into the kerf. As I executed the maneuver, the tree fell precisely as I had planned.

Later, I would hear whispers from an engineer—someone with a degree and a mind for numbers—claiming it was impossible to cut through such a massive tree with a mere three-foot bar on a chainsaw.

Now, standing amidst the chaos of the present calamity, the weight of the agency's degradation pressed heavily upon me, haunting me with the critical need for qualified personnel who could handle such emergencies. The consequences of bureaucratic inertia—of failing to act decisively and swiftly in times of urgency—loomed large in my thoughts, an ever-present specter as nature unleashed its fury upon the land.

What struck me most was the lack of goodwill and integrity coming from this federal bureaucracy and a whole dynamic based on fallacies:

- **Straw Man Fallacy:** misrepresents his opponents' arguments to make them easier to attack, often presenting the opposing side in its most extreme or easily refutable form, as implied by sources noting his structure, which "amplifies binaries," and his tendency to **oversimplify complex issues**.

- **Ad Hominem (Personal Attacks):** His debate style is described by some as shifting toward **personal attacks** or talking down to opponents, especially college students, rather than engaging with their actual points. His reported remark about prominent Black women lacking "brain processing power" is an example of a statement focusing on the person, not the argument.

- **Appeal to Emotion/Rage Baiting:** This tactic aims to provoke strong emotional reactions and dominate the conversation, often at the expense of meaningful discussion. Known as *rage-baiting*, it replaces substance with outrage to manipulate the audience.

- **Misinformation and Distorted Facts:** Some claims were **misleading or factually inaccurate**, which forms the basis for critics who accuse him of deliberately distorting facts to fit his political agenda. One reported example involved promoting a racist hoax about Haitian immigrants.

- **Begging the Question/Circular Reasoning (Implicit):** opinions being **correct by default**, which can set up a debate where the burden of proof is unequally placed, implicitly assuming the truth of his premise.

- **False Dichotomy (Black-and-White Thinking):** Use of a **binary framing** (e.g., "conservatives" versus "radical leftists") can present issues as having only two extreme options, ignoring nuance and complexity in an attempt to simplify the political landscape for his audience.

- **"Moving the goalposts"** is an informal logical fallacy that occurs when someone changes the rules, criteria, or required evidence for a claim *after* the initial requirements have been met or are about to be met, making it virtually impossible for the opponent to win or satisfy the demand.

- It's a disingenuous tactic because the person employing it shifts the target to avoid admitting they were wrong or conceding a point. Query successful

- A "red herring" is an idiom that refers to something that misleads or distracts from a relevant or important question or issue. It can be used in a few different contexts:

- **Logical Fallacy/Rhetoric:** It's an informal fallacy where irrelevant information is introduced into an argument to divert attention from the main topic. For example, a politician addressing a financial crisis by talking about a recent unrelated policy success.

In 2025, a person of courage and integrity finally stood up to fifty years of racism and sexism.

"The Supreme Court on Thursday sent the case of an Ohio woman who contends that she was the victim of reverse discrimination back to the lower courts. **In a unanimous ruling by Justice Ketanji Brown Jackson**, the justices agreed that a federal appeals court in Cincinnati was wrong to impose a higher bar for the case brought by Marlean Ames to move forward than if Ames had been a member of a minority group.

The Supreme Court's cases, Jackson added, also make clear that the test for showing discrimination in a case like Ames's 'does not vary based on whether or not the plaintiff is a member of a majority group.' 'The "background circumstances" rule flouts that basic principle,' she concluded."

Amy Howe, *Supreme Court rules for straight woman who claims she was subjected to reverse discrimination*, SCOTUSblog (Jun. 5, 2025, 12:58 PM), https://www.scotusblog.com/2025/06/supreme-court-rules-for-straight-woman-who-claims-she-was-subjected-to-reverse-discrimination/

Arthur Schopenhauer, Truth

1. **It is ridiculed:** A new truth is first met with mockery and dismissal because it challenges existing beliefs and norms.

2. **It is violently opposed:** As the new idea gains traction, those who hold onto the old beliefs actively and fiercely resist it.

3. **It is accepted as being self-evident:** Eventually, the truth becomes so widely accepted that its validity is no longer questioned, and it is considered common sense.